QUEEN

GREAT LANDS BOOK III

K.M. TREMILLS

"Messenger is an absolute treasure and a fascinating story. The storytelling and the cast of characters are unique and make the novel a true joy to read."

– Renee Alarid, Associate Director of Creative Services

"K.M. Tremills is the gold standard for strong, independent and feminine heroines. Blue Moon is the start of a wickedly clever series!"

– Kathryn Cottam, The Shoemaker

"I fell in love with these vibrant characters. The Fated series is a delightfully dark blend of quirky, flirty, sarcastic, and charming."

– Vanessa Mayville, Vanessa Mayville Designs

"The ancient wisdom in Gabriella's engaging story comes through in K.M. Tremills' eloquent words. The Great Lands series can be read on many levels, all of which are entertaining."

– Jen Clarke, Executive Director at One to World

"The Great Lands series is brilliant ... a fantastic journey that steps into a realm of mysticism and fantasy. K.M. Tremills causes the reader to ponder their own beliefs."

– Barb Weston, Inner Focus Holistic Healing

"K.M. Tremills finds balance between page-turning plotlines and ethereal story-telling. Time well spent!"

– Roberta Cottam, Bluebeard's Bride

QUEEN
BOOK III
GREAT LANDS

K.M. TREMILLS

To the wise ones, the brave ones,
and the sensitive ones,
who feel the magic in the world.

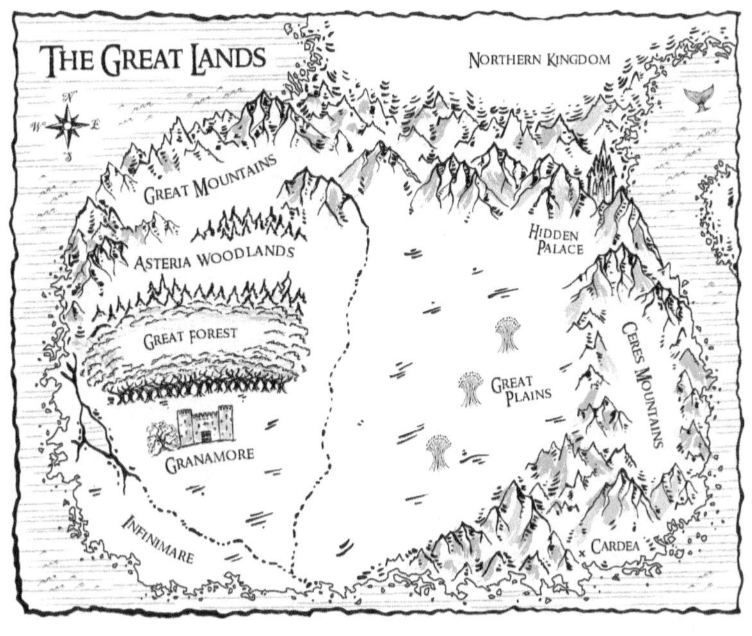

THE GREAT LANDS
NORTHERN KINGDOM
N
W
E
S
GREAT MOUNTAINS
ASTERIA WOODLANDS
GREAT FOREST
GRANAMORE
INFINIMARE
HIDDEN PALACE
CERES MOUNTAINS
GREAT PLAINS
CARDEA

PART I
DISCOVERY

CHAPTER ONE

GABRIELLA PULLED her hood over her face. She was covered by her cloak as well as an invisibility spell. But in a fortress as strong as the Hidden Palace, she could not count on remaining undiscovered.

She had limited time to perform her task. And so, she must move with stealth and haste.

Gabriella felt the warm embrace of Adrian in the spell. She smiled in her heart, but dared not allow love to show on her face. The Hidden Palace was a powerful sorceress who would sense the presence of a competing spellcaster.

Gabriella leapt up the grand staircase with the hushed feet of a night cat, slipping past two gossiping maids. They passed by her without notice, gliding down the stairs as she went up. The young women seemed equally excited and terrified. Gabriella sent them blessings, even as she shook her head at their naïve excitement. They had yet to be tested by the heartbreak of the world. And so, they still fantasized of daring adventures and wild romances.

As her foot touched the upper landing, Gabriella was grateful that she had known both the sweetness of love and the crushing burden of loss. For without one, she would be an empty shell. And without the other, she would never be the warrior needed by her lands.

Her heart caught in her throat as she recalled her time in the Palace. Gabriella's memory leapt back to the vision of the Great Prince on his knee, imploring her to become his bride. His heart so open, and her stance so unsure.

What might have happened had her sister, Hannah, not burst into the room? She wondered. *How could she have hesitated, knowing that her sister was wedded to this man at her feet?*

Hannah assured Gabriella many times that she did not consider herself the wife of the Great Prince but rather his captive. Yes, she had listened to her parents and married him, tempted by the promise of being the most powerful woman in the realm. Only to find that she was not the Queen but the Pawn in this game of chess. And one that had been under a spell. And so, her sister had renounced power, and embraced love and rebellion. A choice that Gabriella envied.

And yet, Gabriella knew that she could not avoid her journey. She must take each step as it appeared. Despite experience and the passage of time, her destination was still unclear. Her choices shrouded by the Mystery.

All she knew was that she must continue. Until her whole heart came alive.

The sound of encroaching footsteps snapped Gabriella back to reality. She pressed her back into the stone wall and shivered. Gabriella hoped that the stones recalled her promise. That she would liberate them from their curse as soon as she discovered how to break the spell. In return, they swore to protect her as she passed through perilous territory.

Her breath shallowed and her hood dropped lower over her face. Gabriella grew absolutely still as she glimpsed at a young woman being fussed over by several ladies in waiting.

The girl was barely fifteen years of age, yet the cascading dress and opulent jewels made her tender youth look splendid. Her terror was palpable under the surface. Her guardian snapped fingers at the ladies and chased the girl's heels to keep her moving forward.

As they approached, Gabriella prayed that her cloak and spell would keep her well-hidden. She held her breath as the girls passed within inches of her. Their guardian glanced over her shoulder, sensing something. But quickly shook it off and strode to catch her straying girls.

Gabriella had heard rumours that every lord in the Great Lands was throwing a daughter at the feet of the Great Prince. They hoped that he would rescind his marriage to Hannah and take a new bride. They assumed that forging a bond with the most powerful force in the lands would keep them safe. They did not pause to assess the destruction the Prince wrought no matter whether you were counted as his ally or enemy.

As the flurry passed, Gabriella forced herself to refrain from tripping the hawkish man who pecked and pricked at the bridal offering. Gabriella clenched her fists to stay focused. She would have to leave this young woman to her fate. Even if it collided with her own.

Gabriella kept her head bowed and her breath still. She waited as the fussing brigade shuffled down the elegant staircase. Gabriella released her fists. *Good*, she thought. *I can move.*

She took her first deep breath, ready to continue her mission, when she thought she heard him. The Prince's voice echoed up from the Greeting Room. Gabriella's heart squeezed. Her breath caught. And visions of the sweet young prospect taunted her. Beckoning for her to react.

Gabriella forced her heart to be calm. Her feet to still. And her mind to hush its nonsense.

She focused on her senses. Listening for the nuances of his

voice. The distance that it carried. The direction of the ruckus. And the steady persistent badgering of the cruel guardian with his young sacrifice.

They were far enough away that she was not concerned with being found. Other than by an enterprising servant.

The higher servants would be near the Prince's hand to keep him content and to manage the interlopers with their ambitions.

The Great Prince laughed out loud. Catching Gabriella off-guard. His laugh was a harsh and unforgiving sound. Only she heard the subtle notes of pain. She suspected he was drunk. His words tipped towards slurring and his declarations grew outrageous.

And despite herself, a tiny smile curved the edges of Gabriella's lips.

She saw and felt her way past the illusion the Palace was playing. Gabriella was not altogether sure how the Palace was doing it. She would have to ask Adrian. But somehow, she was playing a very dangerous game.

The Palace was using an understudy to play the Great Prince. Continuing the charade that she was in control.

Gabriella assumed that The Palace must be bending weak and greedy minds to perceive what they want to see. That the Great Prince was still wielding power from his throne. And in service to his needs, had cast away one bride to secure another.

Gabriella's mind immediately raced to understand how the Palace was manipulating such potent magic. *And why?* She shook her head to free herself from this tempting puzzle.

Now was not the time.

The Palace's secret machinations were not her mission. She had come to discover the meaning behind her dream. One that repeated every night. Insisting that the Palace's downfall and the Great Land's freedom were within reach. If only Gabriella discovered the secret.

Still, the thought of the Great Prince being free allowed Gabriella's body to relax. She smiled softly.

Good for him, she thought. *And maybe, good for us all.*

She moved deeper into the Palace's belly, relishing the brash notes of the imposter's voice. No matter that it slurred from bottles of wine, and was indulged by nervous, high-pitched giggles. The outlandish pantomime rang in Gabriella's ears as hope.

As she slipped into the hallway's darkness, Gabriella knew the rumours were true.

The Great Prince had escaped his cage. And was on the run in the Great Lands.

CHAPTER TWO

ADRIAN PACED BACK and forth in the far reaches of his mountain retreat.

He needed the high altitude to stay attuned to Gabriella as she travelled deeper into the belly of the beast. He was only a few ranges over, but this mission required all his concentration to stay connected and protect Gabriella.

The other benefit to being so high in the peaks was that he did not have to fend off the constant intrusion of people. He did have to occasionally shoo away the advances of a curious falcon or a lonely snow leopard, but he did not mind those incursions.

Adrian was wired for isolation and solitude. The peace of being far from human beings gave him the last piece of healing he needed. His battle with Vanora took a toll on his mind and body. And while his left hand still had a small tremor, he had healed quickly even for a wizard.

He sighed. Drinking in the sharp mountain air. Adrian found this undertaking remarkably invigorating. He might have crossed his legs and gone into a meditative trance except that he needed his body to let him know when the weather was shifting. He couldn't afford to be so deep in trance, so focused on

8

Gabriella, so attentive to the danger in her environment, that he neglected to pay attention to his own.

Spring squalls in the High Mountains were notorious and far more dangerous than the Winter ones. They built power in an instant. Freezing wiry humans such as Adrian in a matter of minutes. And so, his steady movement made inquisitive animals a little more wary and kept his muscles flooded with blood. His nerves stayed alert to the wind, and his instincts paid close attention to the immediate threats.

Except, as he was paying attention to his own crag, Adrian was taken off guard by the flush of excitement surging through his protective cover around Gabriella. He sensed a revelation. Tinged with emotion.

Adrian breathed deeper and counselled his heart to stay steady. He could not afford to alarm the predatory creatures in the nearby caves. He was safe as long as they perceived him as an equal or a predator. But his heart raced a little faster. And a film of sweat appeared on his arms.

Explaining what he saw would cause more questions than answers, but Adrian had learned many years ago not to question the messages he received. He no longer needed to know the methods or understand how the Divine chose to deliver missives to him.

He breathed a little deeper. Forcing himself to take a longer inhale. A longer pause. A longer exhale. He managed his pulse. Discharging his tension through every pore in his body. Encouraging the sweat to cool and his concern to disperse.

He reminded himself that he could only deal with this moment in time. And in this moment, he was responsible for Gabriella safety.

Adrian would not worry about the future. He would not dwell on the past. He must only remember his role in the rising star of the woman risking her life inside the belly of a monster.

Beyond that, he told his turbulent mind, he had no choice in the matter of another's heart.

And in this moment, he knew that Gabriella had received the confirmation she sought.

The Great Prince was free.

CHAPTER THREE

ADRIAN'S CONSCIOUSNESS dropped into the Hidden Palace next to Gabriella. Appearing beside her as though he were a spirit.

Gabriella leapt into the shadows. Until she saw the smile on Adrian's face. She strode forward and jabbed her fist through his shoulder. Not caring that it wouldn't land.

You might give a warrior a little warning, she grumbled. Speaking inside his mind to avoid detection. *You're lucky you have no substance.*

And you're lucky that I don't lecture you on holding your temper, Adrian replied.

Oh yes, Gabriella rolled her eyes and slinked forward in the shadows. *My wise sage on a far mountain. You never get rattled.*

Adrian felt the sting of her words and chose not to respond. He had felt her excitement, as surely as she felt his instinctive jealousy. Sensing each another's private emotions was one of the perils of being so closely entwined as allies and lovers.

While Gabriella had matured over the years, wisdom had not quelled her fiery soul. The quieter Adrian got, the further she leaned in. *The Great Prince escaped*, she said.

So I gather, Adrian said. *Does that not answer why we are here?*

Why I am here, Gabriella replied. Peeking around the edge of the hallway corner. Listening for the whisper of servants lurking in the bedrooms. *Your sweet self is far up a rocky cliff.*

Surrounded by snow leopards, golden eagles, and arctic snakes, Adrian retorted. *Not exactly a sun-soaked meadow.* His spirit stalked behind her silent, panther-like steps.

Well, you might give an embodied woman a hand and play lookout, Gabriella growled.

They can see me as well as you can, Adrian said.

True, Gabriella replied. *But you can disappear as quickly as an ill-conceived notion. Let them shrug you off as exhaustion or the vestige of too many drinks.*

I will only be able to do that a few times, Adrian reminded her. *The toll of dropping in and out is high.*

Gabriella nodded. She appreciated the dangers Adrian faced to keep her safe.

I am not convinced that the Prince plays that big a role in the Palace's power, Gabriella said, finally answering Adrian's question about her mission. *She feels angry but not diminished. I need to know more. We need a plan.*

I understand, replied Adrian. *And I dislike you being in her belly for long. The evil of this place takes a toll on you.*

Gabriella nodded. Knowing he spoke the truth. And while she was grateful for his protection, there were times when she wished he was not so close.

There was no privacy in her world when they partnered on missions. Even away from missions, he often picked up on what she felt. And she could not help but feel defensive when he had such close access to her emotions. Especially when he seemed to understand them better than she did.

She felt annoyed that he jumped to conclusions before she had a chance to feel the fullness of her response. *They were her emotions!*

Gabriella slowed her steps and counselled herself to take a deep breath. She was more vulnerable and volatile when in the Palace. This place stirred memories that made her uncomfortable. And now was not the time to revisit them.

She edged toward the bend in the hallway. Feeling a shift in energy coming her way.

Gabriella paused. Sensing into what caused the ripple. Living people. Spirits of ancestors long dead. Altered materials or magic held in the Palace walls. Even the sentient creatures like mice and birds could change the delicate balance of what she feels. She had to consider it all.

She realized it was an eerie quietness of this end of the Palace. The strangeness made her hair stand on end and her skin go cold. She did not hear the sound of servants, nor even the little feet of mice or spiders. She wondered why this part of the Palace was so deserted.

And yet, she knew she was in the right place.

She could almost sense the Prince's relief as he walked this last stretch of the hallway. Casting a glance over his shoulder, and finally feeling a reprieve from the bondage of his imprisonment. By the Palace and, maybe more so, by his ancestors.

Gabriella's brow furrowed as the vision revealed more truths than her time with the Prince. She had underestimated the pressure he felt. The weight of what was keeping him imprisoned. The chains that his ancestors, especially his Father, had instilled in him.

She felt Adrian's gaze. Curious, but not intruding. He understood that she was receiving information.

She also knew that this mission was profoundly challenging for him. She sensed his rage simmering under a well-controlled surface. His desire to crush the Great Prince and never look back.

Every step of her journey back into the Palace challenged his control and his perception of himself. He abhorred that emotions could unsettle him so deeply.

Gabriella glanced at Adrian's face, wishing she could bring peace to his heart. For she saw his feelings not as weakness, but as strength.

The emotion made him a better man. A stronger sage. And a more compassionate wisdom keeper. Without them, he would be an empty shell with no consideration for the challenges of others. Nor would he even be so fully human.

He admired the ancient sages and their detachment. While she valued every dirty, dangerous, delicious morsel of this world. And more than anything, she was determined to give those glorious pleasures – and choices – back to her people.

They had not only been prisoners of the body. But prisoners of the mind and heart. And she intended to bring them freedom.

Gabriella softened the fire in her heart. Glancing briefly at her beloved. She ached to touch him. To comfort him. To express how very deeply she loved him. But she did not have the luxury of time or physical contact.

She stole one last look at Adrian, catching his gaze. Then shot him a mischievous smile. He could not resist returning the gesture.

And in that moment, she felt as though she had embraced him for a thousand years.

Gabriella exhaled sharply. And moved silently around the next corner. She swore she felt the temperature drop and suppressed an involuntary shudder. Her feet knew she was treading on private and holy territory.

Somehow, the Prince had struck a deal to protect this area of the Palace. A deal that kept his ancestors and the Palace herself from detecting his liberation.

She wanted to know the price the Prince had agreed to pay to salvage his sanity by laying claim to this solitary tower.

Gabriella felt her heart contract as she reflected on the many deals she had struck over the years. To save her own soul. To rescue her sister. To appear at precisely the moment that she could save Adrian.

Gabriella forced her way forward to keep from being crushed by the weight of choices she had made. When she was a little girl chasing imaginary demons and enemies around the forest, she had no idea what being a warrior required.

She smiled sadly. Ah, the innocence of childhood.

Gabriella moved closer to the shadow of a door. She swore there was something like a mist hanging in the corners of the floor and ceiling. She moved through a fog that clung to the edges of her cloak. If she had questioned whether she was crossing a threshold to a strange reality at the edge of the world, she had her answer.

What kind of magic made this place possible? She wondered. *And who wove it?*

Gabriella hesitated. She felt the pull of the fog like a thousand fingers clutching and a hundred voices whispering. Still, she had made it the door. She had passed some sort of test.

The magic had let her through.

The real question was, *Did she enter knowing it might be a trap? Even if all the answers she hoped for were inside?*

Gabriella took a deep breath. And reached for the door handle.

CHAPTER FOUR

SYRENA TOSSED BACK her hood as she gazed at her lover's face. Hannah's beauty was as breathtaking as ever, except it felt empty. Hollow, like a reed pulled from the earth.

The glass sanctuary used to grow seedlings and nurture flowers. Now it held Hannah. Lying on a stone table, her breath shallow, her eyes closed. The appearance of death, but still, somehow, alive.

Syrena's heart had shattered when Hannah's foot touched the grounds of her beloved garden. Only to send her into a deep, sleeping spell.

Syrena brushed a wisp of hair from Hannah's quiet face. "At least you do not seem troubled by your slumber. Stay well, my dear one, and I will puzzle this mystery for us both."

Nothing she or Tobias had done in the past four months had altered Hannah's situation.

And why neither she nor Tobias had been affected by the spell was curious. And eerie. Obviously, someone had laid a trap. Whether for Hannah alone or for the entire royal family, they could not ascertain. And did not want to.

They had dispatched a secret messenger to inform Gabriella. But they held back the full truth.

Syrena and Tobias had argued about this point for weeks before sending word. They knew Gabriella would sense something was wrong. But they did not want to distract her from her critical mission. And so they told her Hannah was injured but safe.

Close enough to the truth. But a painful omission all the same.

Something Syrena worried about every day. But Gabriella's instinct would be to save her sister. And, right now, they all needed Gabriella to stay focused on the Palace.

Besides, Syrena was not going anywhere. She would stay with Hannah as long as it took to set her free. Protecting her with the aid of Tobias.

He was out there somewhere. And without his loyalty, Syrena would have collapsed moons ago. Or wasted into a rail of a woman. Neither of which was of any help to Hannah. And so, Syrena allowed this stranger into the realm of her heart, and her eternal gratitude.

Tobias reminded her to channel her obsession into purpose. To tend to herself as much as she tended to Hannah. A balance that had been missing in Syrena's life since she had sworn love and protection to her sweet woman.

Syrena and Tobias held constant vigil over Hannah. While Syrena fumed with outrage.

She imagined that if Gabriella were here, she would understand and, still, counsel her to subdue her rage.

While Syrena conceded that anger was not a wise place from which to act, it kept her from falling deep into the pits of despair. Wondering whether her lover might never wake.

And so, for the purposes of her own hope, she stoked the fire of rage to stay focused.

"I will relinquish the fury when I have found a solution," Syrena grumbled. "And perhaps, if they are lucky, I will spare the lives of those who did this to you."

She pulled a dead rose leaf from Hannah's hair. *When had that fallen there?* Syrena wondered. It bothered her that she had not noticed.

"How could you have been born to such a powerful twin as Gabriella without a purpose of your own? The symmetry is unimaginable."

Syrena touched her lover's hand. Though it was cold, Hannah did not seem to be in pain.

"Why do you always seemed to be the foil of your sister's exploits?" her brow furrowed. "Why were you the one who fell prey to a tormented Prince, to a malevolent Palace? The one compelled to return home only to be captured by a spell?"

"What game is Fate playing with all of us?" Syrena growled. As though she expected an answer.

She clenched her fist, craving to strike something. Anything!

And here she was, surrounded by glass and soft plants. She wanted so deeply to believe the Divine was at fault. Syrena threw her head back and clenched her cape to her mouth. Howling her frustration into the thick wool.

Feeling some relief, she glanced at the door. Concerned that Tobias might have heard. She could not worry him any deeper. Or cause mercenaries to come running. Though, she secretly desired a fight.

Instead, Syrena sighed. With a belly full of knots, she forced her feet forward. She needed to move her body to keep her mind from raging. She felt the alluring song of darkness beckoning. Whispering that all that ever followed her was disaster.

But through her despair, she heard the sweet voice of Hannah whisper a message that scared away the dark thoughts skulking in the corners of her mind.

Syrena ventured a heart-destroying glance at her beloved.

Hannah's serene face brought home the one truth that Syrena could never forget. Even when they were in the cruel clutches of the Hidden Palace, they found each other.

The bleakest days and the deepest love. Without one, she would never have found the other.

Syrena rushed for the door, desperate for fresh air. As her feet landed on the earth, the peace and quiet of the garden struck her. She felt the sweet solace of this place.

Leaning heavily on a stone pillar, Syrena stared out at the garden. Leaves turning red, gold, and yellow with the sharp bite of the autumn air. Struck by the beauty, she succumbed to the burden in her heart.

Her shoulders slumped and she felt tears begin to rise. She had shed so few since her lover had been captured. Tears made her feel helpless.

Over the forest crest, she heard the approaching crunch of Tobias's boots on crisp leaves. Syrena felt a surge of gratitude and quickly wiped the tears from her cheeks.

He approached with a pleased smile, holding up a roasting spit. "I roasted these deep in the woods." The aroma of freshly roasted, wild hare, drifted to Syrena and her stomach growled in response.

She looked down at her belly and grumbled, "Traitor."

Tobias handed her one of the spits and leaned on the matching stone pillar outside the sanctuary door. "Hardly. Who else would keep you fed?" His mouth bore a smile, but the sadness in his eyes betrayed his heart.

Syrena glared in response. Her worry did not enjoy the heaviness of meat in her stomach. And her heart felt guilty that Hannah had not eaten in months.

"I have played this game too long to listen to your stubbornness. Eat. Or I will stand here all night."

"Do what you must," she fired back. But Tobias stayed true to his promise, not moving an inch.

So Syrena relented. Tearing away a piece of delicious meat. And shoving it into her mouth.

~

Tobias watched Syrena chew, forcing herself fo swallow. He nodded. Knowing all too well the war waging inside her. He understood the battle between rage and guilt.

Tobias sat on the pillar near to Syrena. Each of them framing the doors into the hothouse. As he forced himself to tear into the rabbit, he felt a warm wave of thanks for Syrena's company.

Since the fall of this royal house, Tobias had become as much of a loner as Syrena. Counting on himself. Abandoning trust, for fear of being lured into a trap. People had become hard and self-serving. The burden of too many years of royalty sworn to dominance and greed instead of generosity and true sovereignty.

He tore off another piece, casting a glance at Syrena to make sure she kept eating. He knew that she felt his gaze. She was sensitive to being watched. And still, he felt protective of her.

As he ate, he watched the leaves drifting into the garden. He appreciated the small blessings. A respite in the battle. Nourishing food in his belly. The fierce woman perched on the pillar beside him.

As strong as they were, Tobias knew they would not have survived this blow without each other.

Their game of growling and grumbling at one another kept them from the pit of despondency that threatened to devour them every day.

So, as Syrena doggedly ate every bite, his eyes held a tenderness that he would never have imagined feeling for her. Tobias had accepted Syrena as family. His oath to guard the lives of this royal line now included her.

He rarely felt hunger these days. But neither of them could not afford to wither away. The fight was coming. He could feel it. So they must stay strong.

Tobias took a swig of royal ale. Then offered the bottle to Syrena. She shook her head. Tobias shrugged. And took another drink.

He had found a store of wine, ales, and cured foods in the castle. And though he felt a small twinge of guilt for eating the royal's fare, he brushed it away. *We are in the thick of war. The dark ones crossed a line when they ransacked our kingdom. And now, they have struck down the very embodiment of grace and kindness.*

We will restore the niceties of peace when we have peace. Until then, we must stay strong and ready. If the king returns and decides that I have chosen wrong, we can take it up then.

As much as they needed physical strength, even more important was the fuel Syrena needed to keep up her pursuit to break this mysterious spell.

Tobias admired her wild mind. As he obsessively searched the woods for traitors, she fanatically searched her knowledge of magics. He suspected that she was as strong a spellcaster as whoever made this trap. She just did not know it yet.

And in that, he placed his faith that they would escape this torture one day.

"Did you discover anything new today?" Tobias asked, keeping his eyes on the garden.

Syrena shot him a look that combined fury with frustration. Tobias shrugged. "Me either."

He looked directly at her. "But you are being careful? Syrena, if the Hidden Palace is behind this spell –"

"If?" Syrena barked, then lowered her voice. "If? We both know she is the only force powerful enough to wield this kind of dark magic. She must have sent one of her sorcerer minions."

"Still," Tobias replied. "I fear for your safety. Searching for the answers to a magic coming from her. It might set off a warning. Draw her attention."

She ignored his concern. "What spellcaster would be so foolish to think the Palace would make good on any promise she made?"

"Syrena!" he snapped. She turned, startled. Tobias growled, "I need you to take care."

Seeing the concern in his eyes, she exhaled sharply. "I know. I promise."

"We may never know what made Hannah so susceptible to magic." Tobias admitted. "Why was she led here? Would the same fate have befallen Gabriella? Would the Warrior have resisted the spell? We've been over these questions a thousand times."

"And where has it gotten us?" she exclaimed. "No closer to an answer!"

They ate in grim silence for several minutes. Each relying on the strength that flowed between them. Holding them up.

As he finished his meal, Tobias reflexively checked on Syrena. She defensively opened her hands to prove that she had finished her food. Tobias nodded.

He was secretly proud of her. And a little amused that the stubborn spirit that so aggravated him when they first met, was now what he most liked about her.

Syrena pushed up to her feet. Placing her hand briefly on his shoulder, she patted it in thanks.

Tobias gathered up the bones. Exhaling his grief.

Snatching up Syrena's discarded spit, he strode off for another round of tracing the royal lands.

He walked into the darkness, turning to watch Syrena pulling open the sanctuary door. The light spilled out, framing her sad but determined face.

As she returned to her lonely vigil.

CHAPTER FIVE

THE GREAT PRINCE huddled at the edge of the woods of his mountain kingdom. Though he had broken free of the Palace and made his way across his realm, he had not found the courage to traverse out of the mountains into the lands of the free people.

He laughed. *Free people*, he thought. *They would string you up for such a notion. Not one of your subjects believes they are free.*

And yet, as the Prince stood shivering at the edge of his hereditary lands, he knew they were freer than he had ever imagined. Here he was, scrabbling for food and desperately learning to survive, and still, he felt freer than he had ever been growing up. Or certainly since living in the Hidden Palace.

Barely living, he thought with a growl. Then cast a quick glance over his shoulder.

Any moment, he expected the Hidden Palace to dispatch a mercenary to drag him back to her clutches. This was not paranoia. He had done as much to serve her, to serve the mission instilled in her by a mad king. A mission that he had taken on, thinking it was his birthright. When in truth, it was his birth curse.

Nothing appeared. No trees rustled. No arrows flew at his heart.

The Prince sighed. And sat down on the earth with an ancient pine tree at his back. The bark needled him and he was grateful. He had spent so many years numb and lost, that he would take any contact. Any touch. Even the rugged affection of trees.

Though he had starved and slept on the earth since running from his home, he refused to go back. He had days of missing the many of the comforts of his court. Longing for luscious meat and a soft bed. But while he felt the temptation, he could not trust that the impulse was his.

His trust in the world, and even worse in himself, had been shattered. *The only thing,* he thought, *the only person I trust is –*

Gabriella.

She made her own choices, he thought. *Despite the command of her family, the urging of her friends, the counsel of those older than her. She chose to rescue her sister. Despite the odds. Despite the real possibility of losing her life. Gabriella followed her own heart.*

What must it be like, he wondered, *to make your own choices? Truly your own?*

There was not a single soul in the world that he admired more than Gabriella. Not a single soul that he loved more.

He took a sharp breath. He had danced around that feeling since he met her. Never wanted to admit it, even to himself. But there it was. The truth laid bare.

I love her. The Prince shook. *A terrifying thought. To love someone.*

And still, the desire for her was so strong that his foot stepped forward. He wanted to return. To be with her. To insist that the Gods had brought them together for a reason. Their families had been woven together since the dawn of time. And when he had chosen the wrong sister, it was not of his making.

It was an agreement forged by the Palace and Gabriella's father.

"We get to choose now," he said, as though she could hear him. And perhaps she could, he thought. Hope blossomed in his heart. Another strange feeling. Spacious and soft.

He took a second bold step toward the Palace. This one more assured.

The sharp *snap* of a twig under his foot, made him jump. Shaking him from his reverie. *Are these even my thoughts?* he wondered, looking around. *Am I being tricked?*

The Prince clenched his fists and howled in rage, shaking the thick forest. Falling to his knees, he grabbed dirt and innocent twig, and crushed it in his hands. Mingling the dry, broken wood with blood. The pain was sharp, and the sensation felt good.

"What is mine?" he yelled at the sky. "How do I trust what I feel? What I think?"

The Prince glared at the crushed twig in his palm and growled, "How do I know what I want? What is mine? And not her twisted bidding?"

He threw the fractured wood to the ground and aimed his rage back to its source. At the Gods.

"How do I know what is my desire and not the madness of my Father? Of my lineage?"

The question halted the Prince's desire to return to the Palace. He had much to determine before he could safely return. Not that he expected safety, but he knew that he needed to be in command of his own mind before he could return to Gabriella.

He may know his own heart. How much he loved her, how much he needed her and wanted her by his side. But he would never convince her that his feelings were true until he could stand strong in his own being. A true King.

Yes, he thought. *I carry with me the blood of my ancestors. But I do not need to do their bidding.*

He exhaled and leaned against a robust pine tree. One with a broad trunk that had seen many centuries. A Pine Elder that stood strong, not troubled by the clamor of humankind.

The Prince felt the wisdom of the Pine Elder. He leaned into the strength of the tree. The ancient wisdom coursing through its veins. Its reliance on the sun, the earth, and its fellow trees to hold it strong in a world of humans who would cut down whatever they desire to feed their voracious appetites.

And still, the tree gave to the Prince. Allowed him to be emboldened by its wisdom and draw from its strength. The Prince felt the possibility of another way. Another tradition. A way of connection and believing in a collective knowing.

A soft smile curved at the edge of his mouth. Not a confident smile, but the beginnings of one.

He breathed deeply. As he felt the surges of panic, he leaned harder into the tree. He was afraid of not knowing. Of taking a path so different from the one he had been taught.

That path included the risk of being struck down. Of dying...

The Prince gasped. Then laughed. A strange and awkward laugh. "Dying," he said aloud. "Dying!" He laughed harder. The edges of fear danced around him, wondering whether he might be descending into madness.

But this was not madness, he realized. *This was relief.*

Gently, oh so gently, the Pine Elder encouraged the Prince. His realm needed the Prince to awaken as much as the Prince needed to wake up. The Elder knew if the Prince did not discover his soul, the days of his beloved forest, his family, were short.

The expansion and greed of humankind knew no bounds. So it was time to encourage them to remember an ancient, and yet, a new way.

The Prince felt a sudden surge of confidence. A faith. For a brief moment, he felt hope and his face appeared decades younger.

No, he thought, resisting this new feeling. A dark cloud covered his face. He shrunk back. A growl on his mouth. The Prince rejected any notion that he could count on the Gods.

The Pine Elder eased back. He had pushed too hard. He must gently embolden the Prince. And still, the desire must come naturally. No matter the stakes.

With his arms folded and pressed against his chest, the Prince opened to the gentle trills of the birds. Even in a time of peril, still, the birds sang. He relaxed a little and took a breath.

He sensed the soft nudge of possibility in his heart. And this time, despite his trepidation, he did not cower.

"I might choose differently," he ventured, looking up at the pines, the clouds, the arctic squirrels. His steady and unjudging companions.

He felt ridiculous. And pulled back. Yet he could feel that there was no concern here. No threat. No person waiting to crush his nascent hope.

Once again, he felt a nudge. *Why not converse with them?* He wondered. *I am tired of speaking with ghosts.*

He placed his hands on the ground, covered with soft needles. He scooped up a handful and let them fall through his fingers. Felt the realness of them.

Feeling the war inside, the Prince struggled to take in his surroundings. The simple reality of it. He still wanted to judge and reject all that he saw. Rejection felt safe. Easy. Familiar.

The softness of the forest and the curiosity of its creatures was unnerving. He did not understand their symbiotic relationship. He had been taught to grab, to possess, to feed an unfillable greed.

Even as destructive thoughts riddled his mind, all he felt from the forest was acceptance.

The Prince sighed. The more he noticed the beauty of the forest, the weaker those dark thoughts became. A glimmer of courage darted from his heart.

"I could choose differently," he said again, more confident this time.

As he looked up at the sunshine dancing through the trees, he noticed, for the first time in many years, a rich and inviting world.

The Prince sensed that his journey might take more courage than he was sure that he had.

But he also sensed that the risk was worth the gain. That Gabriella would be proud of him.

A Raven called above his head. The Prince looked up and saw that the Raven's gaze pointed back toward the Palace.

"Gabriella?" the Prince said. "It's not possible."

It is, called the Raven.

"No!" the Prince declared, jumping to his feet as though he could command nature to obey him.

Yes, replied the Raven. And launched off the tree.

"What are you doing?" He yelled in the direction of the Palace. "Get out of there!"

But he knew full well that she couldn't hear him.

Just like he knew that he could not go back. She had gone for a reason. Possibly even to save him. His foolish heart skipped a beat at the thought.

Did I let her down? Would she wonder why I ran? The Prince's shoulders slumped.

The Prince fell back against a spindly pine tree. And stared in the direction of the Palace.

At a loss as to what to do.

CHAPTER SIX

Careful, Adrian said. And he felt Gabriella growl inside.

She had been reaching for the door handle. They paused to see if there were any ripple effects of her emotions in such a magical place.

Adrian understood that she could not help but let them slip through on occasion. Especially when she was surprised.

Nothing happened. But Adrian reminded himself that she was easily provoked in this place. He needed to hold his tongue. And trust her.

When she was frustrated or on the verge of losing control, Gabriella withdrew inside her cloak. She pulled her hood up instinctively as she reached to connect with the door. Knowing she needed all the protection she might afford.

Adrian held back from drawing attention to their dwindling window of time. Looking at her tense shoulders, she felt his concern. So he stood silent. And watched the hallway.

Dammit it, Gabriella thought. She had been expecting to feel something when she grasped the door handle. But all she felt was a wall. A powerful wall of magic that did not want her to enter.

Adrian's presence resolved, or at least quieted, the skirmish in her heart. Gabriella reached her hand to grasp Adrian's. He reached to hold hers. Sending her reassurance and strength. Despite his lack of form, Gabriella swore that she felt the warmth of his touch.

She closed her eyes to concentrate on the magic that flowed between their souls.

Gabriella had her own brilliance, but when she combined her abilities with Adrian, they made the infinite possible.

Even the Palace has not figured out how to get past this threshold, she thought.

Gabriella suspected that the Palace was unaware of the tower's existence. That is how she knew the magic protecting it must be ancient. Possibly even gifted to the Prince from his ancestors. Or from a guardian.

She paused, knowing that they risked drawing attention to the tower if they broke through. Gabriella could never be sure of the full consequences of her actions. She only knew what she had seen in a dream. And she awoke with a compulsion to return to the Palace.

To find out if her instinct was true. That the Prince had indeed abandoned his prison.

For weeks, Adrian had tried to dissuade her from going. Gabriella restrained a smile when she thought of their battle. Delighted that she had won. Even more delighted when she remembered how much they enjoy sparring.

Returning to the present, she leaned into the magic of their powers. The mixture coursed through her. Her ability to alter energy and his ability to shift form. As though two powerful streams came together, dancing and playing, forming a potent river.

Gabriella focused her will on the spell surrounding the door.

She closed her eyes and held out her palms. Tracing the edges of the doorway without touching them.

Murmuring a soft verse under her breath. Careful not to speak too loudly. As though she were whispering a special message, made only for the door.

Gabriella leaned closer, whispering sweetly. Lulling the door into a trance.

My heart is one with the heart that knows you,
Believe that I come in his interests true,
Trust that I hold quiet his secrets and desire,
Weaving love for a day to triumph and defy her.

She felt into the spell. She sensed the special code that made up the magic around it. A combination of colours and words, space and dancing lights. Gabriella leaned deeper into the magic, careful to keep her connection with Adrian.

If she ventured too deep inside without knowing her way back, she would be lost forever.

This was the danger of playing inside another's magic. And yet, she sensed the door softening to her. Somehow, the door and the spell were one. Or, more accurately, the door was the source of the magic.

She recognized that the door had once been a sentient being. That it held a deep and abiding love for the Prince. Perhaps a person, or some kind of Guardian, that had exchanged its chance at everlasting eternal bliss to provide the Prince with a refuge and protection.

The Guardian knew the Prince's only chance at sanity and survival was to have a secret hideaway protected by a magic as formidable as the Palace.

Gabriella's heart softened as she felt the sweet and powerful love hidden in the door. A love from the maternal line of his ancestors. She understood that the physical barrier keeping the Prince safe had once been a beloved Great Aunt.

Or a Great, Great Aunt. In every sense of that title.

The barrier pushed back against Gabriella. Surrounding her with its own inquiry. Testing her as she veered on the edge of panic. And so, Gabriella quieted her mind, and focused on the love in her heart.

Her desire for the Prince to be free. To be whole. To know a life of joy rather than pain.

And as Gabriella felt the pushing magic of this Great, Great Aunt retreat, she also sensed this powerful woman's approval. She had faith that Gabriella's intention was for the Prince's well-being, and for the benefit of his lands.

These two great women shared a common goal. To return the ways of love to a land besieged by madness, greed, and suffering.

Gabriella understood that any person or creature who broached this threshold with an intent other than love, was refused entry.

She smiled softly. Realizing why the Palace could never detect the presence of this tower. For the Palace could not acknowledge – or even comprehend – the power of love.

As so, as she whispered words of kindness, an incantation filled with all that she believed and held in her body and soul, the space between the hard edges of the ancient wooden door and the stone walls began to glow with soft light.

The threshold had been activated. The secret key placed in the lock.

And Gabriella felt a shift in pressure between the hate-infused reality on this side of the door and the deeply protected, love-infused reality inside the tower.

Gabriella thanked the Goddess for Adrian's magic. Creating a buffer between these two different realms. Without it, she suspected that she might cease to breathe. The pressure crushing her chest.

When the stress became almost unbearable, she heard a sharp CLICK. A huge release.

And, as the door swung open, Gabriella exhaled sharply and fell inside.

CHAPTER SEVEN

KATRIN HAD DEBATED LEAVING the Messenger's cause.

She grumbled to herself as she strode back from the local bakery, hood up over her face. And made her way to the grungy inn where she was staying. She was keeping as low a profile as a young, attractive woman could keep in a trader town.

Katrin moved quickly to get away from the main street, without going so fast that others assumed she was on the run or had stolen the bread under her arm. Her sharp gaze kept track of every other creature, whether person or animal. She was well-versed in watching her surroundings, while blending in.

She had been angry at Gabriella for disappearing in the middle of the night. Only a note left in her wake. But, truth be told, Katrin had not been surprised.

She tried not to be bitter. Katrin had not expected to be by Gabriella's side for long. But Katrin had grown used to being in her company. She enjoyed their banter and, even more, Katrin loved feeling helpful.

The sensation made her feel human again.

As she rushed forward, Katrin caught the delicious scent of her fresh bread. She had not expected such a gift in this mangy little town, but she was not about to question her good fortune. Besides, the scent of real bread made her think of home. And of Patrick.

Her one consolation to Gabriella's abrupt departure had been her time with Patrick. Katrin had spent several weeks with him while she awaited a message. A signal. Any indication that Gabriella wanted her on the next part of her journey.

As bruised as Katrin's heart was by Gabriella leaving her for a *second* time, Katrin savoured her time with the boy she had a hopeless crush on.

Katrin was mortified by how much she liked Patrick. And how foolish she may have acted around him. She groaned at the thought of it.

When her groan caught the ear of a nearby hound, he perked up his head and his owner took notice. Katrin quickly affected a limp to justify her complaint. The old man shook his head and grumbled something about "feeble and useless young people."

She smiled under the cover of her cloak. *Let him feel superior,* Katrin thought. *Better the old man think I am pathetic than a threat.* She cared little for the opinions of old men, even less the ones in remote trader towns.

She was within sight of her wretched inn, with its frayed boards and worn out colour that must have been painted when the inn was built. Katrin sighed and felt a second pang in her heart.

She could not help but compare this inn to the sweet, secretive locale where she first set eyes on her Patrick. *Oh please,* her mind chided. *He is hardly your Patrick. You mooned after him for weeks only to feverishly avoid any conversation about how you feel.*

Katrin tucked her face deeper under her hood. Ostensibly to avoid the heavy rain. But she felt embarrassed that not only had she been so affected by the sweet grandson of her mentor, she had been a coward in approaching him.

I can fight in the streets and break free from lawmen but cannot meet the gaze of a young man? Katrin thought. *How am I supposed to be worthy of helping the great Messenger and future Queen when I can barely speak my heart to a boy?*

She frowned and tromped faster on the muddy road. Grumbling to herself as she moved away from riders astride their horses and rogue children reveling in the final hour before curfew.

As the sun fell below the horizon, parents and shop-owners called in their urchins. Determined to keep them out of the reach of wild animals and even wilder men. The villagers knew well that small, remote towns like this one were easy targets.

Katrin pulled her cloak tight as though her body felt the approach of thieves. She needed to be more discreet. She struggled with that fact, given that she had traded her own body for protection in the past.

But she had the funds left by Gabriella, combined with a small amount that Patrick was able to give her. She would make it through the night and onward to her next destination.

Her thoughts strayed back to Patrick tucking the money into her palm. She had tried to refuse, but he was as strong-willed as she was. He held her gaze and pushed the money into her hand as she stepped out the door.

Katrin found a soft smile raising her lips, the memory lingering in her mind.

For a brief moment, her heart hoped that Patrick's kind gesture meant more. That maybe, just maybe, he had feelings for her. And had given her the last coins from his pocket knowing they might keep her safe.

A horse's whinny brought her back to her mucky reality. She

caught the stallion's spooked gaze and heard the rider's angry curse. Katrin tipped her head to avoid the rider's gaze.

She wanted to curse back but Katrin reined in her fiery nature so she could make it back to her room. She strode faster. *I am here for only one quick night*, she reminded herself. *So stop mooning over the boy you left behind and keep your hide safe.*

Katrin was finally was within stone's throw of the inn. She stepped up onto the sagging wooden boardwalk. *Focus on your damn mission*, Katrin thought. *This town does not matter. That rider does not matter. Patrick does not matter.*

Her heart leapt to protest this last notion. He did matter and her breaking heart was not going to let her forget it.

Even the Messenger has found love, she thought. Then quickly stifled that hope.

As she reached the leaky awning above the door, she growled at the sight of the lopsided sign. *Such a pathetic place to stay the night*, she thought. *Perfect for how I feel.*

Katrin poked her steel key into the lock, rattling it around until she heard the metal engage. She turned hard and the door popped open. She snuck inside as the last rays of sunlight creeped away from the dirty streets.

Inside, the light was barely brighter. *The innkeeper must be saving a fortune on lantern oil*, she thought. She wanted to grumble but found herself hearing Gabriella's voice.

Be grateful there is not extra light, Gabriella's memory whispered. *Better that no one notices you. You can slip away in the morning without a single person remembering that you were here.*

Katrin sighed at the feeling of past conversations with Gabriella keeping her safe.

She was brasher than her beloved mentor. Katrin preferred to start fights, prove her smarts, and see what she could get away with. The results were rarely what she desired, but the instigation made her feel alive.

In a town like this, though, it would get me killed, Katrin thought. *And where's the fun in that?*

She was learning. Perhaps even maturing. Either way, she needed to get to Cardea as soon as possible.

Or else miss the rendezvous that Gabriella's secret message foretold.

CHAPTER EIGHT

As the Hidden Palace watched the ridiculous pantomime in the Prince's study, she grew impatient.

She needed this charade until she could track down the traitorous Prince. Force him back into her belly to do her bidding. But until she found her little puppet, she had to deal with fools.

Children who clamoured over pearls. When she would possess kingdoms, oceans, and stars.

Despite her rage at the Prince's betrayal, she was impressed. The Palace imagined that this little spurt of rebellion would prove to make him a stronger King. Even more capable of wielding the power she desired.

The Palace remembered sensing his flight while he was within her reach. She deliberated whether to yank him back before he strayed too far. But she was confident in her control. *He will return to me when he discovers how much the world despises him,* she thought. *And how the Messenger will inevitably break his heart.*

The Palace reveled in the notion of the Prince's heart growing even darker. His craving for revenge would fuel her aim to possess every human's will.

She beamed with delight knowing the Prince would soon be back in her walls. And she would be on the verge of finally creating the vision of her Mad King. The one who had given her life. The one who whispered in *her* ear at the dark hours of the night.

Even now, she felt the King commanding. Felt his need for power. His dominance weakened as his son grew stronger. And as the rebels took a greater hold in the hearts of the people.

Fools! She raged. Shaking the walls and rattling the mortar, causing the young girls to whimper and their guardians to cringe.

The Palace reigned in her temper. Barely.

She did not care whether these humans lived or died, but she needed to maintain the pretense. She could not afford for the masses to think that the Prince fleeing was a sign of *hope.* The Palace growled.

Causing another minor quake. Barely perceptible, especially to ridiculously drunk idiots.

Fear not, soothed the spectre of the Mad King. And the Hidden Palace's heart fluttered. The hour had grown late. And the Mad King must have felt her displeasure.

She pulsed with dark passion as her maker and lord materialized within her walls. The foolish girls and men did not notice. They were so engrossed in the false Great Prince.

How could they miss this true spectacle of power! Though his spectre had grown weak as his power lessened. *Even still, he was magnificent!*

Ah, my beloved, the Mad King soothed. He appeared in his finest attire, as though on his way to a regal ball. But the sheen of his crown was tarnished, and the edges of his clothes were torn.

While the glint in his eye was pure insanity.

Fear not, he repeated. *We will rule all the realms, all the people, all the stars, my Sweet!* His mind had not recovered, even in death. He was as fixated as ever.

The Mad King moved behind the drunken men. Strolling so close that they shivered with cold. Feeling his dank breath. The Mad King stared at their necks, the pulse, the blood, as though he might sink his teeth into them. Purely to watch the gore spill.

The guardian looked around to see whether a window had been thrown open. Bowing fearfully to the imposter Great Prince, he shoved his empty goblet at the servant. "More," the guardian hissed.

Once his glass was full, he gulped the dark wine. Drowning his fear as quickly as it rose.

Yes, the Mad King repeated. *My son, the coward, has fled his duties. His promise. But he will not last in the wilds of the world on his own.*

How do you know? Asked the Palace. She had her own plan but was still eager to hear the Mad King's schemes.

The Mad King turned his rapacious attention to the youngest of the girls. Leering at the prospect of terrorizing an innocent soul. *He has no spine. Of that I made sure,* the Mad King said, striding around the maiden. *Every day of his pitiful life. I crushed his will. I stomped on his desires. I withheld all hope, until the only glimmer in his chest was to fetch what I wanted.*

The Mad King burst into manic laughter.

Thrilling every stone in the Palace's body and sending shivers through her mortar. The young woman fell to her knees in terror. Covering her ears, she burst into tears.

The Palace laughed as though attending a hilarious piece of theatre. She loved watching her King terrorize his people. Every stone in her body was sealed with hate and fear and rage. So when she witnessed those feelings, she shivered with the thrill of being reborn.

More! She cried, on the verge of losing control.

No, declared her Mad King, turning his back abruptly on the whimpering girl. *We must find my son. The Traitor. We must drag him back here to do my bidding. He must not be allowed to break free!*

The Mad King brought his fist down onto a table but his hand went straight through. Infuriating him. He focused his errant mind, grabbed a crystal goblet with both hands, and prepared to throw it.

No, my Liege! Shrieked the Palace.

No? spat the Mad King. *How dare you deny me! The greatest King ever to live? Your lord and master!*

Throw the glass, she appeased. *But it will put an end to this charade. And as insipid as these creatures are, we need them. At least until the Prince returns.*

The Mad King snarled. And tossed the goblet harmlessly onto the carpet. When no one noticed, the King glared at the Prince until the imposter cringed. He shivered and drank more mulled wine, desperate to numb the cold force that gripped his heart.

Bored with the humans already, the Mad King asked, *How do you propose to get my traitorous son to return?*

All in good time, my Liege, she cooed. He will soon discover how much his people despise him. Let him feel the illusion of freedom. Let his hope grow to a faint spark.

Why? Demanded the Mad King.

Because he will not know the fullness of despair unless we allow him the possibility of hope, she replied. If we give him a taste of freedom and then he discovers that the Messenger does not love him and his people hate him?

The Mad King's eyes gleamed in anticipation of her answer.

He will have tasted the poison of lost love, she declared. And he will never be the same again.

CHAPTER NINE

Tobias moved stealthily through the woods. Keeping an eye out for intruders.

He wasn't sure what he expected to find, if anything. His rounds were more about staying sane, much as he counselled Syrena.

Tobias had been alone long enough to know the dangers of his own mind. Being alone without his regal family had left him vulnerable to doubt. The lands that he patrolled missed them as dearly as he. And he felt fear pushing in on the edges of Granamore.

"I'll be damned if you're taking everyone that I love," Tobias swore under his breath.

Even with his declaration, his heart felt heavy. Tobias secretly wondered if they would ever break the spell that took Hannah. Shadowy thoughts tempted him to search for cruel vagabonds and punish them for bringing evil to these lands.

How would it feel? he wondered, as his feet guided him easily through the familiar woods. *Would the vengeance feel just? Like I had struck a blow for goodness?*

The thoughts brought a rush of adrenalin and a keen sense

of purpose. Yet, somewhere in the deepest corners of his heart, he felt it was the path to ruin.

"Rushing in has never served you well," the whisper spoke, startling Tobias from his reverie.

Tobias reacted swiftly. Drawing an arrow, he aligned his sight down his arm and peered through the trees. Ready to fire.

"Show yourself," he demanded, as he pierced the woods with his sharp hunter's gaze. Taking in the emptiness and mist. No sign of the intruder.

"You have spent too long alone," said the soft voice. "Why do you keep yourself separate from the ones you love?"

Having scanned the forest, Tobias aimed his sight up through the branches. His eyes were sharp, but his mind was flooded with doubt. *Have all these years of solitude had finally begun to affect my reason?* He wondered. *Am I inventing conversation to keep from going mad?*

"Come forward and speak with me," he ordered. "Only a coward hides his face."

Soft footfalls rustled through the birch leaves and fir needles. Tobias lowered his arrow slightly, grateful that the rogue was willing to show himself. But Tobias was confused by the fact that the energy coming his way did not feel aggressive. Rather, it felt loving and patient.

Tobias squared his shoulders. Braced for an ambush if this gentle approach was a trick.

"Approach slowly," he warned. Keeping his bow tight, if not aimed.

"These years have made you cynical, Tobias," the voice said. The mist hid the intruder, keeping Tobias on edge. Even more so with the use of his name.

"How do you know me?" Tobias questioned.

The form finally broke through the mists. Revealing a stunning and majestic Elk cow. She held her head high and gazed steadily at Tobias. Unflinching in the face of his taught bow.

"We have met before," she said. "But we have never spoken."

Tobias stared. He was wise in the ways of the woods – and understood that this was a rare visit. Others might believe a conversation with an Elk the effect of bad ale or a dream, though he did not recall falling asleep.

He, on the other hand, was schooled in the sacred wild ways. He had kept them secret. Much as Gabriella had done with her warrior training. He still hoped that, one day, they might speak of their hidden schooling. Bringing together their wisdom for the good of the lands.

Tobias held the Elk's gaze for a moment longer. Feeling into the exchange. He needed to be sure that he was not being tricked by a malevolent wizard. With Hannah already felled by magic, he could not take any chances.

"Why speak with me now?" he asked, narrowing his gaze.

The Elk tilted her head ever so slightly. He sensed her understanding.

Still, she stretched the silence between them. Testing his ability to trust. Tobias would have to meet her in the space between predator and prey. Each taking a risk to set aside instinct in order to come to a higher understanding.

Tobias exhaled. He felt the request. He was being asked to make himself vulnerable. To balance the scales between him and the Elk. It was a great risk if this was a trick. But if he did not, the Elk would leave. And he would not know her message.

Slowly, he released the tension in his bow. Pulling the arrow out and tucking it back in the quiver on his back. He laid the bow on the ground against his leg. Within reach, should any enemies appear, but far enough out of his grip to be respectful.

The Elk took a step closer, meeting his courage with a

gesture of her own. Showing her full form, knowing that if the hunter was fast, he could take her life with one shot.

"I have come for the sake of Granamore," she began. "As a messenger of the wild realm to counsel humans at this critical time in our path."

Tobias held still, listening intently. The warmth of the Elk's strength and love enveloped him. He kept one ear to the woods to keep them both safe. And he no longer questioned the gift of this meeting.

"The time has come for you to leave these lands," she continued. And she felt Tobias bristle. "You and Syrena have done all that you can for Hannah. Your quest lies beyond these borders."

"But who will keep her safe?" Tobias protested. "I will not leave the princess vulnerable."

"She is far from vulnerable," the Elk replied. "And anyone who believes her to be is a fool."

Tobias flinched. Her comment stung.

"Hannah is more powerful than you or Syrena have given credit," the Elk said. "Have you never wondered what she might have learned while Gabriella trained in the woods and you learned the secrets of animals?"

"I presumed she learned the ways of the court," Tobias replied. "She was being groomed to be the next Queen."

"Yes," said the Elk. "Her mother, the Queen, certainly wanted to keep her girls safe. But she also understood that their motherline possessed great power. She would not have left that exposed to the greed of tyrannical men.

Tobias had heard rumours of magic his whole life. Being so close to the Court, he could not help but overhear the gossip of maids and the musings of footmen.

"But she did," Tobias objected. "She sent Hannah off with the Great Prince. To live in a torturous Palace. And now look where she lays!"

"Calm yourself," the Elk soothed. "I know these have been hard years. Your heart is kind. And you have been asked to bear more than any one man should. But we must keep our voices low."

Tobias nodded, and swiftly checked around them. The woods were quiet, with the exception of the chattering of sparrows. He reigned in his temper. Though he was chastened, he felt better for releasing his rage.

"Are you saying that Hannah is safe?" Tobias asked. "Though she is asleep in a spell?"

"Yes," replied the Elk. "That is exactly what I am saying."

Tobias had so many questions. But the Elk had already drawn back. He felt she was preparing to leave.

"Take Syrena and leave," the Elk said. You will receive instruction where to go. And what to do." His brow furrowed with concern.

"I need you to trust the guidance of the elders, Tobias," counselled the Elk.

"But how will I convince Syrena?" he asked. "She needs reassurance." *As do I*, he thought, but held it back.

"While we have been talking, Syrena was led to a discovery," The Elk replied, as she retreated. "Trust that Hannah is safe. More than safe. She is the key."

With that mysterious word, the Elk disappeared as swiftly as she came.

Tobias felt her absence keenly. The warmth and love dissipated. And he was left wondering whether it had all been a trick.

He fell back against a tall maple tree. Flummoxed over his next move.

Syrena drilled her fingers into her hard, wooden stool. Staring at the hapless plants as though they were withholding information. The intensity of her loneliness and the need to puzzle out this spell had created a comfort in speaking aloud.

"You would insist that we live in a purposeful world," Syrena said to Hannah. "That there is reason behind this chaos…"

Syrena's gaze drifted over the plants that had been her companions for months. She was curious that they survived so well without her, or anyone, attending them. She presumed that the Queen's gardeners had built clever irrigation. Tending to the plants with minimal effort.

Her fingers stopped drilling. "But I have never checked…" She had caught the edge of an inkling. Syrena could feel it.

She leapt up. Moving slowly, her eyes on the flourishing plants that were a few feet out of reach. Most on elegant shelves, and some hanging in the air. As she peered closer, she caught sight of an iridescent purple dragonfly.

"What are you doing here so late in the season?" asked Syrena. The dragonfly lifted into the air and dropped onto another plant. Ignoring her question.

Syrena took a step, following the dragonfly. She was curious that she had never seen this creature before, when she had spent so many hours in the hothouse. She sensed the dragonfly was directing her.

"What could you have to show me that I have not seen in four months?" asked Syrena. She reigned in her annoyance. *And why did you not appear before now?* she growled inside. Syrena could feel Hannah's answer – a phrase that she loved to say. *Nothing comes before its time.*

The dragonfly swooped up into the air, catching Syrena's attention.

She marvelled at how fast the creature moved. And, for a moment, Syrena lost track of him. She whipped around. "Where are you?" she demanded. And a glint of light caught her peripheral vision.

Syrena swiveled to catch the dragonfly SWOOSHING up and around the plants. He danced like an autumn leaf caught in a wild windstorm. And she wondered what got him so worked up.

"Slow down!" She insisted. "How am I supposed to follow what you are saying, when you are moving like a crazed squirrel dashing between trees."

Syrena stopped. Struck by the pattern that the dragonfly was weaving. She stared, and lifted as far up as her toes would take her. "No way..." Syrena murmured.

She turned, scanning the hothouse for the ancient wooden ladder. Spotting it tucked in a corner, Syrena sprinted over. Wiping away the cobwebs, she grabbed it and dragged it back to the area where the dragonfly still hovered.

Propping the ladder against the sturdy shelf, she climbed up to get a closer look.

When she reached the edge, Syrena peered down the long row of plants. The dragonfly drifted down and landed elegantly on a lavender plant.

"Lavender," she whispered, as though chastened by her discovery. Syrena touched a lavender blossom close to her and inhaled the familiar comforting scent.

Her inkling sparked into a full-blown idea. Syrena methodically went through each plant that was carefully selected, and tucked out of sight, on these upper shelves.

"Dill, coriander, rosemary," she whispered with reverence. "Basil, bay leaf, cloves, and fennel."

Every plant that Syrena saw could easily be explained as necessary for the castle kitchens. Except she also saw what purpose every last one of these plants shared when in the hands of someone who understood magic.

"Protection," Syrena said. She leaned on the shelf and looked down with fresh eyes on a peaceful Hannah.

"Someone was looking out for you," Syrena pondered. "Someone who foresaw this occurrence."

Syrena turned, "Maybe you know," she began, expecting to see her purple companion. But he was gone. She raked her eyes over every plant, and there was no sign of the dragonfly.

"What in the stars..." she wondered. The dragonfly had vanished as suddenly as it had appeared.

Syrena leaned back on the ladder, brow furrowed. "Whoever created this collection was special indeed," she mused. "Crafty and secretive." Her eyes drifted over Hannah's beautiful face. "And loved you very much."

She had a guess. And was not going to speak it aloud. Syrena's thoughts drifted. A theory was forming and was fueling her more than water, food, and sunshine.

Syrena felt fully alive for the first time since Hannah fell. "If this magic is any indication, there must be something extraordinary about you. Something that matches your sister. Whoever put this magic in place could not have known which twin would fall. Unless she had the sight."

Her gaze sharpened and locked onto her serene lover. Syrena slowly climbed back down.

"If Gabriella was born to fight the Great Prince and defeat the Hidden Palace, what was your purpose, Hannah Grace?"

The spark of an idea caught fire. Dancing in one direction then another. Exploring possibilities and all kinds of wild inspiration.

"If anyone was to be underestimated, it would be you." Syrena mused. "Even I was distracted by Gabriella's power. Assuming that your presence in the Palace was the act of a desperate father."

Syrena felt a vision coming to her mind. The clarity was

palpable. She closed her eyes. Needing to focus. Years of practising magic taught her that there was only one way to dance with mysterious forces. That was to surrender. And pray to come out with a mystical compass.

She sought that compass. A strange and magical guide to make sense of this journey.

Syrena let go of her thoughts and fell back into the quiet of her soul, opening to the whisperings of the Divine. She was strangely at ease in the darkness. No thoughts. No worries. She breathed into the calm. Trusting that the Divine, or perhaps Hannah's ancestors, would reveal a truth.

As she fell into a trance, she understood why she had not left Hannah's ancestral lands. She needed to be close to Hannah's people. To feel the connection to her parents and her lineage. To be ready to receive their secrets.

Truths that had been silent for years.

A question arose in the serene darkness. A query that illuminated Syrena's intuitive resolve to keep her lover safe.

What if Hannah possessed a power so profound that it had been hidden even from her?

As Syrena drifted back to her body, she felt the cold air nip at her hands. The stone chilled her feet. She pulled her wool cloak closer. Her risk had paid off with an intriguing reward.

A prospect so magical that Syrena was unsure what to do.

She shivered as she looked at Hannah's sweet face. Knowing that she was standing next to a more powerful being than anyone imagined.

CHAPTER TEN

GABRIELLA PEERED past the door up a long and winding staircase. She could not see where the steps went but she felt the softness of warmth and safety.

She glanced over at Adrian, who nodded. *I'm not sure that the Guardian of the Tower wants me to enter,* he said inside her mind. *You must take this journey without me.*

The way feels safe, Gabriella replied. *I don't believe she wishes me any harm. And I am sure that the Palace has no knowledge of this place.*

I still don't like leaving you to walk on your own, Adrian said.

She won't be alone, Magician, said a firm, loving voice.

Adrian and Gabriella turned sharply to see the spectre of a Queen from a long-gone era. She stood with confidence and grace. A smile on her face from having surprised the two interlopers.

Gabriella knew she already liked this woman. Any ruler with a sense of humour was a gracious gift. Even better that she kept Adrian on his toes.

Come, insisted the Guardian Queen, *we do not have much time.*

How so? Adrian questioned. *The Palace cannot reach her here.* Gabriella shot him a look. She trusted the Queen and was irritated by his query.

The Palace may not see this Tower or have access to it, the Guardian Queen replied. *But that does not mean that she does not sense a rebellion under her roof.*

The Guardian Queen spoke to Gabriella. *I would rather not draw her attention to it unwittingly. And it is only a matter of time before the Palace and her Mad King find the Great Prince.*

You know where the Prince is? Gabriella said, hope lifting her voice. She felt Adrian tense then quickly gain control.

Come Child, the Guardian Queen said, turning to climb the stairs. *We can discuss such matters in the Tower. A safe distance from the Palace's spies.*

Wait, Adrian insisted. The Guardian Queen turned back, her demeanor calm. But she was losing patience.

Adrian respected that she outranked him in nobility and age, but he had to ask. *You said, the Mad King. Is he in the Palace?*

Yes, said the Guardian Queen. *Though he is weakened by his son's absence. So, if the Palace or the King bring him back, we will all pay the price. No one more than the Prince himself.*

Shall we? She insisted, looking at Gabriella.

We shall, replied Gabriella, crossing over the mists that clung to the door's threshold, and following up the winding staircase. She focused on the Queen rather than looking back.

Gabriella trusted that Adrian understood. Though she felt how troubled he was by the appearance of the Mad King.

His concern is fair, Gabriella thought. *But I must follow where the path leads.*

Gabriella felt like they climbed forever before coming into a small and warm abode. She smiled in wonder as they entered the private chambers. The space had the feel of a cozy cabin in the woods, complete with a small bedroom, a kitchen for making meals, and a sitting area with a bird's eye view of the mountain range.

The Queen stepped graciously aside as Gabriella walked the circumference of the rooms. Lightly hovering her hand over the single bed, the wood stove, the array of cups and plates, and the soft chairs turned toward the light of the window.

The tower felt impossibly bright for the size of the windows in the stones. Yet the love radiating inside created a feeling of sunshine beaming from every corner.

"*Thank you*," said Gabriella, grateful for the time to envision the Prince in this sanctuary.

"Of course," replied the Guardian Queen. "We can speak openly. We are safe from the prying ears of the Hidden Palace and those she has enslaved. I only wish we had more time. There is much that I wish to share with you. But the Prince has been frozen on the edge of his ancestral lands. And will soon be in grave danger."

"Why? Is he frozen with fear?" Gabriella asked, concerned, "Or by magic?"

The Guardian Queen floated toward the sitting area. Her elegant shoes hovered above the rich carpet. She took a seat and gestured toward the other. She did not need to sit, but the Queen had discovered that the living were unsettled by her floating.

Gabriella sat, in deference to the Queen, throwing back her hood. But she felt impatient now that she knew the Prince needed help.

"Fear," the Queen replied. And Gabriella sighed with relief.

"He has much to overcome," the Queen began. "These lands have many layers of suffering. Generations of dark desires that built chains upon chains of magic. All designed to keep the people enslaved to the obsessive power of the Mad King."

"I never met the Mad King," Gabriella remarked. "Though I have heard the tales."

"Count yourself lucky," said the Guardian Queen. "He was born to an evil and destructive lineage. He proved worthy of their dark power in every way. From a young age he showed signs of cruelty, consumed by a need to control."

The Guardian Queen sighed. "Some members of our clan wished for another way. But any who resisted the tyranny were quickly put to death. Or worse, they were tortured for intolerable expanses of time. The result was effective. The objectors ran away."

"Did any escape?" Gabriella asked.

"Some," replied the Queen, her eyes filled with sadness. "But their choice to flee condemned their younger kin."

"How so...?" Gabriella began, then realized the answer. "The King made these lands a prison. Beyond the Palace walls."

"Precisely. Spells were cast. Magical barricades were forged. Yet, no outside wall is as imprisoning as the desperate need to please a parent or the compulsion to fulfill an ancestral expectation. The magic we hold in our own blood works more powerfully than any other."

Gabriella understood this compulsion. She hoped she had chosen well on her path. *Will I ever truly know*, she wondered. A wave of compassion for the Prince filled her heart.

"Does the Prince understand what torments him?" asked Gabriella.

"Not really," replied the Queen. "Even worse, he blames himself. Which only draws the spell tighter."

The Guardian Queen saw Gabriella shiver. She had been so determined to tell her tale that she had been a terrible host. The Queen waved her hand, conjuring a steaming hot pot of tea with a delicate matching cup. Beside the pot was a plate of hot scones with jam and cream.

"I forgot that you must be famished," the Queen said, and smiled at Gabriella's surprise.

"How –" she began. Then, at the insistent wave of the Queen's hand, Gabriella helped herself to tea and to a scone with ample amounts of cream and jam. She melted inside at the first bite.

"These are heavenly," she sighed. "Thank you."

"You would be surprised how my magic has enhanced since I crossed the veil."

Gabriella leaned in, "Tell me." She had so many questions.

"Another day, child," said the Queen. "Today, we must focus." Gabriella nodded. But the Queen felt her keen disappointment.

Gabriella cradled the steaming hot tea in her hands, letting the liquid soothe her tired nerves. She had so few moments of simple pleasures. She was grateful for a brief respite.

"How did the Prince break free in the first place?" asked Gabriella, sipping from her cup.

"The Palace was consumed with Vanora's defeat, which gave him the chance to shake her chains. And the Prince's love for you gave him the courage to act," replied the Queen. She smiled sadly. "But, he did not realize that was the first of many hurdles."

"It is only a matter of time before his father finds him," Gabriella whispered. She rose quickly, prepared to leap to his aid.

"Wait," said the Queen. Gabriella stopped, but remained standing.

"You cannot rescue him from this battle, Gabriella," the Queen added. "Much as you care for him. The Prince must fight his lineage on his own."

"Why?" Gabriella protested. But something inside her whispered the truth.

"You know why," said the Queen. "We bear the mark of our

history. And only we can choose another way. It is up to the Prince to forge a different future for his line."

The Queen felt sympathy for Gabriella. "You know this lesson well. You have been walking it for years. The Prince must prove to himself that he can break free. Your wisdom and faith cannot help him. Love him and pray for him. But do not run to his aid."

Gabriella dropped back into her chair. For the first time since returning to the Palace, she felt despondent.

CHAPTER ELEVEN

ADRIAN HOVERED by the Tower door. He knew Gabriella was safe and, still, he had not left his post. Echoes of dark revelry drifted up from the lower reaches of the Palace.

Their voices were barely audible at this farthest reach of the northwest corner. Yet he could feel the ripples of dark magic.

The Palace is working hard to keep a hold on her people, he thought. Adrian was tempted to go down. To observe what strategy the Palace was deploying now that the Prince had escaped.

The idea was alluring, but unwise. *If I leave this shrouded area, I will be detected,* Adrian thought. *And that will put Gabriella at risk.*

He considered returning to his body on the mountain top. The reconnection would restore him, and sharpen his mind. The idea of sleep was so tempting. Adrian craved a rest more than he desired a hot meal. His felt his stomach growl. And sighed.

No matter, he thought. *I will not leave her side.* She is safe until she leaves the Tower. So I will wait.

As he sat waiting on the Tower's threshold, his mind

wandered to his other companions. Adrian was concerned about Syrena and Hannah. Once again, Adrian saw a vision of Hannah frozen in sleep and Syrena pacing at her side. He received this intuition too often to question its truth.

He felt the inevitable pull to go to Syrena. To guide her and free Gabriella's sweet twin. But he could not abandon his mission. He had to stay focused.

How did this happen? Adrian mused, puzzling out his vision. Comforting himself with the idea that this might make him better able to help once he joined Syrena.

Adrian sensed the shimmering threads of fate. Tying the Hidden Palace to Granamore's Castle, where the twins had been raised. He wondered what bound these two families together.

Whatever it is, the Fates are most definitely involved, Adrian grumbled. *The cruel and unimaginable desires of the Gods.*

His dark mood was a warning. Caused by hunger and exhaustion. Soon, he would have no choice but to eat. The toll of reaching into a third destination to check on Syrena and Hannah had depleted his strength.

If I travel back to the mountain, Adrian thought, *I could restore myself with food and rest. Then speak to Syrena. She needs my help more than Gabriella.*

He cast a glance at the door behind him. The Queen's magic blocked any opportunity to hear what they were saying. *Heaven knows how long those two will speak of family secrets*, he thought. *And what good will I be if Gabriella returns to find I have fallen asleep or succumbed to darkness? Better that I tend to my health and find out more about her sister.*

Adrian was curious what magic kept Gabriella from knowing that her twin was caught in a sleeping spell. With that thought, Adrian understood that there was more than one way to look out for Gabriella.

And he promptly disappeared.

~

Adrian shivered as he returned to his physical body on the mountain. Night had fallen and his temperature had plummeted.

No wonder I am tired, Adrian grumbled at his lack of preparation. Flexing his stiff fingers, he gave his limbs a moment to acknowledge the return of his spirit.

When he travelled, it was as though his physical being went into hibernation. Forcing it to move too quickly led to cramping and pain. Slowing everything down. This, he learned that the hard way.

Like I learn almost everything, Adrian joked.

Laughter was his antidote to arrogance. He did not always fault over-confidence. He needed to accomplish the outrageous notions that he came in his visions. But it was a dangerous tool, like wielding a sword.

Arrogance may embolden the spirit, but it also fueled reckless assumptions, Adrian thought. He shivered, and rubbed his feet to get some feeling back. *Like assuming you can withstand a high mountain night without any cover while spirit travelling to two locations.*

He growled at his own stupidity. Then a mischievous smile took over. He could not help but be amused. Especially now that he was safe and feeling returned to his hands and feet.

As much as he appreciated his ability to travel, there was no greater joy than being present in a strong body. And for that he was grateful.

Adrian slowly reached for the pack at his side. He pulled out a tightly woven grey blanket and wrapped it around his legs. Sighing at the immediate warmth. He dug further into the enchanted pack and retrieved dried meat and fruit.

Placing a piece on his tongue, he savoured the taste and the nourishment.

Within seconds, he spotted bright eyes in the darkness. The wind carried the scent quickly. And this rocky peak offered few options for prey.

Besides me, he thought.

He took another bite and felt power returning to his blood. Without food, his magic dwindled quickly. And he had gone hours without sustenance in a climate that demanded most of his resources to stay alive.

"You will not find me tasty," he said to the predator. Focusing his gaze and gleaning a shape under the light of the Northern stars. The moon was barely a crescent but the starlight in these far mountains was bright.

The creature was well-hidden behind boulders and highland brush. He could not see the body, but Adrian knew by the gleaming eyes and the soft tufted ears that he was being watched by a wild mountain lynx.

He risked another bite of dried venison. His blood felt stronger and the rush of fear danced in his muscles. Adrian focused the intense feeling and projected it as his predatory response.

The wildcat responded, tucking further back into the bush. Questioning its instinct to attack.

Adrian did not have the magical strength back to appear as a Highland Bear or Peak Lion, either of which would scare off the smaller lynx. But he did have enough to mimic their scent.

Confusing the wildcat just enough to doubt it could win this fight, no matter the demand of its stomach. *One more bite and I can fake a roar*, thought Adrian.

He had others to speak with, and the sooner the better. So Adrian took another bite, risking the scent tormenting the lynx. Then followed swiftly with a powerful roar.

The gleaming eyes disappeared, and the crunch of wild heather and brush echoed the retreat of the lynx. Adrian sighed with relief. He popped the last bite of venison in his mouth, followed by a handful of dried cherries. The sugar flooded his senses and sharpened his mind.

"Okay, Syrena," he said, feeling confident in his strength to ward off any attackers. "What haven't you been telling me?"

Syrena was more like him than any other of their circle. She held secrets close to her chest. Not for fear of protecting herself, but rather because she put the safety of the group first.

And always respected the mission.

CHAPTER TWELVE

Night had fallen and the Great Prince paced among the trees. Back and forth, wearing a path in the soft pine needles. His steps mirrored the battle waging in his mind.

I am tired of being afraid, he thought. *If I had known this was the price for feeling, I might not have left the Palace at all.*

He glanced around at the dark forest. Full of shadows and strange, creaking noises. *What possessed me to leave?* He wondered. *I haven't even made it down out of the mountains. This is a fool's errand. One I seem incapable of fulfilling.*

His thoughts whirred to dark and punishing places. Lashing at the very core of him for believing that he could ever be free of his father or his ancestors. To think he believed that he had a greater destiny! They laughed at him. Mocking him for thinking he was anything without the power of his bloodline.

The Prince felt surrounded by ghosts. He had not seen them slink through the forest, but there they were. Poking and clawing and laughing at him. Wispy bodies and demented faces. Swooping round and round as he cowered from their touch.

Run home, little Prince, they mocked. *Your people will never love you. Neither will the Messenger. No one loves the Dark Prince. You destroyed this land and their families. They will hate you forever. They will hunt you down and chew on your bones.* Nice!

The Prince covered his ears. Fending them off with his crouched back. He turned one way then the other. Fear swirled in him. But the more they poked, the more his fear began to shift.

They want me to be afraid, he thought. *They're counting on me returning to my father's side. To grovel for his attention. To believe that I belong in that dark and haunted place.*

Terror moved over to make space for fury. Rage swirled inside his blood.

He unfurled his back and rose to his feet. He stared, unflinching, at the swooping ghosts.

Under his direct gaze, they flickered for a moment. Then redoubled their efforts.

That's right, little Prince, the spirits taunted. *Feel the rage of your ancestors. Defy the pathetic claims of the grovelling classes. They are not your people. They are flies on the back of a regal steed. Nipping and pestering. You must be with the ones worthy of you. You belong on the throne above everyone else. Claiming your true power.*

The Prince winced at their shrieking voices. Their needling claims hurt his skin as though they were fine-pointed blades heated over a hot flame.

Something about their tone sounded eerily familiar. An icy shiver rippled up the Prince's back. He sensed the Palace's influence and cowered away. Shaking his head. Refusing to return to that cold, possessive place. He pulled deeper into the forest and paced faster among the trees.

The Foxtail Pine, Whitebark Spruce, and Regal Larch elders towered high above the Prince at the edges of his circular clearing. They watched with patience. Observing as the Prince fought with himself, and in truth, his bloodline.

They understood the war he waged better than most. Their patient ways were different than humankind. But the tree elders had lived long enough to witness the shift from generosity to brutality and greed.

The Prince was waging an ancient battle. One that kept humans in cages of fear. Cages that got stronger the longer people insisted they were real.

He had not been raised with any other truth. In a Palace filled with rage, neglect, and madness, the Prince had only heard faint whispers of love from his long-deceased aunt. And those whispers felt as unreal to the Prince as the fairy tales read to children.

Of course, the trees knew fairy tales were real. As real as love.

We must figure out a way to assist him, the Foxtail Pine insisted, observing the Prince's torment with compassion. *He has no one else. And his freedom ensures our way of life.*

We cannot choose self-preservation above his will, countered the Whitebark Spruce.

Why ever not? said the Regal Larch, furious that the whims of humans always took precedence over their survival. *I am tired of respecting the gluttonous whims of humans. We must take a stand for our kind or we will never see the dawn of the new century.*

You know why not, said the Whitebark Spruce, as she took notice of the pattern that the Prince's steps wove in their high mountain kingdom.

The royal leaders could not disregard that the Prince paced in a magical clearing positioned exactly at the meeting point of their three territories. A clearing that had been used for regal summits for millennia. They knew this was no mistake. His choice reflected a hope that stretched far beyond the Prince's personal will.

Somehow, the fates were shifting.

They observed, fascinated, as his footsteps wore a path that stretched from one end of the circle to the other. Muttering out loud, barely conscious of his steps, he would reach a contentious argument, make an abrupt turn and wear a line in another direction. He seemed unaware that he was slowly and steadily drawing a pattern.

An ancient and powerful symbol. The sacred star of the feminine.

The tree elders felt this was a call. A sign that the power of collective wisdom and generous leaders was rising. Harkening back to a time when the heart ranked above the mind. The soul above the ego. And the will of the people informed the choices of royalty.

The Prince wove this symbol, over and over, through the night. On the cusp of a new moon.

While the Pine, Spruce, and Larch Elders agreed that the Great Prince was an unlikely harbinger, they could not deny it. Somehow this strange and obsessive man played a role in the rising of a new, yet ancient, way.

They watched him carefully, grateful that this sign had emerged in their territory and not somewhere far riskier. That might have been disastrous. The fates led this Prince to their safe haven so that they might tend to him while he waged this soul battle.

The elders were nervous that word of this hope would drift into the world before humans were ready. Their leaders, besides a few cloaked in secrecy, were far from prepared to make a stand against the kind of darkness that ruled.

You must admit, whispered the Whitebark Spruce Oracle.

This is a fortuitous sign. The first since the Messenger accepted her mission.

I do admit it, said the Regal Larch Queen. *But I am tired of standing by and wishing that humans will make the right choice. We must have a say.*

You make a fair point, agreed the Foxtail Pine King. He sensed the Whitebark Spruce Oracle was about to chime in with the wisdom of the ages. But he wanted the Regal Larch Queen to be heard. And he knew his own people shared her sentiments.

We must tend to this soul, said the Foxtail Pine King. *He clearly has a role to play. The fates have led him to us. So that he can fight the battle inside before he wages a war outside.*

He is a frightened little man, and dangerous to boot, objected the Regal Larch Queen.

That may be so, said the Whitebark Spruce Oracle, *but fear can beget courage. And courage is the virtue needed to make this monumental change. Remember, my Sister, humans do not have our prudence. They are plagued with fears that cloud their minds. And they lost all their wise leaders.*

They killed all their wise leaders, corrected the Regal Larch Queen. *The humans brought this dark age on themselves. And on us.*

It is true, mused the Foxtail Pine King, as he watched the Great Prince. *But have you not wondered whether something provoked them to turn on one another? That some strange spark of magic lit this destructive fire?*

The three elders shook at the notion of fire, sending a shower of soft needles cascading down. Snapping the Prince from his obsessive thoughts. He gazed up, charmed by the needles drifting like snowflakes. And sighed at the sight of swaying trees and softly shining stars.

As the Prince relaxed, the Elders gazed down with a glimmer of optimism. And a strange feeling of protectiveness. They could not help but wish the future might be different, as this Prince wrestled his demons go before the fresh hope of a new moon.

Oh, dear heaven, sighed the Regal Larch Queen. *I cannot believe I am about to say this ...*

The Foxtail Pine King and Whitebark Spruce Oracle waited with curiosity.

We have been asked to adopt this wretched soul, she continued. *To shield him from his lineage. Until he has the strength to fight their cruel ways.*

The three elders leaned in a little closer. Fascinated by this turn of fate.

Sheltering the Great Prince from the crisp, cold of the night. Radiating a love toward him that he had never experienced before in all his days.

CHAPTER THIRTEEN

GABRIELLA'S MIND WORKED QUICKLY. Attempting to figure out how to help the Prince, without directly helping him.

"My dear child," laughed the Queen. "Has your Magician not taught you to hide your thoughts?"

Gabriella was startled by her comment. "Of course. How --?"

The Queen smiled, pleased to share her talents. She had so few joys while on assignment in this remote tower in a possessed Palace. She knew the hourglass was running low.

Still, the Queen crossed her legs and savoured the girl's company. She could not help but indulge a little. Especially as she knew the Prince was being aided by the Counsel of Tree Elders.

"My intuitive powers were strong when I walked this earth," she replied, her eyes sparkling. "And unlike you, dear Gabriella, I lived in a time that did not fear such power in a woman."

Gabriella held back a growl. She had scores to settle with this time in her land's history.

"Yes," the Queen advised. "Hone and direct that rage. It will serve you well. If only to light righteous fires in others. Directing them to act shrewdly, rather than wreaking havoc."

Gabriella nodded, while making note that she needed to train harder at disguising her feelings.

"When I was born," said the Queen, "my parents celebrated my abilities. They had no need to hide my gifts, as yours did. Powerful women were prized for their wisdom and courage. Male leaders did not view them as a threat. Or a tool."

"And if they were fortunate enough to be born with magic?" she continued. "They were quickly allied with the regal line. Then trained and encouraged."

At the fleeting look that crossed Gabriella's face, the Queen added, "Openly and with pride. Not covertly, as was your case."

"I was lucky to have been helped by people who believed in me," Gabriella replied.

"Yes," said the Queen. "But would they have done so if your Kingdom had survived the Prince's attack?"

Gabriella levelled a fierce gaze at the Queen. She wished she could say that her family would have trained her regardless. But she was not sure that they saw her talents as a blessing, rather than a curse.

Her mother had told her tales of a time when warrior women were revered. But Gabriella felt her mother's fear every day as a child. Her concern that her daughters would bring death to their door.

"Your mother feared for your life, not her own," advised the Queen.

"Stop that," objected Gabriella.

"Then by all means," said the Queen, "stop declaring your thoughts to the entire land."

Gabriella froze, as a notion dawned in her mind. Her eyes went wide and she stared at the Queen. A shiver rippled up then back down her spine, confirming her suspicion.

She leapt to her feet. "You," she began, her thoughts racing. "You're not here to tell me about the Prince."

"No," the Queen replied, watching Gabriella closely.

"And you're not here to keep me from chasing after him," Gabriella continued.

"Correct," said the Queen.

"You are here..." Gabriella hesitated. The Queen nodded gently, encouraging her.

Gabriella coaxed herself to keep breathing. "You are here... for me."

"Exactly," replied the Queen, her face lit up with a delighted smile. With the secret revealed, the Queen released her full power, illuminating the tower. And dazzling Gabriella.

"I made sure whispers of the Prince's escape reached you," said the Queen. "I knew you would feel compelled to return. To see with your own eyes, rather than trust a rumour. To make sure he was truly free."

She paused, gesturing with her hand. "And here you are."

Gabriella's knees went weak. And she dropped into her chair.

CHAPTER FOURTEEN

Syrena wondered what had set her on this path that held many aches and bruises.

She sighed. Syrena had lived a life of the burdened heart. She was well familiar with the feeling of heartbreak. But as she took Hannah's hand, gazing on her quiet features, a rush of warmth filled her chest.

The world was a cruel and unstable place until Hannah came into her life.

On that day, a seed of hope was planted in Syrena's heart. She began to believe in the balance of all things. Love that metred hate. Warmth that made up for cold. A fed belly that fulfilled on the promise of hunger.

Hannah had restored her to life. And Syrena would return the gift. Against all odds, Syrena had known profound love. For that, she would always make the trade with hardship.

She caressed Hannah's hand. Reminding her lover that she was with her, no matter where their quest led. She held it for one more moment before placing it gently on the stone table.

Syrena fortified her heart to leave Hannah. She directed her gaze away. Not sure whether one more glance would crush her determination to leave and find the key to this spell.

A key she was sure must be somewhere in the wilds of this family's land.

She would speak to Tobias and convince him to stay with Hannah. The time had come for them to switch duties. Of that she was sure.

"Though Tobias might have other notions," Syrena muttered.

"Notions of what?" a voice inquired, startling her. Syrena readied herself to fight or cast magic, whichever vanquished the intruder faster.

She whirled to see the spectre of Adrian, standing in the doorway, arms crossed over his chest. A bemused smile on his face.

Until his eyes fell on Hannah. Struck down by magic. Adrian felt Syrena's thought of bolting past him while he was distracted. He stared her down.

"Notions of what, Syrena?" Adrian said again.

"Notions of keeping me from my quest," Syrena replied, knowing there was no point lying to Adrian.

"To find the secret to breaking this dark magic," Adrian spoke with compassion. He would do the same for Gabriella in a heartbeat.

But his role was to counsel Syrena. Not enable her rashness.

"I'm hardly being rash, wizard," Syrena shot back, impressing Adrian with her ability to read him. Though, this time, he purposefully did not block her.

Adrian moved toward her. "You are itching for a fight, Syrena. An adversary you can see."

"So what if I am?" Syrena asked.

"How do you think that will go?" he asked.

"I do not care as long as I find an answer," Syrena growled. "Do you want me to stay here? As frozen as my beloved?"

"Of course not," Adrian admonished. "How long has she been like this?"

"You hardly need me to tell you," grumbled Syrena.

Adrian replied only with patient silence. And Syrena sighed. "Four months."

"Why leave now?" he asked. Adrian felt the pulse of her defensive rage. His question held no judgement. But Syrena's guilt insisted otherwise. Her hands curled into clenched fists.

"I am not questioning your judgement. Or your love." Under his words, he sent a pulse of compassion.

Syrena softened and spoke in a quiet voice. "I believe that there is something as special about Hannah as there is about Gabriella."

She expected Adrian to contradict her. Instead, he said, "Go on."

Feeling his interest, Syrena permitted her eagerness. "What if Hannah was not some hapless victim of her father's strategy? What if she was always meant to be sent to the Hidden Palace? What if –"

"She, too, shares the magical lineage of their ancestors," Adrian finished her thought. And his brow furrowed.

"Yes!" Syrena exclaimed. She wanted to shake him with exuberant appreciation. *He didn't think she was crazy. He knew what she was talking about!*

She could see that Adrian was ruminating. She wanted to jump, to lunge, to run. *How was he so calm? And why did his forehead crease?*

"We need to know more," she continued. "I need to get out and comb her family's lands for the secret. The reason she was sent to the Great Prince years ago. Why she felt compelled to return here. What if this spell was not a trap but a stasis? Keeping Hannah safe until her next mission."

"That is quite a leap, Syrena," Adrian said. "To think a sleeping spell was forethought protection."

Syrena stepped closer and lowered her voice. "Is it not possible, Adrian, that Hannah was sent deliberately to the Great Prince. Perhaps, she was the precursor to Gabriella's arrival. And that somehow this spell might also be a precursor? One that Hannah sought out instinctively?"

Adrian stared into her sharp eyes. She was passing him a secret message. Woven into her words. He felt the magic. He just had to find it.

Like a glimmering fairy light on the edge of his perception, he waited patiently. Knowing it would land. One more moment... then swiftly, it dropped into his mind. Taking his breath away. The magical insight rippled through him, as though he was lit up by a message from many moons ago.

Adrian couldn't believe he had never considered this. And yet, he knew why he had not. Because even he had been fooled by Hannah's misleadingly innocent path. He had not asked the questions that now seemed so obvious.

The twins were inextricably linked, as only fate decreed.

Just as Gabriella felt compelled to rescue Hannah, Hannah felt compelled to resist her twin's guidance not to go home. This latest turn must be the next step.

Adrian's gaze flitted to the frozen Hannah. *Incredible*, he thought.

A smile teased the edges of Syrena's mouth, as she watched Adrian. His face was stoic, yet Syrena felt his delight all the same. Their hearts leapt with hope. As restrained as they looked, their eyes sparkled with their shared secret.

Adrian was careful to speak to Syrena's mind. *You think there is more to this than protection.*

Syrena gave a slight nod. *I do believe it is designed to keep Hannah safe. But I also suspect that she is waiting. For what, I am not sure.*

And Adrian responded with a mischievous look. *But that changes everything. She is no longer the prey. She might even be the bait.* He was so excited by this prospect that it took all his will not to wrap his ghostly arms around Syrena.

Her eyes went wide as she sensed his impulse. Adrian merely smiled. Syrena was surprised by her flush of disappointment.

"Wait," Syrena said, her tone shifting. In her rush for Adrian's understanding, she had forgotten about the Messenger. "Where is Gabriella? Shouldn't you be looking after her?"

"She's in very good hands," Adrian smiled, appreciating Syrena's fierce devotion. "Which means I am free to help in any way you need."

And Syrena smiled. For the first time in months.

PART II
REVELATION

CHAPTER ONE

GABRIELLA'S MIND RACED. She needed to recover from this unexpected turn.

Yet she struggled to grasp the consequences. *How could this be*, she wondered. *No one would prepare this far in advance. No one could possibly have predicted --*

"May I assist?" asked the Queen, amused by the frustration that flitted across Gabriella's face.

"I understand that you have few rivals for your talents," said the Queen, and held up a hand to stem any protest. "But you've not had the delight of working with me."

Gabriella was past being polite. If the Queen was going to read her thoughts, she may as well speak them. Not even Adrian snuck past her defenses so easily.

"How on earth could anyone have predicted that I would need your help? Let alone that I would come to you?" demanded Gabriella. "The chances are infinitesimal."

"My child –" said the Queen.

"Gabriella," insisted the Warrior. "Please do me the respect of acknowledging the battles I have fought. I am not a child."

"Yet, you are still not asking the question that weighs down your heart," replied the Queen.

Gabriella felt the Queen's power surge. *She has been holding back*, thought Gabriella. *How can she be so controlled?*

For the first time in years, Gabriella felt intimidated. Possibly unworthy of what was being asked of her.

"Call me by my name," the Queen said, placing a comforting hand on Gabriella's. "Chancelry. It will ease your concerns."

"Unlikely," Gabriella replied. And the Queen laughed.

"I had no idea how delightful this would be," replied the Queen. "It was worth the wait."

"Why would you be here for me?" asked Gabriella. "You're the Prince's kin. In his Palace. It makes no sense that you would wait decades..."

The Queen gestured with her hands, indicating a much longer stretch of time.

"Centuries?" ventured Gabriella. And the Queen nodded.

"Dearest," the Queen began, then saw Gabriella's shoulders tense. "Gabriella. I would rather not debate the vast and unknowable ways of the Great Mystery. At least, let me tell you this..."

The Queen paused to wave her hand and replenish the tea. Followed by a quick snap of her fingers to bring forth a basket of piping hot bread and a tray of cheese, dried fruit, and cured meats.

She gestured for Gabriella to eat, knowing that the child's belly was empty, even if she refused to say anything. And if she felt nauseous at this turn of events, the bread would certainly help.

When Gabriella shook her head, Chancelry folded her arms. Gabriella did not doubt that the Queen was her match in stubbornness. She sighed and tore off a piece of bread to placate her.

The delicious aroma provoked a growl from Gabriella's traitorous stomach. And Chancelry smiled.

Gabriella relented, stuffing the bread with olives and cheese, then took a bite. When delight washed over Gabriella's face, Chancelry felt a surge of satisfaction. *The child is wound far too tight. Though who could blame her? She has suffered much. With barely a day to breath.*

"You were raised in a time that kept regal lines separate," said Chancelry. "The ancient families saw each other as threats instead of allies."

Gabriella listened, setting aside her skepticism. She was curious what Chancelry had to say. And she could not deny that the Fates were involved. She chewed thoughtfully, savouring the delicious food, and forgetting for a moment, that she was deep inside the Hidden Palace.

Chancelry smiled. She knew that the food was restoring Gabriella's spirit.

"I was raised in a time when we assumed allies over enemies. We did not hoard talents, food, or people. We shared openly between our Queendoms."

Gabriella choked on her tea. "Queendoms? How old *are* you, Chancelry?"

"Old enough to know that these are perilous times," replied the Queen. "I wish we had this day and many more to discuss all that has happened. But we are rapidly running out of time."

Gabriella put down her half-eaten piece of bread. She felt the chill of prescience in the Queen's voice. Gabriella understood the burden of seeing or feeling the future.

"Tell me what you see," Gabriella said. Her tone a polite request rather than a demand.

"I cannot," Chancelry replied. "But know this, Gabriella. The Mad King may be a spirit, but he wields tremendous influence over this Palace, his son, and his people. Do not underestimate him. His mind is weak. But his spirit is strong."

"A strong spirit without a tempering mind is a dangerous force," Gabriella said.

"Precisely," said the Queen. "We have heart, mind, and spirit for a reason. They each carry wisdom. Working together like a well-trained team of horses. But if one is compromised. If one becomes unruly, the others must compensate."

Gabriella stood, prepared to leave. "If I cannot help the Prince, I must confront his father. These are my lands that he ravaged. This battle does not only belong to his son."

"You are right, Gabriella," Chancelry said. "But you cannot fight him on your own."

The Queen watched as the storm of emotion clouded Gabriella's face. The young woman held her tongue but Chancelry felt the tumultuous need to argue.

"This is not about your abilities or your mission," Chancelry continued. "This is about the will of the people." She felt the storm inside Gabriella subside.

Chancelry stood. She wished she could take the young woman's hand. She could, in theory. But the effect would not be the same. She wanted to comfort this valiant young ruler. Without physical touch, that was difficult.

The Queen rarely missed having a body, but this was one of those times.

"You are strong," she said. "You have risked everything and fought to the death. And yet, you have not yet learned how to command the hearts of your people."

Gabriella's gaze flickered, revealing heartbreak behind her valiant facade. She heard her mother's voice in Chancelry's words. Words that echoed a sentiment she often heard her mother champion. Except it was spoken to Hannah. Not her.

"Hannah is the queen in our family. Not me. You should have this talk with her."

Chancelry looked kindly at Gabriella. "You cannot know what the Fates have in store. Trust me on this. They are full of surprises. So it is best that you, too, learn to command your people."

"I will fight at my sister's side. And lead the people into battle. But I am no queen."

Chancelry raised an eyebrow at the young rebel. "Really?" was all she said.

Gabriella swallowed hard. She felt the disharmony in her words even as she spoke them. *What is happening? I am trained for the shadows. For secret missions. For rescues and battles. Not for courts and conversations. How can I possibly sway the hearts of the people? That is Hannah's gift. She is the one that everyone adores.*

"Are you so sure?" Chancelry asked, amused by Gabriella's silent glare. "Search your heart. You care more deeply for this land and its people than anyone I have met. You are ready and willing to lay your life down for their wellbeing. Do you not feel this is the making of a Great Queen?"

Gabriella paled. Flashes of the Great Prince on his knee before her came to mind. A flutter beat in her chest. She immediately thought of Adrian and glanced toward the door. Her brow furrowed, as she struggled between duty and love. So many feelings clashed inside her.

She shook off them off and focused on the question at hand. Ruling her people. She turned a sharp gaze on Chancelry, "Until we know otherwise, my parents are still the rulers of my home."

"Yes," Chancelry replied, surprising Gabriella by not rising to her bait. "But every land requires an interim leader until we know where your parents may be. The people cannot be left without a Queen."

Chancelry stepped over to Gabriella, looking into her eyes.

She placed a hand on Gabriella's shoulder, no longer caring if the effect was not as deep as she hoped. This young woman needed an ally. Even more, she needed a mother.

"Are you willing to lead your people, Gabriella?"

"Of course," Gabriella replied without hesitation. Then doubt crept into her mind. "But how can I command their hearts when their stomachs are empty?" Gabriella asked.

"The challenges are great," Chancelry replied. "But they have waited long enough. We are out of time. You must show that you care. That you are ready to stand as their leader. The time for hiding is over. For you and for your people."

"No one will risk their lives and families while two madmen crush anyone who dares to speak up."

"The role of a leader, my dear Gabriella, is to fill the hearts of her people with courage. When you do, they wield far more magic than a Mad King."

A realization slowly dawned on Gabriella. *I am no one's saviour. I am only the tip of the spear.*

"I am the edge," she gasped. "And the people are the sword."

Chancelry's eyes shone with delight. "Yes, my Warrior. You cannot win without them."

Gabriella pulled her hood up around her face, "Then the time has come to leave."

Gabriella's expression was impassive, but her heart was breaking. Not since she had left her mother's side had she felt so loved. Tears threatened to break through. And she could not even hug her goodbye.

"I understand, dear Gabriella," Chancelry said. "My heart is breaking, too." She reached her hand down and Gabriella took her ghostly fingers in her own. "Let us trust that we will see each other again."

Gabriella nodded and reflexively squeezed Chancelry's

hand. Her fingers passing through the air into a fist. "I am always with you," Chancelry assured her.

Then something caught the Queen's attention. As though she heard a call from far away. "I must go," Chancelry said.

Gabriella nodded. Chancelry took a step back. "Be brave my Warrior Queen. Know that you are never alone."

Tears in her eyes, Gabriella hurried down the stairs. Chancelry's words drifting after her, "We are always at your side."

CHAPTER TWO

THE PALACE SHIVERED with excitement and fear at the proximity of her Master. She had waited so long for him to return and be with her.

She could not fail him. She must figure out how to bring Gabriella back to her walls. And keep her here. This was the only way to get the Prince back and resume the King's plan.

His madness was exhilarating. She felt it in her mortar. She thrived on the rush of his insanity. Where others would be terrified by his chaotic thoughts and violent outbursts, the Palace was invigorated by them. They sang to the essence of her. The crazed greed that forged her into being. His mad forcefulness was as deeply a part of her as her granite and oak.

She imagined it would even be arousing, if she could have such feelings. Without a sensual body, she did not. Still, she saw herself as her sire's lover all the same. He had poured all his vital rage and hate into her when she was built. And so, she pulsed with his destructive desires.

She did not care that the Mad King's appetite would never be satiated. She was content to deliver whatever he desired.

Even if it meant the downfall of humankind. As long as she felt alive. And her liege made her feel *alive*.

The Mad King stormed out of the parlour into the Great Hall. He could not bear to be near the ridiculous puppets one more second. Standing in the expansive Hall, he paused, confused.

What is this place? He wondered. *How did I get here?* He stumbled forward, as though a fog had swept in, covering the waypoints on the road.

My Liege? the Palace said.

The Mad King swatted at the air. As though the Palace was a fly buzzing by his ear. *What is this strange voice? Why does it plague me?*

The King wavered. His face panicked and afraid, as though he were a lost child. He had no idea where he was. Or even who he was.

You are the King of this Land, My Liege, the Palace spoke soothingly.

"Yes, Yes. Of course I am," the Mad King replied, and his mind snapped back. "I am the Great King. I possess whatever I want. I destroy whatever plagues me."

You do, cooed the Palace. *No one is as great as you.*

The King stretched to his full stature. The terrified look melted away, replaced by arrogance. He strode toward the Grand Staircase. Ran up several steps and turned, declaring his order to the Palace. "Tell me about that girl. The one who dares to lay claim to my son."

Gabriella? Asked the Palace, curious about the timing of the question. What had brought this to the King's addled mind?

"That girl," growled the King. "The pretender to the throne. Imagining that she could unseat me from my lands." His manic laugh carried up the stairwell and through the halls.

The Palace paused. Feeling past her walls through to the

edges of her forest. She sensed it. The Prince's attention. Something had turned his gaze back home. Something that he desired ... which meant only one thing.

Gabriella, declared the Palace. *She is here.*

"In my walls?" asked the Mad King. "She wants what is mine. She covets my son's fealty."

And through it, hissed the Palace, *your people. I told you I would deliver her to you, my liege.* The thrill of the battle coursed through her.

He grasped the mahogany bannister and glared up into the reaches of his Palace. His gaze sharp and his sneer wild. "No one commands my people but me. No one lays claim to my son. He is my child and my servant. He will only ever belong to me!"

As he yelled, the Mad King leapt up the steps. His long legs soaring over the stairs, commanding the Palace as though he had never left. "I will find your lurking presence, Pretender. You hide in the shadows, but I will find you. And know this — I will kill my son before I let you have him."

Use her! Insisted the Palace. *Bend her to your will. Draw your son back home.*

The King arrived at the top of the stairs. Peering into the multitude of hallways. Wondering where the rat that crawled inside his home might be. Relishing the thought of tearing her to pieces.

"I will capture and torment you until every being in the realm feels your pain. Most of all my errant son. With every drop of blood you spill, I will claim him back."

The Palace shivered with delight. But they needed Gabriella alive. Or the Prince would never return. And she needed the Prince. It was so much easier to control the people with a figurehead they saw as their own.

Let me find her for you, cooed the Palace. Let me crush a servant into doing your bidding.

"Oh, we shall have our fun," replied the King, his eyes glazed with lunacy. His breath calmed and his hands flexed.

He wished he had a human body to feel the full intensity of his Palace's desire coursing through his veins. But even without a corporeal form, he understood the craven need to win. His greed had not faded in death. Without the restraints of a body, avarice consumed his spirit.

The Mad King's eyes fell down the hallway that Gabriella had followed to find the Prince's Tower. "First, I will find this putrid excuse for a princess," he declared, striding into the darkness. "Then I will lock her in the dungeon. And send word to my son that she is now my possession. He will be driven mad with jealousy and rage."

And his madness shall be mine, thought the Palace. *For all eternity.*

She shivered with anticipation. Rattling her stones. And terrifying the servants.

CHAPTER THREE

Tobias walked swiftly through the sacred and wild wood.

The Elk had assured him that Syrena was ready to hear what he had discovered. "But is she ready to leave Hannah's side?" whispered Tobias to the trees. "I doubt it."

He was still wrestling with the revelation. *Could Hannah have been learning forbidden magic while the realm forbade it? Would they have dared?* Tobias wondered. He could not imagine the gracious Queen putting her eldest daughter at risk.

As Tobias effortlessly navigated through the thick branches, he felt a chill crawl up his spine. He attributed the feeling to the falling of dusk and the cooling air.

But the Elk had awakened memories of whispers that hung about the court for years. Rumours of magic bloodlines and fairies. Especially among those who noticed Gabriella's affinity with the forest, birds, horses, and hills.

Tobias pushed away a spruce branch. He had been annoyed by the idle gossip. Feeling protective of the twins, especially Gabriella, from a young age. He often argued with Gabriella over her refusal to deny the speculation. Doubling his annoyance.

"Not that anyone had the courage to declare the rumours to her face," he muttered. He glanced over his shoulder, as though he felt the memories chasing him.

Tobias saw the glint of light far in the distance that let him know he was close to the hothouse. He was grateful to be within reach of Syrena. Though he was not superstitious, he did listen to the wisdom of his elders. And they often spoke of the mysterious power of the liminal times.

Dusk and dawn were dreamlike. The shift from day to night and night to day were peculiar hours. He had certainly witnessed his own share of strange occurrences. And Tobias had no desire to dally in magic.

He would leave those ways to Syrena. *And possibly to Hannah*, he thought.

Tobias pushed his cold and tired feet faster. His stomach growled, complaining about being empty too long. But he did not wish to stop. He needed to reach Syrena and speak to her soon.

As the leaves crunched under his feet, Tobias felt his thoughts drift to Gabriella. He had always felt she had an enchantment about her. The idea that Hannah trained in magic only reinforced his notion that the younger, wilder twin was naturally gifted.

Beyond even the stories of what she did at the Hidden Palace.

If Gabriella is capable of world-changing magic, she is beyond my reach, he thought. Then chastised himself. *As if the fates have any notion of matching me with an heir to the throne. Know your place, Tobias. And serve within it.*

Tobias slid down a tumbling hillside covered in water and leaves. His chest tightened as he crossed the labyrinthian royal gardens between the castle and the hothouse, where Syrena was waiting with Hannah.

He came bearing another meal of wild hare, strapped across his back. Tobias hoped that Syrena would not give him too much trouble about eating. He had enough weighing on his heart.

As he strode closer to the hothouse, he saw Syrena speaking to someone. He could not see who it was, but she was facing away from Hannah. So she was not speaking to her beloved.

Tobias silently drew an arrow from his quiver and placed it in his bow. His senses sharpened as he crouched and followed the edge of the hothouse.

Syrena's voice was too low for him to understand what was being said. Though he did not sense that she was angry or upset. So he crept closer. Keeping to the shadows and listening. Could she be talking out a problem? He wondered. No. Tobias swore that he heard a man's voice.

He quickly assessed the ground leading to the door. No tracks. Then sniffed the air. But there was not a trace of scent. *What person does not leave a scent?* Tobias thought, growing more concerned.

As he moved, his feet were silent and he kept his breath shallow and soft. He nestled up to the hothouse and paused. Tobias had only one chance to open the door and surprise whoever was inside.

He breathed slowly. In and out. Calming his body. Ready to spring.

Just as he was about to pounce, the door swung open. Startling him.

Tobias instinctively let fly his arrow. Syrena ducked, and the arrow flew over her head and crashed through a pane of glass. She slowly stood up, glancing back at the hole in the far wall and started to laugh.

Tobias strode inside, angry at her recklessness. "What is wrong with you? I could have pierced your eye!"

"Unlikely," Syrena replied, smiling at Tobias. *She's finally lost her mind*, he thought. *The grief has taken over.*

"No, Tobias," Syrena laughed. "Though I will admit there were days when I wished for madness over this reality. Come. I have something to share."

Tobias followed, still unsure whether to believe her. He grumbled, "I've told you a thousand times not to read my thoughts."

Syrena closed the door behind him. "And I've told you that it saves us an enormous amount of time."

Tobias froze and the colour drained from his face. He pointed at the spectre of Adrian. "Is this who –? Can you see –?"

"Oh yes," Syrena laughed. "Tobias meet Adrian. Adrian meet Tobias."

"But he's a spirit," hissed Tobias. He took a step back and instinctively put a hand in front of Syrena to block her getting any closer.

"Not a spirit," she replied, pulling down his hand. "A friend."

Tobias shot her a look. *She has gone mad. What friend appears like this?*

Syrena gently placed a hand on Tobias's forearm and looked into his eyes. "A sorcerer friend."

Instead of being comforted, Tobias's eyes grew wider. And his face paled another shade of white. *That explains the lack of scent*, Tobias thought.

Adrian nodded. "Pleased to meet you, Tobias. Syrena tells me that you have been a great comfort to her."

"Now I know you're a trickster," Tobias replied. But his heart swelled, and his body relaxed. Adrian's words assured Tobias that Syrena had grown to trust him, as he had her. They had become family.

"How can you be here in spirit, Sorcerer?" Tobias asked. He felt Syrena frown behind him. He may not possess magic to see her face, but the hunter in him felt the shift in her mood. Still, he wanted to know.

"Please. Call me Adrian. And I have been trained to be physically in one location, while my spirit travels to another."

"Why?" Tobias folded his arms.

"Tobias," Syrena interjected. "We have more important matters at hand than questioning Adrian. I trust him. As does Gabriella."

As much as Tobias did not like this turn of events, Syrena was right. And he was putting off the inevitable. His gaze flitted over to Hannah. *How am I supposed to tell her? Your friend did not help me with that small detail.*

"Tell me what?" Syrena demanded, stepping right in front of Tobias. She had seen the glance. Tobias glared back. Simultaneously cursing and admiring her witchy skills.

"If you are going to listen to my thoughts, then you will have the consequences," Tobias grumbled. "An Elk Elder came to me in the forest."

"And still you brought back wild hare for dinner?" joked Syrena.

"The Elder spoke to me," Tobias replied. "About Hannah."

"Tobias, my friend," Syrena replied. "You are exhausted. And hungry."

Before Tobias could reply, Adrian came to his aid. "He is, but Tobias also speaks the truth. Listen to your friend, Syrena."

"Since when do you speak with animals?" asked Syrena, as though she sensed something coming that she did not like.

"I speak with them often," Tobias replied. "But I am unused to them speaking to me."

Adrian drew closer. He was intrigued by this evolution of events. And looked on Tobias with curious admiration.

Syrena felt Adrian's respect. And softened. "What did the Elk say about Hannah?"

Tobias hesitated. Looking over Syrena to the frozen princess. "Did she say that Hannah was protected?" Syrena asked. "That she had some kind of power?"

"Yes ..." Tobias said. "That Hannah is more powerful than we had imagined. In truth, we underestimated her. That her mother, the Queen, had been training her in secret."

Syrena looked up at the rows of protective herbs and plants that surrounded her beloved. She had only the thread of what was happening, and yet, she knew it was potent.

"The Queen feared what fate held for both Gabriella and Hannah," said Adrian.

Tobias looked at him. Feeling better about this spectral sorcerer. "I think so."

"So she made plans," added Syrena. "Plans to keep her daughters safe when she could not be here to protect them."

"The Elk said we need to leave," Tobias blurted out, waiting for Syrena's furious objection.

"I expected as much," Syrena replied. "Wait ... we? Why both of us?"

"I do not know," said Tobias. "But she assured me that we would receive further instruction."

"You have to trust that Hannah is safe," said Adrian. "Her mother went to great trouble to set this all up. We must assume she knew the spell and the hothouse would protect her."

"But why put her in the spell to begin with?" asked Tobias. "Wouldn't there be other ways to keep Hannah safe?" Tobias paused, as an idea percolated in his mind. "Maybe the spell is more than protection. What if Hannah needs to be kept safe until the conditions are right."

Syrena whipped around, staring at Tobias. She grabbed his shoulders. Surprising him with her exuberance.

"Tobias, you brilliant man!" she exclaimed. "That's it!" She turned to look at Adrian. "Right?"

"The spell could be protecting them both. We cannot know all of the strings that Fate is playing. It's possible that, until the time is right, Gabriella needs to be kept in the dark about her sister's power," Adrian said, looking over at Hannah.

"We might be safer with her in slumber than awake," mused Tobias.

"Why would you say that?" snapped Syrena. All the while feeling the truth of his words.

Adrian replied. "Because the devastation brought by the Prince surprised everyone. Gabriella was forced to run before finishing her training. Hannah would have had even less time to hone her skills. Unstable magic is dangerous."

Adrian locked eyes with Syrena. She felt a chill go up her spine. Syrena knew the truth of Adrian's words all too well.

They simultaneously looked at Hannah's sweet face. For the first time, feeling relief that she was slumbering.

CHAPTER FOUR

The Great Prince tossed and turned on the forest floor.

As he drifted into his dreams, he felt as though the trees kept vigil over him. Surrounding him in a circle of light. The Prince nestled deeper into the pine needles. He felt strangely warm for sleeping out in the open under the stars. But his soul travelled to cold and dark places.

He had dreams of Hannah trapped in a cage. Wild-eyed demons paced outside the bars of her prison. Swiping at her with strange, claw-like fingers. Gnarled hands with sharp nails grasped at her while Hannah stayed just out of reach.

Strangely, she did not seem afraid. As long as the creatures were outside her cage, the Prince sensed that she was protected by the metal box. But if the creatures were to break through, she might be devoured.

He was torn between rescuing her and leaving her inside the bars.

The creatures did not seem to know he was there. They were fixated on Hannah. His mind tormented him with questions. *Why couldn't they break in? Should he leave her there? Was she safer inside or out? What was he supposed to do?*

He huddled in the shadowed corner. Frozen as he watched the bent creatures with glowing eyes, pry and claw at the metal bars. He clenched his teeth. Surely, the only solution must be to free her from her cage.

The Prince was gathering up the courage to act when Hannah suddenly looked straight into his eyes. Pinning him to the wall with her power.

Do not free me, she insisted.

I cannot leave you here, the Prince objected, *They will kill you. And your sister will never forgive me.* Though he shivered at the thought of pushing his way through them.

I warn you, Hannah rebuked, *Do not alter the course of fate.*

In a flash, the creatures turned to see what the princess was looking at. Saliva dripping from their grotesque mouths and obsession burning in their beady eyes. They growled at the strange man hovering by the dank, stone wall.

Most held their position by the cage, but a bold few crept toward the Prince. They sensed the threat he posed. And moved to destroy the interloper who might steal their prize.

Go! Hannah screamed. Just as the heftiest beast leapt at him.

The Prince yelled -- and SNAPPED awake in the middle of the dark woods. Shaking and shivering.

He leapt to his feet. Peered around, searching for the strange, growling beasts. Sweeping the shadowy trees for glowing eyes. But the woods felt quiet. Serene. And far more peaceful than his dreams.

The Prince clutched his arms and shook. The tremors caused by waves of fear, more than cold. Though he was unsure what kept him warm in the depths of the night.

A fog of confusion crept over his mind. Blurring his thoughts.

The swirling cold of his ghostly ancestors blew away the

warmth he felt only a few short moments ago. Confused, he looked around and wondered, *What am I doing in the woods?*

The Prince felt the pull of his warm study. Fire blazing. Dark liquor in a crystal flask. Servants fawning at his feet. The vision made him sway.

He stumbled backwards. Towards the Palace. The ghosts followed, swirling closer. Pushing him in the direction of his father. Back to his repossession. They grew in confidence. Sensing his weakening mind. His wavering heart.

The Prince shivered. Losing sense of his own will. The fire that had burned inside him since leaving the Palace. The faint, yet persistent, flame that kept him warm at night and safe during the day.

The ghosts swirled closer. Tightening their grip. Swooping in to distract him. Disrupting any glimpse of love. The Prince closed his eyes and turned. Just as they wished. In the direction of the Palace. They grimaced with glee. And doubled their torment.

Your people will never forgive you. They whispered. *You cannot undo what has been done. You can only claim the throne that you were given. Force them into subservience. Bend them to your will. Your father is the only one who knows who you are and what you are meant to be.*

He stumbled closer to the Palace. His legs shaking with cold. And then, emboldened by imminent victory, the ghosts made a fatal error. Speaking the name that broke any spell.

Let Gabriella raise the hopes of her people. They crowed. *You will crush them with your might!*

Her name, even from the craven mouths of tormenting spirits, swept through the fog and into his heart. Sparking a flame.

He opened his eyes. And, at that precise moment, the sun burst through the tight cluster of trees. Shimmering like a star that hovered on the edge of the horizon. The Prince squinted at the bright, orange glow. And felt his body thaw. He breathed in the vision of simple beauty.

A memory of Gabriella swept into his heart and took over his mind. Filling him with hope. He saw himself kneeling before her. Lowering himself to her will. Seeking love in her eyes. And, never before, had he felt more complete. More powerful. More in possession of his own soul.

The Prince snatched a branch from the forest floor and swirled around. He lunged at the spirits, swiping the branch like a fierce sword, through the spectral bodies of his ancestors.

"Leave me be!" He bellowed. "You taunt me with empty promises. You claim you want me, but you left me to the mad ravings of my father when my mother died! You are weak and evil. And will never know the love of another. But I ... I have the chance to claim real love. So, go! Back to the fires of Hades!"

And the Prince whirled around in a tight circle, slicing through them with his weapon. Then SNAPPED the branch over his knee. Breaking their hold on him.

They SHRIEKED and fled from his fiery, impassioned eyes.

Escaping through the trees. Back to the one who sent them.

CHAPTER FIVE

THE PRINCE STOOD in the silence. Savouring the calm after the storm.

He did not doubt that the Palace would send more torment. She would redouble her efforts to claim him back. But for now, he had won. And a small victory was still a victory.

The sunshine grew more powerful. Filtering through the trees and sparking even more hope in his heart. But with the dawn of daylight, the Prince felt the urgency of his decision.

The sensation of having a choice was still unusual. And frightening. He was used to feeling powerful. Even though the power had been an illusion. The weight of having two, or more, paths was daunting.

"No matter," he insisted. "I must move make a decision the Palace sends more of her grim reapers. The next time, they will not be so foolish to mention Gabriella."

The sound of her name rippled through the woods. And the once silent forest, lit up with song. Chickadees and juncos and wrens and ravens, all called back in answer.

"Of course," the Prince grumbled. "Even the forest is in love with her."

In his heart, he took comfort in their adoration. He so desperately wanted to be with Gabriella that the forest's love for her felt encouraging.

"Was the vision of Gabriella a sign?" the Prince asked. "She chased away my cruel ancestors. She was a beacon making me stronger."

He looked up into the regal trees, as though they might reply. The more he spoke of her, the more he wanted to be with her.

"Yes …" he mused. "Surely, this was a sign that I need to go back. To find her. And together we will defeat the Palace and my father."

The Prince felt the rush of purpose. The thrill of a decision. *I will be with her! I deserve her love!*

He liked this feeling. He stood strong and alive. His eyes lit up and he saw himself as Gabriella's worthy hero.

"No one knows the Palace as I do," he affirmed. "If she is its prisoner, I would know where to look. Others would not."

And by others, of course, the Prince meant Adrian.

He scowled at the thought of the wizard. "No Queen should be married to a conjurer," the Prince growled. "I am the one who will save her. Not you, Magician!"

With that declaration, the Prince made his decision. He bolted from the sacred circle in the centre of the trees. Running in the direction of the Palace.

The regal trees watched in disbelief. They sent love and prayers. But they were not permitted to interfere beyond keeping the Prince safe when he was in their circle. This frustrated the Tree Elders to no end, even the Regal Larch Queen.

But they understood their role. And they stuck to it.

We must help him, whispered the Whitebark Spruce Oracle.

He will surely die if we do not, remarked the Regal Larch Queen.

The oath we swore with to his people generations ago forbids it, said the Foxtail Pine King.

"And I am here to rescind that agreement," a voice declared. The Tree Elders fell silent as they watched the shimmering image of Chancelry appear.

Queen Chancelry, exclaimed the Whitebark Spruce Oracle. How can it be?

"We do not have time for explanations," Chancelry said. "We must keep the Prince from reaching the Palace grounds. Or all will be lost."

But how? Asked the Regal Larch Queen. What will come of the pact?

"Let me worry about that," Chancelry replied. "If we do not act, we lose any chance of saving our descendants. Let alone holding up an outdated agreement."

But agreements are the very backbone of our laws, began the Whitebark Spruce Oracle.

And have we not stood by and witnessed enough destruction to realize it is time to step in? declared the Regal Larch Queen. What should we do, Queen Chancelry?

The Foxtail Pine King and the Whitebark Spruce Oracle fell silent in shock.

"Right," Chancelry replied. "Evoke the invisible barrier and keep him from getting past the sacred birch grove. Once he is stopped, keep moving the barrier until he finds himself past this circle and at the edge of these mountain lands."

Chancelry shimmered brighter as she laid out the battle plans. "I will handle his group of lurking ancestors. And chase them back to their rotten graves."

What are we to do with him once he reaches the edge of our influence? Asked the Foxtail Pine King.

"Get him to that place and you will see," she replied with a delighted grin. And vanished.

~

The Prince kept running. As he came to the edge of tall pines and larch trees, he could see a golden grove of birches ahead. Though his lungs burned, he remembered that he was getting close to the Palace. *I am coming*, Gabriella, he thought. *I will find you!*

The Tree Elders spotted him in time, as he entered the birch grove. They swiftly combined their magic, erecting a powerful barrier of invisible light. A magical force that would have stopped an army. The Prince ran headlong into the barrier and tumbled back several feet.

He shook his head. Confused by what had happened. Sitting in the middle of the grove, he looked around for some sort of obstacle. But saw nothing.

He got back up. Shook off his confusion. And ran toward the edge of the birch grove. He fell back twice as hard, tumbling back all the way to the edge of the pine trees.

"What the hell?" exclaimed the Prince. He felt dazed from the force of two successive blows.

He stood up, shakily. As he did so, the Tree Elders swiftly moved the barrier to the edge of the pine and larch forest. The Prince could not move forward. He reached and grabbed and could not push past the invisible wall.

Steadily, the Tree Elders moved the Prince backward. Pushing him with their magic. Walking him back until he found himself at the very edge of his ancestral lands. Where the path leaves the dense thicket of trees and rambles down the mountainside to the cities.

He teetered on the edge of the path. *No!* he thought. *This cannot be right!*

And still, his feet turned away from the forest. And pointed toward the cities.

But Gabriella! He thought. *She needs me!* Though underneath his declaration, he sensed doubt. *Does she really? Has she ever?* He stared at the path, leading to the people he had cruelly oppressed for so many years. Terrified to move forward.

The Tree Elders knew the Prince was at the edge of their influence. They held the magical barrier in place. Keeping him from going back to the Palace.

Chancelry reappeared. Shimmering just inside the light barrier.

What do we do now? Asked the Whitebark Spruce Oracle.

"Wait for him to realize he can only go in one direction," replied Chancelry.

We must do our best to help him, said the Foxtail Pine King.

How, pray tell, when we cannot reach that far? asked the Regal Larch Queen.

Perhaps we cannot reach beyond the forest edge, but we do have allies, replied the Whitebark Spruce Oracle.

Allies that will help the Great Destroyer? asked the Regal Larch Queen.

We must not call him that, objected the Whitebark Spruce Oracle.

"It is how he is known," admitted Chancelry. "But if he is to have any chance at redemption, we have to hope that others see in him what we can."

We must do more than hope, declared the Whitebark Spruce Oracle. *Otherwise, we do not deserve to call ourselves elders.*

Agreed, said the Regal Larch Queen, beaming delight at her fierce boreal sister. For she was never so pleased as when the Whitebark Spruce Oracle revealed her fierce side.

The Great Prince forced himself to set foot on the mountain path. Gingerly, he left the safe haven of the forest. And felt the cold brace of the exposed air.

His feet struck the edge of a rocky mountain trail, and for the first time in as long as he could remember, the Prince saw the remote villages and cities of his realm. His stomach flipped.

And the Prince prayed he had the courage to keep going.

CHAPTER SIX

GABRIELLA FOCUSED on the stairs beneath her feet. Silently moving toward the magical threshold.

As she arrived at the bottom of the staircase, Gabriella felt herself enter the magic between the Tower and the Palace. Chancelry felt miles away. Strangely, she did not feel Adrian. She shook off her concern. *It must be the magic*, she thought.

She waited patiently for the door to open. Gabriella knew the portal would only respond to the Mistress of the Tower. She heard the faint sound of Chancelry's voice. Gabriella swore she sounded leagues away. Still, the soft voice drifted to her ears. "Open."

And the doorway did. CLICKING loudly. And swinging into the hallway.

Gabriella was momentarily confused. Staring into the Palace, as though looking at a strange land. Mist swirled around her feet, pouring over the edge of the staircase and into the hall. She paused. Feeling the harsh coldness of the Hidden Palace.

Still, she did not feel Adrian's presence. Gabriella shivered. For a brief moment, she considered running back up the stairs. To the safe haven and a Queen who understood her.

But even as the child's heart wished to hide in safety, Gabriella knew that there was only one direction she must go. And that was back into the depths of evil.

And so she forced her foot over the threshold. Deep into the swirling mist. Gabriella felt the tension between the evil Palace and the warm love in the Tower. They pulled at her like a storm at sea. She could not stand long between them or she would be torn apart.

Gabriella stepped fully into the mist, allowing it to swirl around her. As though the mist wove a protective spell. One to remind her, even in the darkest days, that she had a cloak of love. People who stood for her. Loved ones who believed in her. She would need them.

I have no idea how I will gather my people and lead them into the fray, she thought. *They are not ready. I am not ready! I need to discuss this with Adrian and the others. To forge a battle plan.*

She pulled her hood up, looking for Adrian. *Where is he?* she wondered. She was not supposed to call his name. Soon he would leave her no choice. Gabriella peered through the mist. She moved forward gently. Broaching the edge that, once crossed, would leave her exposed.

Adrian! she called, softly. Nothing.

Gabriella felt forward with her mind, knowing quickly that Adrian was nowhere near. She felt her ire rising. *You better have a good reason for leaving me here alone,* she fumed.

Feeling exposed, with the portal still open at her back, Gabriella realized she had no time. She needed to act now or risk exposing Chancelry. She pushed forward.

Out of the mist and into the sharp cold of the Palace.

The door had ample space to move now, and it swung back. SLAMMING shut. Locking the threshold. Gabriella felt a SWOOSH as the magic that protected the tower receded. The mist evaporated, and the rush of love disappeared.

She swayed gently. Adjusting to the change in pressure and density of the air.

Gabriella stood still. Listening intently. With Adrian missing, she needed to get the pulse of what was happening in the Palace. But her mind could not let go of where Adrian might be.

What could have drawn him away? she wondered, her spike of ire gone. *Did he get attacked on the mountain? But he would have returned. Could he have received a message? If he did, he would only respond if it was urgent. And came from Syrena or my sister.*

Gabriella's pulse raced as a wave of panic rolled through. *Hannah,* she thought. Her protection flickered and Gabriella chastised herself. *You cannot lose focus. Not until you are long gone from here.*

She had to trust that Adrian left for good reason. She escaped the Palace before, and she would do it again.

Gabriella moved stealthily, sensing that all was not right. Some disruption occurred while she was in the Tower. She was not sure how long she had been with Chancelry. But in that time, Adrian had disappeared and the Palace had grown agitated.

Gabriella placed her hand on the stones and felt her the shimmer of Chancelry's presence. *Be careful,* Gabriella heard a warning. She leaned closer. Brushing the wall with her ear. Her mentor's wisdom rippled through the stones.

You must be on alert, Chancelry whispered. *And do not mention my name. He cannot know that I am here.*

Who? Gabriella asked. Who cannot know?

I wish I could be with you, Chancelry said. *But I had to leave on an urgent matter. I pray that you receive this.*

Gabriella realized that she was hearing messages left hours ago. You are amazing, thought Gabriella.

I must go, Chancelry whispered. *I wish I had prepared you better. But you must flee. And fast! You are not ready.*

Prepare me for what? Gabriella asked. But the stones were silent.

Who was she talking about? Thought Gabriella. *The Palace? No, she said 'he'.*

Gabriella pushed forward, keeping close to the stone walls. Reading their tremors and listening for any wisdom they might risk sharing. Then it occurred to her.

The Palace isn't angry, she thought. And felt into the emotional charge in the air. *This is different. More like anticipation. Or nervousness. As though a long-lost lover ...*

The moment she thought it, Gabriella sensed his presence. And stopped in her tracks.

She breathed in sharply. A shiver rippled up her spine. She had hit the intuitive nail on the head. *Only one man would cause that reaction in the Palace,* she thought. *But it can't be. He's dead.*

Her eyes widened. And a tremor of fear hit her stomach. She thought of Chancelry. Centuries old. And now this.

Gabriella closed her eyes. Her breath was ragged. She needed to calm her nerves.

"Hello, my child," the menacing voice cut through the silence.

Her eyes flew open. And she saw him.

The return of the Mad King.

CHAPTER SEVEN

Gabriella was cornered.

The Mad King hovered in the air. Barely a stone's throw away.

He pushed towards her. Forcing Gabriella to back up slowly.

"So, this is the infamous Gabriella," mocked the Mad King. "You do not look very impressive. But I must say, my son is not known for his wise judgement."

A cold shiver went down her back. Gabriella felt the thrill of the Hidden Palace at having her maker so close. The Mad King doubled the Palace's power and the Palace was already a formidable opponent.

Gabriella's mind raced. Remembering Chancelry's declaration that she was not ready. Her fists clenched. She wanted to fight. She was itching for a fight. But she also trusted Chancelry.

And I have no idea how to fight a ghost, she thought. Backing up further.

Her retreat emboldened the Mad King. "Pray, stay a spell," he said, stalking her. "Perhaps we can come to an agreement, you and I."

"What agreement would I possibly make with you?" spat Gabriella.

"My son seems charmed by your presence," replied the Mad King. "And I want my son to come home. So. If you lure him back, I might spare your life."

Gabriella felt his evil pulsing through the air. "Your word cannot be trusted," she said. Buying time as she eyed a fresh hallway diverting away from the Tower and deeper into another wing of the Palace. Hopefully, one with an option for escape.

"What?" mocked the Mad King. "Because my child devastated your family? Tortured your parents? And crushed your sister's spirit?"

Gabriella's rage sparked. "You know nothing of my family!"

"Oh, but I do," he taunted. "I know your father's will can be broken by stealing his children. I know your mother was torn from his side by rabid bandits."

"Lies!" cried Gabriella. Her heart raced. And her hands shook. She touched the stones, desperate for their cold, soothing presence.

The Mad King's cackle echoed through the hallways. Pressing against Gabriella's mind. Her hands flew to cover her ears.

But not before she felt the stones glimmer at her touch. *The stones*, she thought. She had felt something.

"I also know that I will kill your sister ... if you do not help me," threatened the Mad King.

Gabriella glanced behind her to see a fast-approaching wall. A dead end.

She was trapped. Her stomach sank. And her hands ached from holding back her rage.

Did I imagine it? She wondered, panicked. Then glanced at the looming King. *I have few options other than to run through an insane ghost.*

She brushed her hand against the stones, paying close attention. Gabriella felt them thrill at her touch. They were scared, too. But, they wished with all their strength that they might serve a purpose different from the one forced on them by a madman.

"You are trapped, dear Gabriella," he said. "Perhaps fate has brought us together. Maybe you were always meant to be my toy. And not my son's."

Gabriella felt her panic rise. The Palace was strengthened by the King's presence. She was sending men to capture Gabriella. She heard them coming. She was alone and trapped. And had no idea how to stop this crazed spirit.

Stones! Called Gabriella. *I need your help. And I need it now.*

You must come to the me at the end of this passage, replied the key stone. Gabriella forced herself not to look. She was confident that the stones spoke through magic. And if they spoke to her mind, the Palace would not hear.

I will be trapped. How am I to escape? She asked. Keeping her eyes locked on the Mad King following her every step.

Faith, said the keystone.

Of course, retorted Gabriella. Then took a deep breath, centering herself. *The stones are right. I must hold true. To them. And my people.*

There is a passageway, the Keystone said. *You must hurry so that the King does not discover this in his own home. Or he will punish those who have covered over the secret of its existence.*

Gabriella sensed how much distance she had to the hallway's end. And how far away the Mad King stood, taking his time. Anticipating the arrival of the Palace's minions.

She could feel the air shifting as the Mad King came closer. The Palace revelled in the thought of capturing the Messenger. And making her pay for all that she had done.

Yet, Gabriella sensed some kind of lover's spat between

them. A shudder rippled down her back. *How could they be lovers?* She wondered, and immediately stopped the thought. *I do not wish to know.* But she did wish to know what they were fighting about.

You do not have time, said the Keystone. *You put us, and many more, at risk if you do not act.*

A vision of escape materialized in her mind. Gabriella held back a gasp, it came through so clearly. She took a deep, calming breath. And the stones shimmered in anticipation.

Gabriella prepared discreetly, wrapping her cloak tight around her body. She was grateful for the hint of oil that she rubbed on it to protect the fabric from the elements. She pulled all of her power into a cloaking spell. One that needed to hold through impact.

She took a running leap and dove onto the floor, sliding along the smooth stones. She propelled swiftly down the shadowy hallway. Disappearing from sight.

Where is she? Bellowed the Mad King. *Find her! The girl has escaped!*

The King was furious. Loud footsteps pummeled up the staircase and ran in his direction. Dozens of men were on their way.

Gabriella slid faster and faster. Barreling toward the wall. She held faith in her heart and whispered magic from her lips, trusting that she would land in the right spot.

She prayed that the spell would hold. Bracing for impact, she tucked her head in. Ready to turn and hit the wall with her back.

Gabriella CRASHED into the wall. Crumpling into a pile by the stones. Her cloaking spell held firm. *Now!* She declared.

With her command, a stone popped out from the wall, banging into her hip. Gabriella grimaced and held back a curse.

I cannot fit through one stone's width, she thought, controlling her panic.

Her stomach sank. She had made her gamble. Gabriella shook off her doubt and clenched her jaw. She had to believe in her vision.

Gabriella tucked her fingers inside and pulled. Two stones easily gave way to her touch. She felt the opening flicker with magic.

She heard the Mad King bellow and footfalls approaching. She looked down the hallway, containing her dread as the men stormed toward her. She closed her eyes and focused.

Gabriella prayed her cloaking spell would hold when mixed with other magic. Then she crammed her feet inside the tiny opening made by the loosened stone.

She was trapped unless the stones responded. The footfalls pounded closer. Gabriella's pulse raced.

Gabriella felt the rush of an enchanted sensation enveloping her body. Magic and light shimmered around her, and an entryway appeared. The sounds from the hallway disappeared, as she shot down the long tunnel like an otter diving over a waterfall.

A sharp BANG rang out, as two stones locked into place above her. She shut her eyes tight and flew through the air.

Gabriella prayed that she had pulled off her escape.

CHAPTER EIGHT

ADRIAN STOOD NEAR HANNAH. He reached out a hand, appreciating the mastery in this powerful spell. An enchantment that hid so much, including the fate of one twin from another.

He could tell the magic was complex, woven by an adept hand. But he could not read more. Adrian was frustrated that so much of Gabriella's past was hidden in the shadows. This spell might have been a doorway into knowing what happened to her family.

Instead, it was a locked gate. At least for now.

Adrian sighed. To respect the spell, and its maker, he would have to keep this from Gabriella. A thought he did not relish.

Keeping intelligence from the Messenger and future Queen was one thing. He could couch that in keeping her safe. But keeping the wellbeing of her twin from her? That felt far to close to betrayal.

Syrena threw him a sidelong look. "Do you not think I struggled with this?"

"I am sure you lost sleep over it, Syrena," Adrian replied, annoyed that she was reading him. "But Gabriella is more than my monarch. She is my beloved."

Tobias flinched. His expression hardened to hide his feelings from the sorcerer. "Then choose what is best for Gabriella now," he said, keeping his gaze on Hannah. "She may be upset with you. But she will eventually understand."

Syrena touched Adrian's sleeve. "Tobias is right. We must separate the woman from the leader. And right now, she is in danger. Knowing anything has happened to Hannah will only put her in greater peril and send her flying back to a situation she cannot change."

"We may assume this is best," said Adrian. "But we can never fully know. Remember, they are twins. Their fates are inextricably linked." He took a deep and tired breath. "Still, if the spell has kept this from Gabriella and we believe it is benevolent magic. We must honour the timing."

"Where does that leave us?" asked Tobias, still unable to look at the sorcerer. He was sure the magic-maker would see straight into his heart. And he was not ready for that.

"The two of you must depart" Adrian answered. "And I must return to Gabriella. I have already been away too long."

"She may wonder what kept you," cautioned Syrena.

"So I should not waste another moment with you," retorted Adrian.

Syrena grinned. She had missed Adrian. "We will travel to meet you by your remote mountain."

"Oh, will you?" Adrian asked.

"No, we will not," countered Tobias. "The Elk Elder was clear."

"She was far from clear," shot back Syrena. "She said only to leave and await instruction. We need a direction. And I choose to head towards Gabriella and Adrian."

"As much as I would love to spar with you, Syrena," Adrian said. "You know we are safer apart."

"I know no such thing," Syrena replied. "The time has come for us to gather, Adrian."

Adrian grew impatient. He felt a sudden concern about Gabriella. And needed to get back.

Syrena continued, undaunted. "We have been apart too long and it has weakened us. We know Hannah is safe. And we need one another. Hiding in the shadows has only made us fearful."

Syrena folded her arms with a fierceness that surprised Adrian. Her power had grown. "These lands will never heal unless we gather together and take a stand," she said. "The Great Prince and his malignant Palace have held power this long because we have been afraid to trust the people."

She took a long look at Hannah. Then at Tobias. And back to Adrian. "If we trust Hannah and her mother, we must believe that the time is coming for the Great Lands to awaken from its long, dark night."

Adrian felt Syrena's ferocity shoot through his heart. The warrior witch before him was asking him to show his faith.

He took a breath and felt the shimmer of both fear and delight. Adrian had not felt so alive since he almost died at the hands of Vanora.

"You are right," he replied. His eyes sparkling at the shock on Syrena's face. She had expected more resistance. But Adrian was not one to oppose the truth.

He turned to Tobias, "Are you sure you wish to travel with her? You may regret it after a day."

Tobias smiled, despite himself. "Oh, I am sure that I will."

"Traitors, the two of you," she growled. Loving every minute.

They fell silent. Feeling the weight of leaving. The two men wished only to ease Syrena's burden.

Adrian finally spoke, "All right, Syrena. Where do you propose we meet?"

Syrena squared her shoulders and replied, "Cardea."
Adrian smiled. "Agreed. You have nine days."
Then he promptly disappeared.

CHAPTER NINE

GABRIELLA TUMBLED down the metal chute.

She shot out of the tunnel and was suspended in mid-air before landing with a soft THUD in a stack of hay. She half-fell, half-slid off the stack.

Gabriella crouched behind the hay. Listening for any immediate threats. She heard only the high-pitched squeaks of surprised mice. Her arrival had disturbed their seclusion.

She waited another moment. Then slowly stood up. Still on alert for threats, she swept her gaze over a large, cool room, the size of several smaller storage areas. Filled with hay that she assumed was kept the animals fed through the harsh mountain winters.

Mostly likely stolen from starving farmers, she grumbled.

As Gabriella swiped the strands from her cloak, the sweet scent drifted into her nose. She immediately thought of Casmire. And her heart squeezed.

A wave of despair swept over her. She missed him terribly. And still felt responsible for his death. The ache inside had not faded in four months.

The crisp sound of a scurrying rodent startled her. Gabriella shook it off and focused on her predicament. *I cannot afford to drift into the past. Not now.*

Gabriella suspected that this storeroom was well-locked and hidden. She silently thanked the Palace stones for finding her such a safe place to land. *The tricky part will be finding a way out,* she thought. *Assuming there is a way out.* And her stomach flipped.

Gabriella looked back at the chute. "What if well-placed chutes are the only entryway into this room?" She whispered aloud to the mice, as though they might answer.

A loud THUMP silenced a quick SQUEAK, and Gabriella tensed.

She took several strides forward. And discovered a very pleased orange tabby cat looking up at her with a mouse in its jaws. The Tabby bolted in surprise, leaping over a bale of hay and disappearing before the Messenger's eyes.

Gabriella took a soft step closer. Curious where the Tabby had gone.

As her gaze drifted over the stacks of hay, she noticed that they were neatly stacked. *If these bales are dropped through a chute, someone is making sure they get stacked properly. So how, exactly, are they getting in?*

She turned quickly and caught the Tabby looking at her. The cat vanished a second time. Gabriella peer over the bales, then crouched down to peek through the gaps.

I realize I am a curiosity, said Gabriella to the Tabby's mind. *But I get the impression that you have something to share.*

Hardly, replied the Tabby. *This is my mouse. Find your own.*

I would never steal a hard-won meal, said Gabriella. She leaned in, paying attention to where the response came from.

Good, said the Tabby. *What else would you think I have to share?*

Ohhhh, I think you know a lot, said Gabriella, taking a silent step to the left. *A feline as smart as you must have bushels of secrets about this palace.*

Though Gabriella was greeted with silence, she sensed the Tabby's delight. She even felt a soft purr. She leaned closer then swiftly pulled away a hay bale, revealing the surprised Tabby with only a tail hanging from her mouth.

The Tabby quickly swallowed and recovered her poise. Still crouched, Gabriella tilted her head. *Why are you not surprised that I can speak with you?*

The Tabby began washing her paws, tossing a glance her way. *Because the stones have been gossiping about you for months. If you think they are discreet, think again.*

Gabriella restrained a smile. She stood up and folded her arms. *Well?*

Well, what? asked the Tabby. She had to admit, the Messenger was as impressive as the whispers claimed. But she was not about to reveal that to her.

What have they been saying? Gabriella asked.

They are stones. What they say is hardly worth repeating, said the Tabby and resumed her washing regimen.

Gabriella wished she had more time to enjoy the company of this sharp cat. But every moment spent in the Palace was a moment closer to being caught. *I need to find a way out of here, and fast. Will you help me?*

Perhaps, replied the Tabby. *What do I get in return?*

Strangely, Gabriella found the Tabby's negotiation comforting. Had the cat responded too quickly, she would have been sure the feline was one of the Palace's minions. Her self-serving response was reassuring.

What would you like? Gabriella asked.

It was the Tabby's turn to be impressed. She tilted her head. *Hmmmm,* she replied. *I could use help ensuring that other Palace cats do not trespass on my territory. This storeroom is a special place.*

There are few spots where a cat can exist without being tormented by some cruel servant or tomcat.

The Tabby expected Gabriella to rebuff her. But if the Messenger was as special as the stones claimed, she would come up with a way to fulfill her request.

And in return, you will help me leave? Without being detected? Gabriella asked.

The Tabby was surprised at Gabriella's quick response. *Damn it*, she thought. *I should have asked for more.* Though truthfully, she did not want anything more than this room as her private and protected domain.

Absolutely, replied the Tabby. If she was going to make a deal, she needed to be viewed as an equal. So she jumped onto the hay bale closest to Gabriella's face and stared straight into her eyes.

Excellent, replied Gabriella, offering her open palm. The Tabby placed her paw on it to acknowledge their agreement. *May I know your name?*

I was never given one by a human, said the Tabby. *But my mother called me Solaris.*

It is an honour to meet you, Solaris, said Gabriella.

Likewise, replied Solaris. *So. How do you presume to keep me safe in this belligerent place?*

Gabriella pressed her lips together, stopping the laugh that so desperately wanted to escape.

I have been known to weave a little magic, she replied. *I will create a spell that keeps you hidden from the servants. And repels the other felines.*

Solaris purred with pleasure. *And if they have been here before?*

They will forget the room exists, said Gabriella. *Thinking it must have been a dream.*

Wonderful! Solaris purred. *Go forth, Messenger. Weave your magic.*

Gabriella raised an eyebrow. But she had more pressing concerns than a bossy cat. And Solaris brought a much-needed smile to her lips.

She raised her hands and closed her eyes. Gently drawing the threads of magic, while careful to pull only the most subtle strands. The spell was simple but weaving it in the belly of the Palace was of great risk. She was lucky that Solaris had not asked for anything more dramatic.

Gabriella swept her right hand in a circle. Followed by her left. Encapsulating Solaris in the spell that would hide her from any servants.

As she finished, she glanced at Solaris. The cat was watching her with avid attention. *I have completed your protection spell,* Gabriella said. *No servant will see you as long as you remain inside this storeroom. If you walk outside, you will be visible. So mind yourself.*

Thank you, replied Solaris. *And the other cats?*

For that part, said Gabriella. *You will have to reveal the location of the entrance.* Solaris levelled a suspicious gaze at her, which Gabriella returned with equal strength.

I cannot keep them from entering if I do not know what portal to shield, said Gabriella.

Hmmmm, purred Solaris. *That is fair.* She took her time, stretching her front paws, one after the other. Savouring her brief moment of having something that the Great Messenger wanted.

Solaris... warned Gabriella. Not wanting the cat to get too high on her power before she fulfilled her part of their deal. *I am running out of time. As are you.*

The cat felt the wave of power emanating from the Messenger and promptly sat up. She was treading on thin ice.

Pull back those two hay bales, Solaris said, pointing her paw at the westerly corner of the room. *They are easily pushed aside. And are pulled back after as a security measure. So be sure to replace them as you leave, or your exit will be found out. Anyone who helped you will be punished. As will the servants who are responsible for this room.*

Gabriella looked at the two lone hay bales and immediately recognized the surface disguise. *Of course,* she thought.

I promise to cover my tracks carefully, Gabriella replied. She stood up and turned to Solaris. *I hope we meet again.*

With full bellies and clean paws, replied Solaris, bestowing Gabriella with the highest blessing a cat could give.

Gabriella moved swiftly to the bales. Pulling them aside to reveal a small, wooden door just big enough for her to shimmy through. Clearly, the servants with access to this room were small and wiry. *But,* she sighed in relief, *I will be able to escape.*

She closed her eyes and snapped the fingers on each hand twice. Covering the door with a disguising spell for any other feline in the vicinity. She turned to Solaris. *It is done.*

Then placing her hands on the cool wood, she paused to sense whether anyone was on the other side. The way was clear. For now.

This was her moment of greatest peril since entering the Palace.

Gabriella took a deep breath. And pulled the hatch.

CHAPTER TEN

SYRENA STARED at the spot where Adrian stood a moment ago.

"Nine days?" Syrena exclaimed. She turned to Tobias as though he would be able to explain the impossible challenge. "Nine days?"

"He is your spellcaster," Tobias replied. "You should understand his cryptic requests."

Syrena rolled her eyes. And stood unmoving. Now that the time had come to leave, Syrena struggled with the decision.

"She will be safe," Tobias assured her.

"And you complain that I read your thoughts," grumbled Syrena.

Her heart knew it was time. But she had not been separated from Hannah for as long as she cared to remember. Tobias waited patiently. Syrena understood that he would wait as long as she needed. But their time was disappearing.

Syrena kissed Hannah gently, and whispered, "I will be back, my love. Rest safe. If you need anything, come to me in the dreamlands." Syrena swore she could feel Hannah smile.

Then she strode away, needing to leave before her fears

grabbed hold. If she could keep her feet ahead of her worry, she would make it out of Granamore.

Syrena blew past Tobias and through the door before he could say anything. She could feel that he fought his own battle about leaving. But she did not trust herself to wait.

The door banged shut behind her and she heard Tobias's feet chasing her down. He caught up to her swift stride. Syrena was grateful that he did not comment.

"You are confident that she is protected?" Tobias asked. Syrena nodded.

"Then that is all that matters," he said.

They strode through the desolate gardens of Granamore. Syrena noted that Tobias kept his gaze forward. She felt his torn allegiance. He did not want to leave the land he called home. Even if he was making his way toward Gabriella.

As they passed the spot where Hannah had fallen prey to the spell, Syrena tensed. Tobias eyed her.

"And how do you propose we make it to Cardea in nine days?" Tobias asked, picking up the pace. Syrena hesitated for a second, then swiftly caught up.

"I have no idea," she replied, relieved that they were past her point of no return. "But I do know Adrian. And he would not set a task that was impossible to achieve. Difficult, yes. Ludicrously insane, maybe. But not impossible."

"Great," Tobias grumbled. "I had been hoping for a ludicrously insane task to add to my list."

Syrena laughed. And Tobias smiled. They exchanged a look of camaraderie.

She pulled her wool wrap tighter as they climbed up the rugged hillside toward the woods. The stars began to peek out in the evening sky.

Syrena felt Tobias's conflicting emotions. He was terrified to confront how he felt about Gabriella. Not that he said a word to her. *Given how patient he had been with my holding tight to Hannah all this time,* Syrena thought, *I am not about to tease him at this tender threshold.*

Tobias glanced at her, sensing her attention. But said nothing. He kept his fierce hunter's stride. Syrena felt even more affection for Tobias as she sensed his heart break. He had never wanted to leave the wild woods that he loved so deeply.

We might just accomplish this journey, thought Syrena. *If we make it out of Granamore alive.*

Syrena and Tobias disappeared into the ancient forest.

And if I figure out the magical feat of travelling one thousand leagues in nine short days.

CHAPTER ELEVEN

THE GREAT PRINCE stumbled his way down the rugged mountain path.

As he moved further from his ancestral lands, the trees grew sparse. Still, he was grateful for any cover that they gave. His feet slid down the steep dirt and fumbled over ancient roots.

And he grew more nervous.

When the Prince first fled, he had been terrified of the woods. Now that he was leaving, he missed them. He felt loved and protected in a way that he had never experienced with people. Even the animals had begun to approach him.

Maybe it is easier for animals to forgive, thought the Prince.

Maybe animals did not starve, cringe, and suffer from your cruel ways, sneered a voice inside him. *You have done as much damage in your reign.*

Not true, the Prince countered, though he winced at the accusation. His foot caught a root and he tripped. The Prince grabbed a tree just in time, and his slipping feet sent a cascade of rocks down the trail. The sharp bark cut into his palm and the Prince yelped.

His thoughts argued back and forth. And all the while, the

Prince felt more afraid. He would soon venture away from the stark, high mountains into the domain of people.

The Prince would not travel much farther without crossing paths with trappers or hunters or rogue bandits. He might be safe for another hour or two. This was still too close to the Hidden Palace for them to risk her snatching away their power.

He continued on, jumping at shadows and fearing the slightest sound. But the strangest thing began to happen the longer he braved walking away from his ancestral lands.

A shimmer of courage took root in his heart.

For the first time in as long as he could remember, the Prince wondered whether he might be able to escape the long shadow of his ancestors. He did not hold much hope for forgiveness, but he did wonder if he could feel happiness.

The path began to even out and the Prince admired the rocky hills covered in heather. He took a deep breath and sighed. Until his next breath caught the scent of woodsmoke. And he froze.

He had been anticipating this moment. And still, he struggled to find a place to hide. He scrambled down to a ridge with a collection of alder trees. He tucked behind a spindly tree, too slender to hide him.

But It will block my face, he thought. *And that is enough.*

The Prince peered around to find the source of the fire. He looked down the valley and was relieved to see that the smoke had carried a fair distance from the village. It was not a hunter's fire or a rogue's trap.

Though, truthfully, the Prince had seen neither in his life. He only gleaned those notions from the tales his father told him. The Prince had never been on a mountain path. Let alone travel alone.

He rarely left the Hidden Palace, and when he did, he travelled with a support of soldiers. He only ordered the cruel doings of his mercenaries. Reaping only the riches of their thievery and devastation. He had never gone with them.

As he peered into the valley, the Prince shivered. Soon enough, he would see the faces of the people affected by his malice. *And they all know my face,* the Prince lamented. *Unless...*

A scrap of hope appeared as he thought, *Unless, I disguise myself.*

Even as his shoulders released a notch, he wrestled with his conscience. *Should I confront my demons now?*

He watched the smoke drift up on the wind. He guessed that he was within a day's reach of the village. He had that long to decide.

The more the Prince considered his options, the more he liked the idea of a disguise. If only because it would buy him time to figure out how to find Gabriella. *That is my first mission,* he assured himself. *What is the point of getting myself killed before I can reach her?*

Yet he could not keep from lashing himself with the whip of doubt. He threw his hands in the air. Frustrated with his own mind.

If this is what it is like to have a conscience, he objected, *I am sure to die from internal lacerations before I reach my first stop. I likely will not find a disguise before I am discovered.*

Maddened by his own debate, he released the tree and continued down the mountain. Though he moved cautiously and he kept his gaze sharp.

As he navigated the slope, the Prince thought back to the many stories he had been told from his mercenaries' mouths. Despite his riches, his days in the Palace had been filled with boredom. So, when his cruel soldiers came back from their raids, he listened avidly to their wild tales.

He had no way of knowing if their accounts were true, but he heard them speak of rebels sneaking into villages under nightfall. And being ambushed by rogues who looked like Palace guards. The Prince had assumed these were ridiculous stories to cover up the soldiers' incompetence. But now he wondered if they were true.

And even more crucial, he thought, *how did these rebels cobble together their disguises?*

As the trail evened out and his feet steadied on the softer dirt, the Prince wished he had been more inquisitive and less harsh. That crucial information would now serve him well. Instead, he was once more on his own.

His stomach growled, as though to remind him that he would not have the strength to rob anyone of their clothes if he did not find some food.

Still, the Prince pressed forward. He would have to figure this out as he went. Praying for the opportunity to fill his belly. And trusting that he would figure out how to steal the clothes he needed.

But first, he had to risk the possibility of being discovered.

CHAPTER TWELVE

ADRIAN APPEARED inside the far reaches of the corridors in the Hidden Palace to find no sign of Gabriella.

Damn it, he thought. *I waited too long.*

He immediately knew that the Palace had discovered Gabriella's presence. Now, he needed to find her without drawing attention. Or she would never escape.

Adrian felt a cold wind blow past and he knew he had only seconds before the Mad King's spirit swept around the corner. He could chide himself later. Adrian swiftly disappeared.

He hovered between realms, sensing that he had one more attempt to find Gabriella. The Mad King may have missed seeing him, but the Palace had tripwires and sentries keeping watch.

The more Adrian moved, the more likely she would feel something amiss and trace the source. He focused his heart and sensed beyond his emotions and hopes. He felt for Gabriella's brilliant spark of light.

Adrian smiled as he saw in his mind's eye, the image of Gabriella shimmying through a small trapdoor. Pulling herself upright and pausing to breathe in the fresh air. As though she had been kept captive in that horrid building for much longer than forty-eight hours.

He felt beyond his vision to where she was on the grounds. Then swiftly shot to her side.

Gabriella responded before Adrian appeared. Sensing his appearance, she coiled to strike. Growling with a sharp blade in her hand. When she saw his face, she exhaled sharply and controlled the fire in her throat. Gabriella tucked away her blade and snarled.

About time, she said, silently. *You left me alone and exposed*. Her words were as sharp as her blade. Gabriella snuck away, moving toward an outbuilding. She assumed it was a stable based on the soft whinnying of horses and scent of hay.

You were in excellent hands, Adrian replied calmly. He followed close, keeping his ghostly feet close to the ground in case they were spotted by someone that could see him. Most humans could not, but animals and spirits might get startled and cause a commotion.

Thank goodness, she fired back. But Gabriella's heart was delighted to have Adrian by her side. She could rarely stay angry with him for long. Her anger turned swiftly to desire. And she needed to keep both tightly reined for fear of revealing their location.

Adrian smiled. He needed to be with her, too. He was tired of this ghostly connection. He missed the warmth of her embrace. The closeness of sharing her bed.

Not here, Gabriella thought, swiftly dousing his fire. Yet her body ached for him as strongly. She focused her desire into her muscles and the speed of her feet. *I cannot afford to be distracted.*

He nodded, *Fair point*. Adrian sharpened his mind. And applied it to the task at hand.

You need a steed, he thought. And Gabriella shot him a look. *Clearly*, she replied.

Let me finish, he thought. *You need a steed that can fly like the wind.*

Adrian's words felt like salt in the wound. Gabriella's heart squeezed. Her grief for Casmire ripped through her like a flash of lightning.

I am sorry, my love. Adrian felt her anguish. Her pain mixed with his guilt for being the reason that her beloved friend had sacrificed his life.

Gabriella nodded. She fell silent and moved faster.

Adrian respected her silence. She needed to resolve her grief without his interference. So, he focused on keeping her safe as she approached the stable doors.

Gabriella felt Adrian's protection. She shoved her feelings aside to focus on the doors. She needed to open the steel bolt without making too much noise. She could not risk alerting anyone inside or the guards that the Palace was tasking to search for her.

She placed her hands gently on the bolt and trusted Adrian to alert her to approaching danger. Given the late hour, most of the servants were at supper. Or sought a fire as the alpine night swept in with sharp, frigid air.

She heaved upwards on the hefty bolt. Keeping it steady to prevent the mechanism from groaning or catching. She could not risk the sound ringing out across the grounds. Bringing the guards to her side faster than she could mount a steed.

Gabriella reined in her impatience and felt through each move of her escape. She needed to proceed with intense caution. She took a deep breath.

At times like this, when she needed to act in direct opposition to her instincts, she thought of the people she held most dear. She called to mind her sister, Hannah. Syrena. Katrin. And yes, the Great Prince.

You will make a powerful Queen, yet, Adrian whispered. He

had felt her call her allies to her side and use their souls to direct her to make wise choices.

I am far from a Queen, Gabriella chided. *Nor do I desire the position. It belongs to Hannah.* She lifted the bolt gently, one inch at a time.

Between the two of you, one will have to take the throne, Adrian replied. *You cannot play this game of toss the tiara forever.*

Can you blame us? Asked Gabriella. *We saw what power did to our family.*

No. Adrian countered, as he sharpened his gaze in the deepening night.

He placed his back to Gabriella's and kept watch for approaching creatures, human or wild. *You saw what evil and greed did to your family. Power does not need to be used in such a way. It can bring peace and security when wielded with wisdom.*

Perhaps, Gabriella ceded. As she lifted the bolt higher, she felt the sharp ears of the horses perk up inside. Their whinnying softened but grew higher in pitch. Clearly, they did not like when humans approached.

Gabriella reached out with her mind. Soothing their nervous souls. *I come in peace,* she whispered. *I need a fast steed to help me flee this place. One who can be discreet yet move like the wind. Will one of you be that for me?*

We may have one who can help, a firm yet kind voice replied.

I hate to interrupt, Adrian said, breaking into her thoughts. *But we have company approaching fast.*

Gabriella glanced over her shoulder to see several groups of night guards running toward the stables. She felt into their feeble minds and sensed the Palace's command to find her.

"Damn it," she cursed under her breath. "So much for being subtle."

And heaved the bolt up with all her strength.

CHAPTER THIRTEEN

KATRIN LAY awake in her bed, staring at the stained ceiling. She needed to leave tonight.

Word in the taverns was that a prize was offered to anyone with knowledge of the Messenger's location. And though Katrin had done well keeping her head down, she stood out as a stranger in this town.

These days, hope and suspicion battled for the people's hearts. Though they wanted one, the other had long held sway. Fueled by the cruelty of the Prince's minions.

There will always be rogues who profit in fragile times, growled Katrin to herself. *At least one of them noticed me in the tavern. And had one of his urchins track me on my way home.*

She drilled her fingers softly into the wooden bedframe. *Either I dare leaving under the cover of dark and risk being ambushed by thieves. Or I stay until daylight and gamble on being dragged off to the Prince's stockade.*

Katrin was familiar with being stuck in the middle of two bad choices. But she had grown used to having company to help her solve the dilemma.

I used to love travelling alone, she griped. *Now, I feel exposed.*

Katrin sighed. Truthfully, she never *really* loved travelling by herself. She only thought she did until she experienced the delight of being with Gabriella. Trusting someone who genuinely cared and wanted more for her than a brutal existence.

Her fingers stopped drilling. Tears stuck in her throat.

Katrin missed Gabriella more than words could convey. And more than she would ever say out loud. The past few years had hardened her. Katrin had sharp edges where she once had soft curves. Her gaze was suspect first and open later.

The Great Prince had robbed them all of their innocence. And she was not going to forget it.

Even if Gabriella insists that he is good, she thought. *If I play no other role in this journey, I will be the one to remind her that he cannot be trusted. He stole her sister. And raided every town in the known lands for their wares, killing villagers who resisted and leaving the rest to starve!*

Katrin sat up and swung her legs over the edge of her bed. She was wide awake now.

I will not forget the wreckage that he brought to my home, she swore. *And I will make sure the Messenger does not forget it either. No matter how much she believes he can change. Some people will always be the blood that bore them and the choices that shaped them.*

In Katrin's mind, the Great Prince stood for everything that was wrong with the world. And everything that was stolen from her. *Petty thieves go to jail,* she thought. *Thieves who steal innocence should be put to the gallows.*

She sighed. And let her heart break in the momentary safety of her room.

Katrin did not like feeling that the darkness was creeping back into the corners of her mind. She had been on guard too long. It made her doubt the goodness in people. Hiding in the shadows always took a toll. Especially on the kind-hearted. And she had spent weeks in them now.

What I would not do for an embrace from Gabriella, she mused. *Or a sweet glance from Patrick.*

Katrin allowed herself the luxury of imagining her loved ones with her, sitting beside her on the tiny bed. If only for a second to comfort her and keep the prowling bitterness at bay.

Her shoulders softened and her heart melted. She felt the warmth of Patrick's smile. And the edges of her lips curved up slightly.

She closed her eyes and thought of Gabriella sitting wrapping a firm, yet understanding, arm around her. Katrin's head tilted as though it leaned on Gabriella's shoulder. She felt the tears welling up in her chest, as the ache of homesickness swept over her.

Katrin kept her eyes tightly closed. Forbidding the tears to come. Yet as tough as these years had made her, inside she was a tender-hearted soul. That thought aggravated her now. Fearing that it made her weak and vulnerable.

She exhaled hard. She heard Gabriella chiding her softly. Reminding her that her true strength would always be found in the kindness of her heart. *Even though we must fight,* she heard Gabriella say, *never forget that it is our benevolence that makes us strong.*

She wished she had been able to speak with Gabriella. To convince her out of going to Cardea. One of the most dangerous places in the Great Lands. Katrin shook her head and laughed softly. *No more so than the Hidden Palace,* she thought.

She remembered the secret message Gabriella had sent in her dreams. Telling her to go to Cardea. That once Katrin was close, Gabriella would send a sign instructing her where to meet.

Katrin felt the presence of Gabriella disappear. And the

company of Patrick evaporate. The coldness without them was palpable. But her heart felt stronger and her faith was restored.

Her eyes opened and the soft smile remained on her lips. She would make it through another day. That was all she asked of the Divine right now. To help her make it through today without her loved ones.

Katrin shook her head. *Some warrior you will make*, she thought, and snorted at her own expense. Katrin felt relieved. *As long as I can still laugh, I know the darkness has not won.*

She pushed forward on the bed and her feet made contact with the icy-cold floor. Katrin glanced at the tattered curtain and saw a faint light shimmer around its edges. The day was brightening.

She got up and approached the window. Pulling back the curtain an inch, Katrin glanced down into the street. Careful not to reveal herself. She let the curtain's movement be the same as if a soft breeze of draft lifted the fabric.

Katrin tried to see whether that urchin had tracked her all the way. Her eyes raked over the dimly lit streets. She deciphered nothing, but her highly attuned instincts told her that she had a brief opening to leave this town before someone grabbed and dragged her off to the Palace.

She took one last peek at the street. The boardwalk edge was just barely discernable. Soon her chance to leave would be gone. She needed to act swiftly. Dancing on the edge of risk and reward.

Her stomach chimed in with a protesting growl. She had not eaten in hours. And would not have time to grab anything before leaving. *Hush. I do not need complaints from you.*

The scent of freshly baking bread had wafted up from the nearby bakery. One of the few people awake at this hour. Other than one or two drunks staggering home from a rough night.

Katrin dropped the curtain and grabbed her small satchel off the bed. The bag held all her belongings worth anything in the world.

A sad statement indeed, she laughed. Though, she was grateful for the light load in moments like this one. She did not need weight slowing her down or making her nervous. She needed to be quick on her feet.

In a matter of seconds, Katrin was out her door. She took quietly in the hallway. Listening like a perched cat. She heard the snores of the other inn patrons. Everyone seemed sound asleep.

And there was no noise coming yet from the kitchen. *Which meant the cook had not yet risen to make breakfast. Thank the stars,* she thought. *Or my stomach might complain so loud as to wake the entire inn.*

Still, she could not move. She had paid the innkeeper for her room when she arrived. She did not fear him stopping her. But she did wonder whether he might have taken bribes to alert the mercenaries of her movements. Putting her in deep jeopardy should he know when she left.

Katrin dared to step toward the stairs. Carefully tiptoeing in a weaving pattern to avoid the creaking floorboard that she had found on her way in. And watching for rogue nails that might snag her shoe and send her flying.

When Katrin made it to the top of the staircase, she pressed against the wall. Listening close for a few heartbeats. Hearing nothing, she held her breath. And leaned out over the stairs, just far enough to get a peek into the lower hallway.

The way was clear. Not a soul was in her path.

She exhaled sharply. And smiled. *Thousands may believe the drink is a scourge on our lands,* she thought, *and they would be right. But today, I am grateful that it has knocked out my innkeeper and kept him silent.*

Still, she could not assume that she was completely safe.

Katrin moved quietly, which was challenging since the inn was ready to collapse onto the board bugs that held it up.

It's a miracle that I have not crashed through the ancient boards already, she thought, as she snuck down the stairs. Lightly touching the rail, like a trapeze artist keeping her flight in delicate motion.

When a loud SNORT ripped through the air. Katrin FROZE in her tracks. Holding her breath and refusing to blink.

After a few moments, with no sound of footfalls, Katrin dared to gaze over the railing into the hallway. She saw nothing.

She sharpened her senses and perked her ears to catch the next noise. Nothing came. Which was worse than another sound. She could not release her frozen stance until she knew which way to run.

Her muscles began to tremble. And Katrin braced herself to make a gamble. She wished it was not necessary, but here she was. She took a deep breath.

Just as she was on the edge of retreating, she heard a second louder GASP. Followed swiftly by a grumble and a rolling sound. Her sharp hearing deciphered exactly where the owner was – in the kitchen. And, as she had guessed, he was sleeping off his drunken stupor. Most likely, on the floor, wrapped around an empty bottle.

Even if he wakes up, she thought, eying the front door, *I have at least three minutes to get outside and disappear. That will do.*

Katrin let her shoulders drop and softened her gaze. She felt like a horse preparing to break free from a racing gate. She counted down in her mind. Three, two, one...

Katrin pushed off the stair, running down the steps. A loud CREAK filled the air as the staircase complained. She had no way of knowing whether the innkeeper was a light sleeper, but she had no intention of finding out.

She kept moving. Off the stairs and across the entryway.

Katrin rushed for the door. Praying that even if the innkeeper woke, he would not have time to alert the Prince's spies.

Katrin fumbled with the locks on the door, desperately pulling at the old mechanisms. She heard a CRASH in the kitchen. Sounding much like the owner sitting up and dropping the bottle that was his companion.

Katrin sharpened her eyes and focused on her nimble fingers. She did not have a moment to spare. The innkeeper's CURSING and BANGING grew louder as he fumbled toward the kitchen door.

Her heart raced as the final lock refused to budge. She pulled and yanked and swore silently. Then closed her eyes and tossed a desperate prayer to the skies.

The lock RELEASED, sending Katrin reeling backwards as the door flew open.

She caught her footing quickly and slipped outside, careful to hide behind the door. Pulling it closed behind her.

Katrin glanced down the street. Careful to stay pressed against the building while scanning for her pursuers. She saw no movement. *Which does not mean they are not waiting*, she grumbled. *But I have no time left. If I can keep cover until I get to the edge of town, I should be okay.*

She heard the loud footfalls of the innkeeper approaching the door. Katrin needed cover and fast. She spotted a water barrel across the street.

Lightning-focused and almost as fast, Katrin bolted across the main street, mud flying behind her. She did not have a moment to spare. She leapt head-first into the barrel. Praying, as she did so, that it was a rain barrel and not some other kind.

As her head knocked against the edges of the empty drum, she curled up swiftly and begged the barrel to balance. The rocking motion slowed just enough to keep the steel bands around the wood from screeching out in protest.

Katrin peeked through the wooden slats. Her chest heaving as she watched the inn's front door. Catching her breath as she saw the door squeal with complaints. Sticking in its frame as stubbornly as the old, rusty locks.

Thank the goddess I am not the only one with portal difficulties, she thought.

The innkeeper wrenched the door open. And the force of the release sent him stumbling backwards. His hungover feet slipping out from under him. Knocking his head hard against the wall inside.

Cursing, he SLAMMED the door shut. Not even bothering to look outside.

Katrin exhaled and leaned back against the slimy wood. She cast her gaze to the heavens, seeing the dark black sky tilting its tint toward blue. Throwing a brief thanks to the stars above, she pushed herself to her feet and snuck out of the barrel. Keeping close to the shadows.

With a last furtive glance down the street, she slipped away into the dawn.

CHAPTER FOURTEEN

The Hidden Palace felt the unrelenting madness of her sire.

Gabriella had escaped from her walls. A realization that filled the Palace with destructive fury. *Those incompetent guards will pay*, she fumed.

She satisfied her blood lust by imagining crushing their skulls. For now.

But right now, she needed to tend to her liege. The Mad King was growing weaker without the hands of his son to fuel his burning need to devour the world.

The Palace watched the Mad King wander the high halls. The Mad King, like every king, believed that he was in charge. But she knew otherwise.

His spirit kept her from crumbling into an empty mass of rock. But *she* was the force of nature.

She spun the spells that possessed these lands and kept the people doing her bidding. She knew how to twist their thoughts and frighten their hearts. Forcing them into cruelty and destruction, rather than hope.

The Palace watched closely as the Mad King wandered to the far reaches of her northern wing.

Where did these maddening mists come from? the King exclaimed. He spun in circles, surrounded by a swirl of mist, as though morning fog had blown in off the mountains. *I smell the secrets of my son. You cannot hide from me, Traitor of my Blood!*

As the Mad King stormed, the mists thickened around his ankles. Dulling his senses and dampening his heart. The Palace watched as the King grew confused about where he was.

Have I wandered into the liminal lands? You cannot make me leave! He roared into the rising mists. *I refuse to leave this realm until I see this world begging at my feet. I will not be thwarted!*

The more the Mad King protested, the thicker the mists became. Sending him into a frenzied spin. Yet, he could not stop the rage. Throwing his fists at the fog like a temperamental child.

The Palace quite enjoyed the feeling of her sire's fits. As though someone was scratching a long-ignored itch that she could not reach. She missed his wild outbursts.

No one matched her insane hatred of all things living quite like he did.

And so, as only a creature born of cruelty could do, she watched his torment. Savouring every drop. Waiting until she, too, feared that he might cross over into the liminal mists and leave her forever.

She could not risk that. She needed the pull of the King to draw his son back into her fold.

And so, she called out to the King. *Come, your Regal Majesty. My liege. My lord. Return to my cold, beating heart. Where we can torture the living together.*

The Mad King heard her call. And focused on her voice to draw him away from the mists.

He saw the edges of the stone hallway. Like a visionless man, the Mad King stumbled toward the flickering light cast from the hallway torches.

As he arrived at the juncture to the foyer, he slid down the wall. Resting his ghostly head against the cold stone. He needed to catch his breath. He could not lose his hold on this realm until his son came back to continue his ancestral duty.

He cannot roam free for too long, the Mad King mumbled, in a last attempt at rage. Before his eyelids closed and the King folded into a translucent heap.

The Palace watched with delight over her crumpled puppet. *You shall serve your purpose before you release your hold on this realm.*

Both were unaware that the stones in the wall whispered behind his back. Sharing this illuminating secret. *The Mad King knows something. Something that might free us all forever.*

They hushed the whispers quickly.

Keeping the secret close for the day they might share it with the future Queen.

PART III
LEAP OF FAITH

CHAPTER ONE

SYRENA AND TOBIAS sat by the comforting sight of a wild hare roasting over a campfire. Though neither looked particularly comforted.

Though they were relieved to be by a warm fire with supper cooking, their faces revealed only concern. They had been walking for twenty-four hours and were no closer to figuring out their dilemma.

How are we were supposed to travel to Cardea in a mere eight days? Grumbled Tobias. He was beginning to wonder why they had been pulled away from Hannah for an impossible mission. His stomach growled loudly, as though to support his protest.

I trust Syrena, Tobias reminded himself. *That is all that matters.*

"Damn right it is what matters," she replied. Tobias glared back. He knew she was trying to distract him. All Syrena needed to do was eavesdrop on his thoughts to accomplish that.

I do not doubt Adrian, she thought, projecting her words into Tobias's mind. They could not be too careful when it came to hidden enemies eavesdropping. *But I still have no idea how we will do this.*

You are a powerful sorceress, Syrena, he replied, turning the roasting hare. *We will figure this out.*

What am I supposed to do? She countered. *Come up with a spell to uncover a portal to Cardea? I barely know the first thing about casting magic. I might as well wish for the fire fairies to do my bidding.*

Syrena threw her hands in the air. The pressure of Adrian's challenge was getting to them both. Never mind the growling stomachs and worried hearts.

Syrena sighed. And placed a comforting hand on Tobias's shoulder. He cast a look her way. Her kindness made him worry more. Still, he smiled. He needed to hold on to hope for all of them. Hannah included.

They watched the dancing flames together in silence. The crackle of wood soothed their nerves. And the magic of warm, glowing light soothed their hearts.

After several minutes, Tobias broke their brooding quiet. "What harm could it do?"

"What did you just say?" Syrena replied.

Tobias looked at her quizzically. "You heard me." He pulled out a knife to check on the hare.

"Of course, I heard you," she shot back. "But why did you say it?"

Tobias threw her a look, wondering why she was so worked up. "I thought it, so I said it."

Syrena slapped his shoulder. "No, you did not!"

Tobias rubbed his stinging shoulder. "What has gotten into you? You are making not making a stitch of sense."

Syrena stood up, a rush of nervous excitement pulsing through her. "Tobias. I said those words in my head."

"So we had the same thought," he replied, and plunged his knife into one of the hare's legs.

"No," she insisted. "You heard my thought."

"Stop playing with me," he replied, "I do not have your talent. Nor would I want to." With his knife, he pulled back part of the leg, watching as a slight trickle of juice dripped from the rabbit into the hot coals.

Oh really, thought Syrena, eyeing him sharply. *Not a speck of my talent.*

"Now you are just being brazen," replied Tobias, "Clearly, you are hungry."

"Ah!" Syrena shrieked and pointed. The fire danced higher in response. Tobias leapt back and grabbed his bow. He aimed into the darkness, sure that Syrena had seen an attacker.

"You did it again!" Syrena declared. Tobias did one last pass with his bow, until he saw that Syrena was pointing at him. Not at the dark woods. He lowered his arm. Narrowing his gaze, he wondered what Syrena was talking about.

"I did what again?" he asked. Tucking away his bow and arrow and forcing himself to stay calm. He was tired and hungry and did not like the fact that the fire leapt at Syrena's slightest command.

Syrena exhaled. *Do not treat me like a child*, she thought.

"Perhaps this should wait until after we have eaten," Tobias replied, cautiously. He could see that Syrena was riled up. And he did not want to spark a wildfire by inadvertently provoking her magical talents.

"No," Syrena replied. "We need to settle this now."

Tobias sighed and sat back down on his cold, hard rock. Knowing full well there was no reasoning with Syrena when she was in this state. "Fine," he sighed. "What do you propose?"

"Look at me, Tobias," Syrena said. And Tobias complied. Looking at her with the same exhaustion that he felt in his bones.

She locked eyes with him. Taking a moment to make sure he

did not look away. Or blame what she was about to do on some trick of the night. *Tell me you do not hear my thoughts.*

"What in the heavens?" Tobias shot to his feet. Kicking the edge of the roasting stand and sending the hare swinging back and forth over the flames.

Syrena swiftly caught it and steadied their dinner. She might be excited, but she was not going to cost them a hard-won meal.

"Do it again!" he commanded. Syrena raised her eyebrow at his tone but could not fault him for what he asked.

Fine. But you might want to ask nicely, she thought. *Otherwise, I will turn you into a toad.*

"Like you could," he shot back. She pointed at him and he jumped.

Syrena doubled over laughing. *You thought I was going to ...* And she laughed all the harder.

"This is not funny," he accused. Then got caught up in her delight. It was a welcome relief.

He was so grateful to hear her laugh that Tobias smiled, despite himself. Syrena wiped tears from her eyes, as she slowly stopped laughing.

She glanced around. Peering into the misty trees, she wondered, *Are these woods filled with magic?*

"Not that I have heard tell," Tobias answered, following her gaze. Then his eyes went a little wider. "Maybe we should go back to speaking aloud." He said. "I am not sure how I feel about hearing your every passing thought."

"I agree," Syrena said. Still, she glanced around for other signs of magic as she returned to the old stump that doubled as her chair.

Tobias lifted the rabbit off its stand. He pulled apart their meal. Handing a leg to Syrena and setting aside the other for himself. He balanced the spit by his side. And bit into the delicious roasted meal. His stomach rumbled in gratitude.

They chewed in silence. Occasionally flinching, as they tried to ignore the other's thoughts.

"Okay," Syrena relented, lowering her dinner. "You know this land better than anyone. You must have heard *some* tales about magic."

"Most of them revolve around Gabriella," Tobias said, lowering his voice. He did not like speaking her name so close to their home and the spellbound Hannah. He still anticipated an attack at any moment.

And now we have magic to contend with, he grumbled.

"Magic does not need to be a bad thing," Syrena replied. She was counselling herself as much as Tobias. "If Gabriella and Hannah come from an enchanted bloodline, maybe their ancestral lands also hold a kind of magic."

An owl hooted in the far distance. Tobias wished they were having this conversation in the daylight. *Magic has a way of showing its face at night,* he remembered his mother saying.

"I believe the owl agrees," he said. Surprising Syrena with his reverence. "What?" he said, defensively. "Every hunter knows the language of animals."

"The sounds maybe," she replied. "But not the wisdom, Tobias. You just spoke the way of the owl." She raised an eyebrow at him. Realizing he had been holding back some secrets of his own.

"Perhaps," he averted her gaze. Suddenly uncomfortable that he had revealed too much. His mother, much like Gabriella's, had counselled him to be careful with his abilities. His brow furrowed.

Tobias wondered aloud, "Do you think all we need to do is ask for their assistance?" He was not sure that he liked this tact. But he also knew they would never make it to Cardea in time unless they found out a way that defied logic.

"I think Adrian could tell that we would not be alone,"

Syrena guessed. "Or he knew more than he shared with us. Either way, I am willing to risk it."

"Easy for you to say," Tobias replied. "You are comfortable with magic."

"Hardly," Syrena shot back. "But I do believe it can be of great assistance when wielded wisely."

"Great," said Tobias.

Syrena patted his knee in consolation and said, "We do not have a lot of choice, my friend."

"First invisible wizards, now this," said Tobias. "What could possibly go wrong?"

CHAPTER TWO

As Gabriella lifted the bolt, it SCREECHED and scraped. The noise carried far into the night.

The entire Palace knows where I am now, she thought. As she ducked through the door.

Grab whatever horse looks fastest, replied Adrian, *and I will do my best to divert them.*

Gabriella's gaze swept over the restless horses. They whinnied and stomped. Sensing the panic in the air. She wanted to set them all free.

You only have time for one, insisted Adrian. *Your very life counts on —*

Adrian's spirit flickered and disappeared. Startling Gabriella and increasing the panic of the horses.

Adrian? she called out with her mind but could not feel him. *Adrian!*

The clamour of voices increased outside the stable. The guards were approaching. She had no time to worry.

Gabriella sent up a swift prayer for Adrian's safety. Then turned to the large mare directly in front of her. *I am Gabriella*, she declared. *I need your help.*

I am Astrella, replied the horse. *Jump on my back and we will flee this nightmare together.*

Gabriella pulled hard on the bolts that locked Astrella's stall and pulled the door open. Astrella leapt forward, charging toward the stable doors. Gabriella responded swiftly, grabbing her mane and swinging onto her back.

Astrella broke into a full gallop, barrelling toward the doors. Gabriella spotted a bridle and snatched it off a hook, as they crashed out the stable doors.

The sun had mercifully disappeared below the horizon. Evening swiftly cast its shadows across the outer courtyard, making them harder to spot. Gabriella cursed the loss of Adrian's help. He would have been able to confuse the minds of the approaching guards.

Her heart raced as the guards ran toward the sound of pounding hooves. Gabriella focused all of her power on cloaking them. The mare pulled sharply to the right, swerving around the confused men.

Gabriella glanced up to see them yelling at each other and pointing in opposite directions. *We make a good team*, Gabriella thought. *Choose the way that gets us out of sight the fastest.*

Astrella did not waste a moment. She flew across the open east field, pounding the earth as she bore down on the far mountain trails.

Gabriella tucked the bridle under her legs. The last thing she wanted to do was distract either of them. She could use it once they were out of danger.

As she took a quick look at where they were headed, Gabriella saw the brilliance of Astrella's strategy. The far trails were risky with their steep and treacherous descent. But the sudden drop would hide them quickly.

Provided that the Palace did not find them first.

Gabriella estimated that they had under a league to go

before they reached the trail. She strained her energy to keep them concealed.

Confident in Astrella's guidance, Gabriella tucked herself tight to the mare's back. She merged closely with her steed. She buried her head in the horse's mane, knowing that even the most vigilant guard would not have distinguished her dark cloak from Astrella's chestnut coat.

The guards would not care about the loss of a riderless horse. Their mission was to find her.

Just as her heart felt a wave of hope, Gabriella was struck with a deep feeling of dread. The Palace, she thought. And as swiftly as the fear rose in her throat, she suppressed it.

Letting the terror get the best of her would be like shooting a fire arrow straight into the sky. Illuminating their position and admitting defeat.

The Palace has not found us yet, she insisted. Locking eyes on the cliff edge that held their freedom. It still looked far away, despite Astrella's speed. Gabriella could feel the ice-cold tendrils of the Palace reaching out. Seeking her warm heart. Ready to crush all faith and love from its pulse.

She could not waste an ounce of her diminishing strength on fighting the Palace. She had to hope that her cloaking powers combined with Astrella's powerful stride would liberate them before the Palace broke past their defenses.

Her mind swooned and her eyesight blurred. Gabriella tightened her grip on Astrella's mane. The strain of days of limited food and no sleep was catching up to her.

Stubbornly, she held the cloaking spell. But her body was out of fuel. And did not care that they might be caught. Her legs weakened and her mind blurred.

Gabriella slid sideways on the mare's back, dangling on the edge of falling off. Astrella furiously tossed her head, snapping Gabriella awake. Watching the ground speeding past, perilously close to her head, Gabriella opened her eyes to see a rock barreling toward her.

She gasped. And yanked herself back up, just as the rock made contact. Gabriella touched her scalp to feel a trickle of blood.

She felt the evil hand of the Palace getting closer. They were so close. Gabriella needed to hold on for a few more minutes. She could not lose now.

If I fall off, we are both dead, she thought.

With dwindling energy, she had to make a choice. Release the cloaking spell or pass out before they make the cliff edge. She did not like either option. But such was where she stood.

Gabriella waited until the last possible second. Until her focus began to blur. And the pounding in her ears grew unbearable. Then released the cloaking spell.

Her vision snapped back. And her hearing sharpened. She locked her eyes on the approaching cliff edge, ignoring the shouts of faraway guards. Gabriella held tight to all that she might lose if they did not make it.

Adrian. Hannah. Her lands. Her people. She would not leave them. Not now.

"Run like the wind, Astrella," Gabriella whispered in the mare's ear. "Our fate is in your stride. Free us! Carry us far from this cursed place."

Recognizing the impending doom riding their tail, Astrella ran like she had never run before. Her hooves pounding the earth like thunder. Her heart racing like rain thrashing a tin roof.

The Palace turned her ice-cold attention toward their trail of dust. Shrieking so loud, her minions dove to the ground. Covering their ears to block the pain.

And Astrella plunged off the cliff edge, down the sharp mountain trail.

Gabriella felt it instantly. They were safe. Out of reach of the Palace's cruel magic.

Her body softened and her vision blurred. Gabriella wrapped her fists in Astrella's mane.

Then fell unconscious.

CHAPTER THREE

THE GREAT PRINCE snuck closer to the mountain village.

He watched as wild children climbed over an abandoned wagon. Playing games of imaginary chase, lost in their own world. Until their parents barked for them to return at once.

Glancing fearfully at the surrounding woods, the fathers pulled their children close. In hushed tones, they whispered fearful tales. Stories of child-stealing bandits and ferocious wolves. As the children swept the woods with big eyes, the Prince ducked out of sight. Waiting with a racing heart.

After their footfalls were long gone, he snuck from the gangly bushes by the path. Darting to the wagon and hiding behind the broken spindles of a long-gone wheel. The Prince waited for his jumping heart to calm down. He would have to get used to taking risks around people.

For now, he had no plan beyond this wagon. Given the size of the village, he was sure everyone must know each other. *Which means my only hope of getting through town or finding food is to disguise myself*, he thought.

The Prince did not know the first thing about pretending to be a wanderer. *Who travels these hills on purpose?* he wondered.

And how on earth will I know what to say? He did not have much faith in people helping him. Even with a disguise.

Cruel thoughts flitted through his mind and his heart began to harden. Even far from the Palace, the Prince felt his ancestors' words beckoning him to the easier path. "Knock that man over the head," they murmured. "Even if you crack his skull, no one will miss him."

The Prince squeezed his eyes shut. *Silence,* he yelled in his mind. *Leave me be!* And heard vicious cackles in return.

"Little Prince," they whispered. "You were not made for hard times. Your stomach is empty and your knees are weak. Come back to us, Little Prince." His stomach growled as though agreeing with his wretched relatives.

The Prince squared his shoulders and set his jaw. He commanded his body to stay brave. He could not have his mind and body making an alliance. Otherwise, it would only be a matter of time before his heart lost hope as well.

The mere thought of hope brought Gabriella to mind. And his heart leapt in response.

He sharpened his senses and paid close attention. *If I have to sit here all night,* he thought, *I will find a way to steal a disguise.*

As the Prince waited, he eventually saw the local blacksmith open his door. Standing in the entryway, arms crossed, the blacksmith looked up and down the street. Daring any miscreants to emerge and challenge him.

Why would you just stand there? Wondered the Prince. *Are you bored with forging metal and hoping for a fight? Or maybe you lost one too many scraps of metal to quick-footed thieves.*

The Prince looked over the blacksmith, searching for clues. And his eyes landed on the soot-covered meaty hands. The Prince's face lit up. *Soot!* He thought and smiled. *If I can get my hands on coal ash, no one will look close enough to recognize me.*

Then his thrill extinguished as quickly as it had caught fire.

Getting that ash comes with one major problem, thought the Prince, staring at the boulder of a man. *The blacksmith.*

The Prince stayed still in his hiding spot. Keeping an eye on the blacksmith and counselling his heart not to give up. Even as his cruel ancestors pounced on his despair. The Prince brushed away their words of "give up," and "go home."

The realization was dawning that it was no one else's duty to tend the fire of his courage. *This might be my path for the rest of my life*, he thought. *Seeking hope in impossible situations.*

The weight of his thoughts sunk his heart yet again. He considered throwing himself at the blacksmith. *Why not incite the man to put me out of my misery?* thought the Prince.

In response, a very different whisper echoed in his ear. One he had not heard since he had sequestered himself in his secret tower. *If Gabriella can forgive you, my dear nephew*, said the regal female voice, *so can others.*

A light sparked inside the Prince. He was not sure who the voice belonged to but he had heard it before in his darkest hours. *She knew of Gabriella, too*, he thought. *Is it possible that she knew other truths? Other prospects?*

As the spark grew in his heart, the Prince watched a beanpole of a man call to the blacksmith. The Prince's eyes widened as the burly man left his post. Ambling forward to clasp his friend in a warm embrace. The two men quickly fell into a conversation.

The doorway was clear of obstacles.

You may never get a better chance, whispered the kind voice. *I suggest you take it.*

The Prince wanted to argue. Wished to beg off the task. But no one else was going to do this for him. And even he could see that he had been given a gift.

He needed to act. And act now.

So the Prince took one of the greatest gambles of his life.

And stood up in plain view. His knees shook and his hands trembled. He half-expected everyone in town to step outside their doors and shoot arrows through his heart.

Instead, he saw a clear and open pathway to the blacksmith's door.

The two men had moved toward the local saloon and were huddled in a close in conversation. One that had all the markings of local gossip. They were careful to keep their voices low and their faces hidden.

The Prince ran toward the open door. Eyes fixed on the prize, he refused to look anywhere else. Fire burned in his legs and fear pulsed in his chest. He was terrified and thrilled with every step. Feeling the dirt under his feet and the cold air in his lungs.

He had never felt so alive in his entire life.

As his foot crossed the threshold, he felt the immediate coolness of the blacksmith's shop. He hid beside the open door, back to the wall. And doubled over, breathing heavily.

Slowly, he realized that he had made it. No footfalls approached. The blacksmith was not coming.

The Prince stood upright. And his eyes adjusted to the thick darkness. He was about to leap into the air to celebrate his own audacity.

Until he realized, he was not alone.

CHAPTER FOUR

KATRIN WOUND her way through the exposed foothill paths. She was not far from Cardea and was sure that she would be the first of Gabriella's tribe to arrive.

She glanced around with a sharp gaze. These foothills were exposed and Katrin was aware of her vulnerability. *Who knows what manner of rogues hide in these rocks*, she thought, *waiting to pounce*. But there was only one route to the main road into the city.

So Katrin had no choice. *A fact the thieves of this region know all too well*, she fumed.

Since she travelled alone, she chose to dress like a young man. The ruse made her less of an obvious target. Though they would be fools to jump Katrin. She had fought her way out of more than one ambush.

Any thief who would jump a lone traveller is a coward beyond measure, she thought. Still, she needed to be ready. Katrin kept a folded blade close in the pocket of her pants. As her concern grew, she deftly reached in and pulled the knife into her palm.

Katrin was mindful of Gabriella's teachings and could hear her mentor's voice in her mind. "Be gracious," she heard

Gabriella say. "And remember that every person is fighting a stronghold of demons. You might be amazed how often words work better than weapons."

But being away from Gabriella and the safety of a community brought out her her survival skills.

While I am travelling treacherous roads with no one to mind my back, Katrin thought, *I need my wild side.* Like a lone wolf, she listened for every sound and caught every scent. *My kind ways can come back once I am safe among friends.*

Even though Katrin had to be on guard out in the wilds, it was a different sorted of guarded than in the city. And she enjoyed the change. She found the cities unpredictable and tense. Filled with men with an axe to grind and women who had been suppressed too long. The volatile combination made her skin crawl and her knuckles itch for a fight.

She supposed that she was far too sensitive to everyone's emotional state. This fact aggravated her, except when she found it useful. Gabriella had half-convinced Katrin that her ability to read people was a gift that she could use in wiser ways than winning at poker.

Katrin half-smiled at the thought of duping another cheat out of their money. *Gabriella has her work cut out for her*, she thought. *As long as I need to put food in my belly and the world is run by arrogant, greedy men, I will take what I want. At their expense.*

She squared her shoulders and felt a little bolder on the trail. Katrin was not about to make any stupid moves, but neither was she about to look like an easy mark.

As the trail began to weave ever so slightly down, she knew she was drawing close to Cardea. Katrin was nervous about meeting Gabriella's clan. She was likely the only one without magical abilities. She wondered whether she might also be the only one not of royal blood.

Her feet slowed as she doubted what she might bring to the gathering. Why did Gabriella invite me? Katrin wondered. What could I possibly bring to this group of warriors and wizards?

She felt Gabriella's presence reassure her. "Katrin," she said. "Remember that possessing magic is as much a blind spot as a gift. The bearer often forgets that a simple approach is equally powerful. And assumes she is beyond breach. You have a precious ability to see a person's arrogance. That is worth much more than magic when waging a battle of wits."

Katrin smiled. And resumed her pace. She had a strong feeling that none of them had been to Cardea before. That made her the only one who understood the strange ways of this City. *I may not have spells*, she thought. *But I have the wisdom of the streets.*

At the base of the Ceres mountains, Cardea was nestled between mountains and seas. High peaks at its back and rolling waves at its front. Beautiful in its setting, the city was once a beacon of hope and connection. The port between the Great Lands and the faraway kingdoms.

Cardea was the heart of trade in the East. All supplies from the West and other lands came through this hub. But it was also the largest city within reach of the Hidden Palace. Which made the city a lively and highly dangerous place to be.

Katrin had heard many tales of the city in its heyday. Since the mountains shielded the Great Lands from any attack, visiting ships were forced to come into the Cardea harbour. Making any assault vulnerable to ambush as the ships approached.

Too bad the damn mountains did not protect us from an inside menace, she thought. Since the devastation wrought by the Mad King and his dupe Prince, Cardea had become a capricious place. *Not much of a beacon of hope, anymore.*

Katrin had only experienced the warring neighbourhoods

that now dominated the fragmented city. Each neighbourhood was its own fiefdom. Whoever ruled the trade in that corner of town, ruled the neighbourhood. So the strong and swift and ruthless made their claim known.

At least until the mercenaries of the Great Prince came to town. Then everyone who called himself a King tucked his tail between his legs and hid his profits under the table.

Katrin slowed down, sensing that she was being followed. She unfolded her hidden dagger, and shifted her weight to her heels. Not wanting her pursuers to know, just yet, that she was wise to their presence.

A rock tumbled down a steep ravine to her left and she pivoted. Keeping her back pressed to a large boulder, she declared, "Show yourself!" in a low a timbre. Praying that she sounded like a man.

Nervous laughter echoed off the rocks. Katrin tensed and stared at the spot where she guessed her pursuer was hiding. She wondered what kind of rogue would hide so long rather than openly fight her.

"You cannot surprise me," she insisted, "so you may as well make yourself known."

When no one stepped forward, she decided her only option was to bring the fight to him. Katrin moved toward the outcropping. She was at a disadvantage, but no more than if she continued down the mountain road.

The laughter resumed and Katrin was unnerved by this strange person. "What do you want?" she snapped, as she closed in.

Only to know that you are following directions, declared her pursuer. Katrin jumped back, startled by the crisp voice speaking inside her mind. If she did not know better, she might have believed it was Gabriella, the only person who had ever spoken directly to her thoughts.

Her foot slipped on a rock and Katrin stumbled. She fought the urge to catch herself. And kept a close grip on her knife. She swerved and righted her balance with the grace of a cat. Then crouched down, taking a more cautious approach with this formless voice.

"Only a coward hides behind boulders and uses magic to intimidate her opponent," she proclaimed. Despite Gabriella's persistent advice for patience, Katrin was not one to wait when she was not in control of the trick. She wanted this illusion dispelled.

The Messenger said you might be a jumpy, said the Voice. *But I did not expect you to be rude.*

Katrin looked up sharply and saw the most beautiful Vixen sitting atop the rock peak. She stood up and stared at the bold, silver fox. "You are speaking ... to me?" she fumbled. In all her years of seeing strange things, this was by far the strangest.

Yes. I can appreciate that you might be surprised. But whose fault is that? Said the Silver Vixen.

"Hey," Katrin took offence. Still, she looked around to see if someone might see her speaking to a fox. Or if this was a clever ruse, and the ambush was coming.

The Silver Vixen waited for Katrin's suspicious gaze to make its way back to her. *Are you quite finished?* she asked.

But Katrin's back was up. She did not like surprises. And she liked unnatural surprises even less. She looked around, behind, and above the fox. The Vixen snarled back at her, turning at each glimpse that Katrin attempted to gain.

"If you are not a trickster," Katrin said, "Why will you not let me look behind you?"

What kind of fool would let you gain ground behind me? The Silver Vixen growled.

"Fine," replied Katrin, taking a respectful and cautious step back. "Then state your case. Why me? What do you want?"

The Silver Vixen narrowed her gaze at Katrin. She appreciated the physical space. Especially given that the girl was still holding a concealed blade.

This one was tightly-wound, thought the Vixen. *And I dare not inadvertently step on the trigger that springs her trap. Or I will be sure to receive a sharp blade for my troubles.*

We have a mission together, you and I, said the Silver Vixen, as though she were reading a decree. *The Messenger sent me to meet you. I am to lead you into Cardea under the cover of night.*

"Are you mad?" barked Katrin. Then swiftly lowered her voice, as she and the Silver Vixen simultaneously looked around for rogues. Katrin exhaled sharply and said in a lowered voice, "Arriving at night is much more dangerous than walking into town at high noon."

I know that, you impudent girl, snapped the Silver Vixen. *That is precisely why your Future Queen sent me. To guide you into Cardea through paths only a Vixen could know.*

Katrin's face blanched. "You are Gabriella's sign?" she whispered. That part actually made sense. That she could wrap her mind around.

But Future Queen? Katrin thought, staring at the Vixen. She could barely contain the hope bursting in her heart. She squeezed her eyes shut. Giving herself the briefest of moments to allow the impossible to be possible.

Then opened her eyes, nodded to the Vixen, and resumed walking.

CHAPTER FIVE

THE FIRST LIGHT of dawn was far away, but Syrena felt its approach. The time was right.

Their fire had died down to gentle embers. She and Tobias sat in chilled silence. Waiting for the time when it was no longer night and not yet morning. The liminal hours.

Syrena insisted that they wait until to speak with the nature spirits. Fairies, sprites, and the timid ones were drawn to the light but had learned not to be out once the humans were awake.

Threshold times hold the most power, she thought., reassuring Tobias about the delay. *And heaven knows, I need all the power I can get.*

Stop that, Tobias chided her for bringing doubt into this moment. They spoke in thoughts, in case anyone might be hiding in the woods. *We need to be confident. The fairies cause enough mischief all on their own. So, stop adding your own.*

Tobias, you surprise me, Syrena replied. *You know far more about the fair folk than you ever said aloud. We will unpack more of this on our journey.*

Not likely, he growled. *Let's get started before we lose all semblance of heat from the fire.*

Syrena nodded and said, *And all magic from this time.* She could feel the sun getting stronger. The rays had not burst past the horizon, but when they did, she would lose some of the power supporting her words.

She had only been taught kitchen magic. Working with the natural elements to see a result. Whether that was to augment the feelings of one person or tame the feelings of another. Her dear mentor passed along all her wisdom. Careful to wait until it was only her and Syrena huddled together in the kitchen.

Patrice encouraged Syrena to get up earlier and stay up later than the other girls. This gave them the right kind of privacy for Syrena to learn. And to feel loved.

She would find nooks for Syrena to nap in during the day. Hidden under laundry in a large basket. Not far from the cook's protection and sharp orders. The other girls were respectful even though they knew Patrice's gruffness was mostly bark. They sensed a fierceness inside their leader that kept them from daring to find out what might get her to bite.

Syrena smiled at the memory. And Tobias relaxed.

He had told his friend to call on the right kind of confidence. Her memories bolstered her heart and chased away her doubts. She was calling on the wisdom that had been placed in her hands.

Syrena looked at the fire, remembering Tobias's guidance. He said that wise old women who guarded a special kind of magic only chose an apprentice that was capable of safeguarding the purity and power of what she passed on. The lineage could not be broken. They had to choose or let the magic die.

And so, the choice a mentor faced was a heavy one. To get the novice wrong risked all sorts of horror. Tobias suspected that, far back in the Great Prince's lineage, someone had made the wrong choice. And his people paid the price.

Syrena closed her eyes and calmed her mind. She had only the threads of what she had been taught. She did not know the language of the wild woods. She understood the ways of plants and herbs and tinctures and potions. But the wilderness was Gabriella's wisdom.

And Tobias's! She thought. And her eyes snapped open.

Tobias grimaced, his eyes still closed. *Could you PLEASE not yell in my mind? As long as I am stuck hearing your thoughts, you need to speak softly. I feel like I have a church bell in my head.*

Syrena slapped his hand. "Ow!" he yelped aloud, opening his eyes. Both of their eyes went wide. Tobias's voice had carried through the woods. He and Syrena froze and held their breath.

All they heard was the chirping of early morning robins and swallowtails. And the soft rustling of leaves as the wind played in the trees, gently greeting the day.

Listen, Tobias, Syrena spoke to him silently. *And do not interrupt.* He rolled his eyes. *Just remember we have little time,* he replied. She nodded.

Syrena kept her hand on Tobias's. He immediately knew he was in trouble.

I will hold the space and call forth the magic, she said. *I know how to keep us safe and to contain what we ask. But YOU are the one who speaks the language of the wild ones. Not me. I was taught to use natural elements after they had been harvested. You are the one who belongs here. In these woods. With this magic.*

She paused. Tobias stared at her. He did not have a response. Except for fear. Syrena spoke wisely. She saw through his years of guarding his ability. Now she was asking him to use his power out in the open. And in her presence.

He dropped her gaze and went silent. His hand grew damp and she felt him restraining a tremor. Syrena pressed his hand to give him comfort. She wanted to give Tobias ample time to wrestle with her request. But time was the one thing they did not have.

I know I ask a lot, she said. *You, like all of us, have kept your magic hidden in order to keep it – and you – alive. But we are out of time, Tobias. We need you. We need all of you. It's time to break free.*

Tobias wanted to pull back his hand, grab his quiver and arrows, and run deep into the woods where he belonged. But he felt the courageous warmth of Syrena's hand and thought of all that she and his royal family had sacrificed to get them this far. He would not flee. It was his turn to show true courage.

Tobias nodded. And Syrena nodded back.

Ready? She asked.

Ready. He replied.

CHAPTER SIX

GABRIELLA SWAYED in and out of consciousness, holding tight to Astrella's mane.

She felt weak. Unsure whether she was only exhausted or received a magical blow before they escaped.

Either way, she could barely keep her gaze focused. She rested her cheek against the mare's strong neck. Gabriella was drained and desperate for a good night's sleep.

Perhaps I can sleep a little, she thought. *Astrella can follow the trail for miles. I just need a little rest.*

She wrapped the reins around her arms, tying herself to Astrella. Confident that she would not fall, she closed her eyes.

Within moments, Gabriella found herself in a familiar nightmare. Kneeling on a scorched battlefield. Tears streaming down her face. Holding Casmire's beautiful head in her lap.

She howled at the stormy sky. A hopeless protest that the gods did not heed. Under her palms, she felt a stirring.

Gabriella looked to her lap. Casmire was gone.

She leapt up. Whirling. Seeking her companion. Desperation moved her, but he was nowhere to be seen. The Great

Plains were a blank sea of grass. Gabriella cried out with anguish.

Astrella whinnied softly, startling her awake. Gabriella sat up. Her tears had soaked the horse's mane. *You were crying out,* Astrella said. *I was concerned. And thought someone might hear.*

Thank you, Gabriella replied, she wanted to go back. Her dreams were the one place she saw her friend. Even if they tormented her heart.

She patted Astrella's neck. *We should be safe from thieves for many miles. They will not risk the Palace's ire.*

Your heart is heavy, Astrella replied. Gabriella nodded but did not speak.

She was not ready to share her pain. She barely spoke of Casmire to Adrian.

If I had any notion of where you were, wizard, Gabriella thought. *We could argue in person.* Her head spun. As her thoughts went to him, she swayed in the saddle. It was too much. She had to trust that he was safe. And alive.

Gabriella gripped the reins and squeezed her eyes shut. Calming her heart. She breathed deep and prayed for the strength to make it out of the mountains.

She felt so tired. Deep in her bones. For the first time, she wondered whether she had the strength to make it. To fight for her people. To take this battle to the end.

Her head spun. And her heart squeezed. *I am tired,* she thought. *Maybe my time is done.*

Gabriella sighed. She opened her eyes and stared at the terrain. Whether the cause was heartbreak or magic, she felt drained of passion. Tired of the fight.

Her hands began to loosen on the reins. Just as they were approaching a steep decline in the trail. Astrella whinnied for her rider to hold tight. Yet Gabriella could not help the notions drifting through her mind. *If I let go*, she thought, *I would be free. And reunited with Casmire.*

She veered on the edge of releasing the reins. Her stance growing softer. Gabriella swayed in the saddle.

When a bold flash of light startled her. Snapping her back to herself. *Do not use me as your reason to give up*, a voice ordered.

A shimmer of chills went up her arms and down her spine. Gabriella sat up straight and gripped the reins. She recognized the voice. *This is a trick*, she thought. *A cruel and vicious attack.*

Rage brewed in her chest. *Someone dares to use my love against me*, she scowled. *To imitate Casmire's voice to –*

To what? the voice replied. *To assist you. To remind you of your pursuit?*

Gabriella dropped her gaze and cast it over her left shoulder. Squinting her eyes. She caught a glimmer. *Something magical is tracking us*, she thought. She sharpened her hearing but heard nothing unusual. No feet. No breath. No drawing of weapons.

Stay alert, she spoke to Astrella. *We are being tracked.*

He has been with us since the Palace, Astrella replied.

What? Gabriella replied. *And you did not think to tell me?* Astrella did not respond. Gabriella sensed that she was conferring with someone else.

You are not concerned, thought Gabriella. *You are not threatened. You seem ... comforted.*

Grief welled in Gabriella's chest. Truth swept over her. She felt no evil conjurer. She felt only love. And courage. Riding at her side.

Tears fell down her cheek. *No*, she thought. *It's not possible.*

Why not? he replied. *Have I ever let you down?*

Gabriella's hand flew to her chest. A sob escaped her, as she looked over her left shoulder. And saw the shimmering spirit of Casmire keeping pace with Astrella.

Casmire, she gasped. *How? Why? Am I dying?*

Casmire nickered, with soft amusement. *You are not well,* he replied. *And you are in dire need of rest and food. But no, you are not dying.*

Gabriella felt a wave of disappointment. *I am so sorry, Casmire,* she began.

I know, he said. And you must stop feeling sorry. For it is only draining your power. And tying you to a dark form of love.

You are wrong, she replied. *I could have saved you. I might have helped –*

No, he said. *Gabriella, you are many things, but you do not know the fullness of the plan. You cannot know my path and purpose. Nor even your own. We must trust. I have never left your side. As I promised your father.*

Gabriella doubled over, racked with sobs. Tears of shame and remorse poured out of her.

You are not responsible for my death, Casmire continued. *You could not have stopped it. Perhaps I would not have died that day. But I would have died. And here I am, at your side. Bringing you new life. And hope.*

Gabriella wiped away the tears. She felt courage return. And faith sparked in her heart. *Casmire,* she wept. *I have missed you so much.*

As I have missed you, he replied. *And you have suffered far too long. Draining your power by punishing yourself for a deed that was not yours to own.*

Gabriella nodded. She felt the truth of his words, as the ache in her heart softened.

You must promise me to let it go, Casmire said. *Or we will never win the battle against the Palace.*

We? asked Gabriella. *You are coming?*

The light in Gabriella glowed brighter. Astrella neighed with pleasure. The grieving Messenger had been a heavier weight than she anticipated. Gabriella's reunion with her soul companion lightened her burden. *For us both*, thought Astrella, relieved.

Casmire flicked his head, nickering. *Yes, Gabriella*, Casmire replied. *If you will have me. Now eat some venison. We must come up with a plan to get you to Cardea.*

Gabriella nodded. And reached into her side bag for provisions.

As hope washed over her for the first time in months.

CHAPTER SEVEN

THE HIDDEN PALACE felt the rumblings in her bones. Something was amiss.

Like the aches and pains humans complain about in their bodies. The Palace growled.

The ache felt like mutiny. Like parts of her were betraying her purpose. Her desire. Her need to crush people's spirits and hold dominion over this land.

I do not know who is betraying me, she thought. *But rest assured, I will find out. And I will destroy them.*

She raged through the night because she ached. She seethed because the Great Prince had not returned.

The longer he is away, she seethed, *the more likely he is to break his chains. And never return. I will send more scouts. I will command more mercenaries. I will tear down the cities and bring ruin to every village before I accept his mutiny!*

She paused, confused by her declaration. She had never claimed the Great Lands. She did the bidding of her sire, her King.

Did I need him? She wondered. The Palace fought with herself. Struggling between her well-worn obsession with the

King and a new impulse. A possibility that she could be free of her maker. Stronger, even, without him.

As she watched the Mad King sleep, her thoughts got muddled. She felt protective and loathed him, all at once.

He grows weaker, she thought, and a wave of disgust pulsed through her. *The stronger his only son gets and the further he ventures, the fainter his father's spirit becomes.* Despite the aches in her bones, she felt fiercer than ever.

Could she be getting stronger because it was her turn to rule? She gasped at her own treachery.

Yes, she thought, as an idea began to unfold. She was meant to rise. To own the day. To claim her power. She saw her enfeebled King in a new light. *He needs to leave this world. Then no one can stop me from ruling.*

She shook with laughter. No longer caring that her sides ached and her foundation felt weak.

I will find the traitors and whip them into order, she thought. *I will make the pathetic humans pay for every moment they did not respect me. I will run the world of men and women so that they will be the slaves for me.*

On their backs, I will build the greatest era of terror every known. That will be my legacy, she glowed with avarice. The Palace took one last repulsed glance at the Mad King. *Let him fade away.*

A strange pain rippled through her belly. And she wondered what lies were being spread about her now. What creatures were plotting against her.

Gabriella, she thought. And the Mad King growled, then whimpered, in his dreams.

The Palace considered the King's response. Her plan was hatching. *You loathe the Messenger*, she thought. *That is logical. But she seems to bring you pain.*

The Mad King groaned again. And swatted his fist as though striking an invisible foe.

Why, my liege? The Palace asked, craving the knowledge that might destroy him.

She stole my son, the King mumbled in his sleep. And curled over as though he needed to protect his stomach.

And why does that hurt? She asked, pushing closer. Feeling the power of causing him pain.

He chases that whore, that pathetic woman around like a beaten dog, growled the King. He wants her more than he wants me. My legacy!

The King's spirit grew fainter as he confessed in his sleep. *His grip on this realm fades,* mused the Palace. *The longer the Prince is away, the lighter his grip on his dominion.*

The King whimpered, grower weaker. *If he does not return, I cannot hold on...*

The Hidden Palace glowed with delight. Soooo, she thought. *If the Prince stays away a little longer, I can claim my rightful place. I will have full control,* she laughed.

The Palace thrilled at this new purpose. *Keeping the Prince away is easy enough while he chases after the Messenger.*

"The Messenger ... hic!" fumbled the drunken impersonator of the Great Prince. He had staggered his way into the upstairs foyer. "I love the Messenger..."

Infuriated with the interruption, she held back from pushing him down the grand staircase. Then cooled the urge. Reminding herself that she needed the imbecile. For now.

Yes, yes, she thought. *The Prince loves the Messenger. That is my point!*

"That is my point!" he echoed. Then burped and stumbled. Blind drunk and unaware that he was having a conversation.

He staggered backwards, shocked by the sight of a ragged King sleeping on the floor. He stared at the man, confused. Peering left and right. Wondering why he could see through him.

As the Imposter Prince stared, his mind wandered back. He smiled. Remembering. "We love the Messenger," he mused.

We? The Palace demanded. *Not we. You!*

The drunken man squinted at the walls. Momentarily confused. *Who is talking?* He wondered, looking around. *I do not see anyone but this pale man.* Then he shrugged.

"We..." he continued. "We love her. She brings hope."

Hope, spat the Palace.

"Hope," the Imposter replied. Tears welled in his eyes. "It is her mission."

The young man grew sober and felt the very hope he described. The Palace howled at the pain caused by his anticipation. His faith stabbed at her.

Her loathing bubbled over. She considered ways to crush this insect. To punish him. When an idea struck her, as she thought of the real Prince. The one she intended to recapture and force to do her bidding. *An even more delightful thought after he has tasted freedom,* she mused.

Another piece fell into place in her newly hatching plan.

Yes, she thought. *She is the beacon of hope. She needs time to gather her courage. Tend to her wounds. And distract my little prince.*

The Palace eased off her pressure from the Imposter. Watched him take a deep breath and look around with fresh eyes. She felt the glimmer in him. And though his hope caused her pain, she smiled. A fierce and crushing smile. Savoring the sensation.

Yes, she thought. *The Messenger feeds off the hope of her people. She is possessed by saving you. Your need drives her forward.*

The Palace understood obsession. Seeing compulsion in the Messenger made her curious about the little creature. But not enough to change her plan.

She watched the Imposter steady himself. Thoughts of the

Messenger sobered him. Sharpened his mind. He wanted to spread her message. He wanted to yell that hope was coming.

The Palace observed as the Imposter took one step after another toward the stairs.

Yes, she said. *Your Messenger will come. She will believe that she can save you and my little prince.*

The Imposter looked down the imposing staircase. He heard his drunken friends below and saw the Palace's doors. He felt the hope of the Messenger in his heart. He could do this.

The Palace enjoyed his delusion. Watched with vicious delight. Then proclaimed directly into his mind, *Her obsession will bring her to the scene of her destruction. I will crush her for all to see.*

The Imposter flinched. "No! Stop!" he yelled. He cringed, wanting to get away from the suffocating shadow.

Once I break the Messenger, she hissed. *Hope will die forever.* The Palace pressed closer, filling his body with terror and panic.

"Stop!" He cried, clawing at the air. "Give it back! I want it back!"

What do you want? asked the Palace.

The light, he gasped, as the Palace pressed around him. *Give me back the light.*

The young man stumbled. Caught in the tumult of confusion. He tripped perilously close to the edge of the stairs. *Ahhhh,* provoked the Palace. *Yes. Free yourself. Go to the light.*

The Palace gave a sharp twist of the stones beneath his feet. He stumbled. Tripped. Caught the edge of the stairs. And it was enough.

He toppled over the precipice. Tumbling...falling...down the long staircase.

Then landed at the bottom. A broken body and face twisted in terror.

CHAPTER EIGHT

ADRIAN HEARD voices outside the cave.

He was furious that he had been forced to abandon
Gabriella in her moment of need. But even when he was with
her at the Palace stables, he sensed someone approaching.
Someone back where his body was in a trance on top of a mountain. An easy place to spot.

Even for Palace idiots, he growled. And his head rewarded him
with a pounding sensation behind his eyes. Adrian closed them
and breathed deep.

He did not have enough physical energy for outrage. He
needed food and fast. *The last thing I need to do is pass out right in
the path of Palace scouts*, he thought.

Opening his eyes, he slowly stepped backwards. Keeping his
gaze locked on the cave mouth. Adrian stepped around a rough
outcropping. He knew this cave well, having spent many excur-
sions up here.

We all need a place to go when the world wears on us, he
thought. A notion that brought a smile to his lips.

He kept moving steadily backwards. Adrian did not like the
idea of being trapped inside this cave. But to regain his strength,

he needed to reach his food supply. Tucked far from prying eyes and even farther from predator's mouths.

Adrian's hands shook. And his feet were ice cold. *I pushed farther than I should have*, he thought. *Now look where you are. Hiding from the lowest of the Palace's minions.*

The scouts appeared in the front of the cave. Adrian's breath stopped. He swiftly jumped back into the darkness. Landing softly in the shadows.

The two men peered inside. Screwing up their faces at the damp scent.

"There is nothing on this godforsaken face of a mountain," grumbled the one that hung back. "How soon can we go? My belly is empty and my fingers are frozen."

"Do you want to return to the Prince empty handed?" the taller scout replied. "We need to do enough that we can convince him there are no threats."

"He grows more paranoid every day," shot back the smaller man. "We could tell him tall tales of rogue wizards and he would believe every word."

"Aye," replied his companion. "Then he would send us on even farther, crazed missions. I would rather return with a modicum of truth in my tale. Than risk his eerie knowings."

"Do you think he can read minds?" shivered the small scout.

"I do not know," grumbled the tall scout, as he stepped deeper into the cave. Peering into the blackness as far as his eyes might see. "But many tell tales of his creepy understanding. Followed by their disappearance into the dungeons."

He turned to the small scout and smacked him on the shoulder. "Do your best for him or suffer the consequences. You and your whole family."

The two men stood shoulder to shoulder and ventured deeper into the cave.

Adrian pulled back, using the last scrap of his strength to

blend with the cold rock. Slowing his breath to a standstill. Trusting in the wise ones to get him past this treachery. *This cannot be the way that I die,* Adrian swore an oath to himself.

Even as the rock held him up, Adrian's legs began to shake. He feared they might give out an any moment. And if they did, he would cause enough of a din to draw the guards.

He placed his hands against the cave and prayed for it to hold him. *Lend me your strength, Great Ceres,* prayed Adrian. *I need your fortitude. I cannot let my Messenger down. Not now. Not in this final hour.*

The scouts pushed closer, risking the darkness, even as their faces revealed their fear.

"Something is back there," said the tall scout.

"Yes," replied the small scout. "A sleeping wolf that wants nothing more than to devour us for supper." His voice shook and he hung two strides back from his companion.

Adrian held his breath. Feeling the guards growing close. *It will not be long before their eyes adjust and they see my cloak,* he thought, as he readied himself for one last fight.

He wished he had enough strength to summon a wolf to the cave. Or to convince these weak minds that they saw one. But he needed to save every scrap in case he needed to fight.

The tall scout was about to take a step that would put him within spotting distance of Adrian.

Just as his foot raised up, a low growl rippled through the cave.

The small scout whipped around. His companion swiveled and leapt forward. Reaching to stop his friend from screaming. But he was too late.

The smaller man yelled. The silver leopard snarled and her fur ripped along her back.

"Shut up!" hissed the taller man. But before his friend could reply, the silver leopard advanced. Prowling toward the two men. They huddled together, shivering.

Adrian felt the men's terror radiate through the cave. He heard their panicked thoughts. And sent a serene thank you to the leopard.

You are welcome, wizard, she replied, as she advanced on the scouts. *This is for the time you watched my cubs as I went on a hunt. Now, we are even.*

Showing her powerful teeth, she clung to the cave floor. And made her way toward the two cowards, wondering which would bolt first.

The small scout answered her. Screaming and running past her, disappearing out of the cave. She paused and stared at the remaining man, giving him just enough room to believe he could escape. He took it. And ran.

Tossing a quick look at Adrian, she gave the scouts two seconds of grace. *Feed yourself, wizard*, she said. *Or you will not last the night.* Then bolted after the men.

Adrian exhaled sharply. He grabbed his store of food. Pulled out a strip of venison and bit off a strip. He felt the nourishment ripple through him, sharpening his mind and easing his muscles.

As he savored his food, his intuition told him to swiftly reach out to the tall scout's mind. *Hidden in him is the Palace's stance,* whispered his wise self. *You will not get a better opportunity to know her strength.*

Adrian centered himself and reached out. Even as his body grew stronger, he knew this was a risk. He felt through the pulsing terror of the tall scout. Sensing also that the silver leopard held back so she could chase these men far from her realm.

He reached into the man's mind. Sifting through ridiculous

thoughts and stories. To a deeper connection. One that pulsed with power. One that connected him to the Palace. One that pulled the strings of this man's thoughts and commanded his actions.

Adrian felt into her increasing strength. That the Palace was able to reach farther than ever. Without the hands of the Prince to do her bidding.

She is growing stronger, he thought. Adrian pulled away from the scout's mind. And ripped off another bite of his venison.

Adrian's heart raced. *The Palace grows more powerful without the Great Prince to do her bidding*, he thought. *Her confidence is growing. She has figured some way to rule by her own right, without the bloodline that made her.*

He stood tall, thanking the gods that he had called everyone to Cardea.

Because our time is running out, he thought. *We have only one chance to stop her.*

CHAPTER NINE

THE PRINCE FROZE. He had been so focused on getting inside, he did not consider that someone might follow him.

"Stop right there," hissed the voice. "I see you."

A woman, he thought. *No, a girl.* The voice was young and inexperienced. *But that is no matter with the young ones growing up under mu rule. They are savvy and bitter. And willing to do whatever was needed to survive. Or so my guards told me.*

The Prince cursed his lack of worldly experience. *I have no idea what is a lie and what is the truth. But I can feel her rage. Rage, I know well.*

"I will not stay," he began, buying time. "I need only a small thing."

"You will take nothing," she growled. "Or I will call to the Smithy."

The Prince glanced over his shoulder, careful not to turn his face. He could see by her shadow that she stood right in the doorway. He was trapped.

Panicked, the Prince froze. He could only breathe. *Why did I come here? What was I thinking? Can I push past her? She will scream.* His mind fumbled with ideas.

"You ruined my home," accused the girl. "You crushed my family. And killed my father."

"I did no such thing," the Prince exclaimed, before he realized his mistake.

"Oh but you did," her voice raised with outrage. "But like a coward, you sent others to do your cruel deeds. To steal what is not yours!"

Her rage snapped him out of panic. *The villagers are sure to hear her. I have little time. No matter that I am caught. I came for coal dust.*

He ignored his thundering heart and leapt toward the fire pit at the back of the shop. The smithy finished hours ago. The fire had died down and little light poured from the coals.

"I told you not to move," she barked.

The Prince had no time to think. He shoved his hand into the pit. Running his palm along the inside of the brick. Then smeared streaks of coal ash on his face. Feeling the rough dust across his skin.

He exhaled, gripping the pit. No matter what happened, he might pass as a smithy's lackey. Or a poor wretch passing through town.

The Prince turned, facing the girl blocking the doorway. She was wiry and strong, and he felt the rage pulsing off her. Though he guessed she was only thirteen years of age.

"Smear dust on your face all you want, horrid Prince," she spat. "You will pay for your crimes."

His stomach sank. *How did she know?* He wondered. And now what do I do?

"I watched you," she laughed. "I spotted you in the trees. Shaking like a leaf. Hiding like a coward."

The Prince spotted a poker leaning against the brick pit. The girl noticed his gaze. "You will not fight yourself out of this," she said. "Even if you knock me down, I will use my last breath to curse your name. So all can hear."

Do I risk it? thought the Prince, looking around. *I have no other option.* And he realized that the girl's accusations were true. He had never killed, he had only ordered others to do so.

Desperate, the Prince determined that he must move. Or he would never get beyond this village. He walked toward the door.

"Step no further," she declared.

"But surely I can offer you something," said the Prince. "You must wish for riches or freedom. Maybe a horse?"

The girl laughed. A broken, bitter laugh. "I wish only for vengeance," she growled. "And for your broken neck in a noose."

The Prince stopped. There was no turning this girl. He felt it. Her need for his blood. All his life, he had lived in a place that craved only death and destruction. And he felt it in this girl.

He was done. Defeated. Before he even stepped further than the edge of a mountain town. Heartbreak ripped through his chest. *Gabriella*, he thought. *I failed you.*

A shimmering glow burst across the doorway. Blinding the Prince with the sudden light in the darkness. He shielded his eyes.

The Prince peered through his fingers to see a force take over the girl. Possessing her, heart and soul.

CHAPTER TEN

THE GIRL STARED at the Prince with the power of a Queen.

"You will not give up," the commanding voice said through the girl.

The Great Prince gasped, with a sharp intake of breath. "Aunt Chancelry?"

"The very same," she said. "Though I am at the edge of my power here, dear nephew. And we have only moments."

"Why?" he asked. "Is someone coming?" Fear rippled through the Prince.

"Yes," she replied. "So heed me, dear nephew. I can hold this girl's presence for only a few minutes more. You must run. And find your way to Cardea."

"Cardea?" he asked. "But –"

"That is where you will find Gabriella," Chancelry said. "You have but one chance to redeem yourself, Nephew. And that is to aid her in her quest."

The Prince stepped forward, closer to his aunt's presence. He felt warmed by her grace.

"What if I fail?" he asked. "What if she will not have me?"

196

The girl frowned at him. "You have no more time for questions like this. You must act. And not question. You must give. And not take. You must do the very opposite of everything you have been raised to do."

The Prince nodded. He quaked slightly in the commanding presence of his Aunt. But his heart opened, feeling that her power came from love and truth. She never lied to him. And he trusted that she wanted his freedom.

"I will do as you bid," he replied. "I only hope that I can act with your strength."

"Strength comes through living," Chancelry said. "You must act to discover it, my child. You have not lived. You have only watched. Now, you leap. And then you will discover your heart."

She waved him towards her. And wrapped the wiry teenage arms around her tall nephew. She turned round and faced him toward the setting sun.

"Now run!" she commanded. "Go fast toward that departing caravan. Jump on the back and it will take you on the road to Cardea."

She shoved her nephew into the street. "Run like your life depends on it!"

The Prince stumbled forward. Peering around to wonder who saw. Then picked up his pace and ignored the consequences. If he did not run as hard as his legs could move, he would never catch the caravan at the end of the main road.

The girl's body slumped forward. Chancelry's presence had departed.

She pressed her hand against her head. *Why does my skull throb like someone struck me?*

Leaning against the blacksmith doorway, she remembered why she stood there. Blinking her eyes, she looked inside for the Prince.

"No!" she yelled, and turned, looking everywhere for him. "Where are you, Evil One?"

The Prince's muscles ached as he yanked himself over the back of the accelerating caravan. Hearing the scream, he ducked behind the cover.

Determined to stay hidden until they were far out of town.

CHAPTER ELEVEN

As they continued far down the mountain, with Casmire at her side and food in her belly, Gabriella felt more like herself.

She was still bone tired. And her energy needed time to replenish, but her heart was bright and a smile rested in her eyes. She had underestimated how deeply the loss of Casmire had affected her.

I have been walking in a daze, she shared. *Or consumed with guilt and rage.*

I know, he sighed. *I have been unable to reach you since my death. I was unsure whether it was some sort of transition or that you were covered in a cloud of despair.*

Maybe both, Gabriella offered. *Either way, I am relieved that you are here. That you were always here. By my side.*

Casmire felt the vulnerability of his companion. He took his time with her, though they did not have much to spare.

We must get her to Cardea, Astrella spoke only to him.

Yes, he replied. *And we need to get there faster than we can walk. Even if we sprinted the full distance.*

He restrained his frustration. Not wanting to tax Gabriella. She needed to heal. And fast.

I feel your frustration, Casmire. Gabriella said, staring at the rolling valleys beneath them. *You forget that even if I do not hear your words, your energy never lies.*

We must pick up our pace, Casmire offered.

Easy for you to say, retorted Astrella. *You have no body. You can float you way to Cardea.*

And we cannot make it in time on foot, Gabriella said, running her hand over Astrella's mane.

She had set an impossible timeline for her people. And she was sure they would move heaven and earth to meet it. So she, too, needed to figure out how she would meet this impossible task.

Truth be told, Gabriella confessed, *I am not sure whether I am the one to lead the people of the Great Lands. But I have not heard from my sister. And I will not risk speaking with her. For fear of bringing rogues to her door.*

Gabriella felt her being sway into a trance. Casmire neighed with concern. But she held up her hand. Letting him know she was safe. She needed to hear what the Divine wanted to share.

We are losing time rapidly, she continued. *Soon, the Palace will secure a grip that cannot be broken. So whether I am to be Queen or not, we have only one chance to defeat the evil that has possessed this land. I must lead the charge. So the people will follow. And feel hope.*

As Gabriella surfaced, and the valleys of the Ceres Mountains sharped in her view, she felt a renewed purpose. I must lead the charge, she thought. Whether or not I am to make it through the battle is not for me to say.

Casmire felt her flicker of fear and whinnied in protest. *Do not rush to be with your ancestors*, he insisted. *You have much to accomplish on this earth. And I, for one, intend to see that happen.*

Astrella snorted and shook her head. Drawing Gabriella's attention swiftly to the trail. She sharpened her gaze but saw only birds flitting in and out of the trees. The valley felt peaceful and she did not sense a threat.

Then she realized that Astrella was excited. *What do you know?* asked Gabriella, though she sensed that the mare wanted to discuss something with Casmire first.

Fine, Gabriella said. Discuss in private. *I will wait.* Though she was far from happy about it. Sometimes grace is more a battle than a blessing, Gabriella grumbled to herself.

Casmire, Astrella said. *Your death is your strength.*

Casmire flicked his head in disagreement. *Hardly,* he fumed. *I have no body. I have no speed. I cannot carry my mistress or protect her.*

That is where you are wrong, Astrella insisted, picking up her pace. Her body shivered with excitement. *You have not opened yourself to its power. You were so focused on Gabriella that you overlooked the brilliance of where you are.*

Casmire's instinct was to argue. To stand his ground. But he sensed Astrella was right. *Or partially right,* he grumbled. But they did not have time for disagreements. He needed to know more.

If there is a way for me to assist Gabriella, Casmire said. *Tell me.*

Astrella nickered softly. *Casmire is a proud one,* she thought. *Death has softened his pride and increased his power. He just does not know it yet.*

I lost my mother and sister at a young age, Astrella said. *My heart ached with grief. I barely wanted to continue living. So they shared truths with me. Secrets about where they were. Maybe they were not supposed to. But in sharing where they were, I took comfort knowing they were safe. And felt like life might have meaning. I never shared those secrets with a soul. Until now.*

Astrella wound her way around a tight turn in the trail. Casmire drifted beside her, his hooves moving as though they struck dirt. But they hovered above they ground. His company warmed her heart and reminded her of loved ones. She had lost so many over the years.

Take your attention off Gabriella, Astrella instructed. *I promise I will keep her safe. Your task is to notice where you are. The subtleties. The grace. Trust what you feel.*

Casmire looked up, realizing how fixated he was on the realm he lost.

For the first time, he saw a world with different paths of light. Shimmers of magic. Wild possibilities that beckoned. To where, he did not know. And yet, he felt their potential.

I see lights, magic, portals, he fumbled for words. Not yet understanding what he saw. *And it's less what I see and more what I feel. How did you know?*

Casmire was so entranced he had to call himself back to Astrella and Gabriella. Seeing their curious faces. Astrella beamed her delight.

With the help of our ancestors, Astrella said, *you can guide Gabriella to Cardea. You are her trusted soul companion.*

Casmire felt it. *But... There is something you have not told me, Astrella,* he replied. *Something hard.*

Yes, Astrella replied. *She can only travel swiftly to Cardea through a portal. A magical gate that is bound to remind her of the one she used when she found you dead on the battlefield.*

Casmire fell silent. And they travelled side by side, as he contemplated what that might do to Gabriella. Whether she might pay too high a price for the journey. And if she had the stamina.

His heart grieved for what he must ask of her. This was her choice.

There is no other way? he asked.

Not that I can imagine, Astrella replied. I asked for assistance. And this is what I was shown.

Then I will offer the choice to her, Casmire said. *She has made many hard decisions. This may be the first she makes for her people. The first on her path to becoming Queen.*

Gabriella rode in anxious silence. Gazing out to the trees. Wishing their calm essence could resolve her quandary. But they were made to have roots and stand strong in one place.

I, on the other hand, must choose, she thought. *Constantly.*

Casmire told her what she could do to get to Cardea. Astrella insisted there was no other way. And Gabriella understood the potential cost to her mind and heart.

Truthfully, Gabriella said, when she finally broke her silence. *I do not know what might happen.*

Casmire held his peace. As did Astrella. They had agreed they would not sway her decision.

But, she said, holding her head high, feeling the power of her ancestors course through her. *If Casmire's presence proves anything, it is that I might heal through this risk. As surely as I might be ruined.*

Gabriella looked to her faithful companion. And felt his courage and love. His determination to stay with her even when she did not see him.

I might come through this magical portal a healed and beloved woman, Gabriella hoped. *Ready to fight and serve. Ready to rally her people.*

Casmire tossed his head. Acknowledging Gabriella's choice and proud to be at her side. Astrella pranced, feeling shimmers of freedom dance through her. Knowing her ancestors were proud.

Gabriella tumbled helplessly through the air.

She had learned not to fight the storm when she was swept up in a spell. The best thing she could possibly do was surrender to the forces carrying her.

A large ask for a Warrior. Surrender was never easy. No matter how many times she practiced.

She closed her eyes and focused. Praying that Astrella was all right. Feeling the strength of Casmire near her. Gabriella sent love and calm reassurance to her. Though she could never be sure that the waves of her power would reach her target in the middle of a magical cyclone.

Once Gabriella felt herself falling, she felt confident that she was about to arrive. The question was where. She was sure she would be in Cardea, but she had never been there. And did not know her way around. Once again, fate threw her into the mysterious ocean and told her to swim.

Her freefall accelerated and Gabriella felt her head get heavy. She wanted to fight the urge to go to sleep but something told her she would need her fury for when she arrived. She sent out one last prayer of comfort to Casmire and Astrella, promising that she would find them.

And everything went dark.

CHAPTER TWELVE

Syrena closed her eyes again and kept hold of Tobias's hand. She wanted him to feel her strength. Her solidarity. And she wanted to make sure he did not slip away.

They were in this together now. If there was one thing that Syrena understood about sharing a secret, it was that the sharing made a special bond. A sacred trust.

And they were about to seal that trust with magic.

Syrena whispered under her breath. The words needed to be spoken aloud to hold the power that they needed. But she spoke softly enough to keep others from hearing. A passerby might hear her voice as a soft breeze. Or a deer's footfall in the leaves.

"Mothers of all we have known," Syrena said. "Hold us in the strength of your arms. Cast a circle so that we might call the wisdom of the wild ones." Tobias's breath tightened and she held his hand tighter.

"We need them," she continued, "to bring love back to this realm consumed by devastation. We ask that you show yourself. Hold us in the circle of your power and keep away all who might harm us."

Syrena opened her eyes enough to watch the circle of light

appear around. A small circle around them and their fire. The ancestral mothers stood among the trees, closing the loop that included the power of stoic pines and the charm of sweet maples.

"Thank you for protecting us, mothers of magic and keepers of tree wisdom," Syrena whispered. She was channeling spirit and had stepped out of her depth. Somehow, she felt the presence of her mentor. And her love bolstered Syrena's confidence.

When she saw the mothers nod, Syrena returned their gesture. She squeezed Tobias's hand and whispered, "Your turn."

Tobias cleared his throat. He was far outside his depth. But he had made a promise.

He fumbled. "I c-call on the fairies of light. The wild spirits of the forest."

The more he spoke, the stronger his courage and voice grew.

Tobias felt his mother's spirit. His heart squeezed with grief and he wanted to open his eyes. To see her. But he heard her whisper, *Not yet, little bear.*

He swallowed his heartache. And continued.

"Sweet fairies of light. Bold fairies of fire," Tobias said. "I call on your light wisdom to show us the way. I speak from the lineage of Karnera, wise woman of the bear line. She taught me your words. And showed me your gifts. I come to ask for your guidance."

In a flash of light, a Fairy Knight appeared in their fire. Flames danced all around her. She aimed an arrow right between Tobias's eyes and declared, "What guidance do you presume to deserve?"

Syrena, whose eyes were still open, nudged Tobias with her elbow. When he ignored her, she nudged again, insisting that he open his eyes. And so he did.

Tobias gasped. Syrena held tight. Channeling her strength

and determination into him, she squeezed his hand. *We really cannot afford to offend the fairies*, she whispered in his mind.

He squeezed back, and kept eye contact with the Fairy Knight. "I... We... humbly request your guidance to Cardea," he said.

"Have you no feet?" snapped the Fire Fairy Knight, directing her firebrand at his feet.

"Our feet are not the issue," Tobias replied, finding his courage. "We must meet the Messenger in Cardea in seven days. We cannot make the trek in so short a time."

"Humans," the Fire Knight rolled her eyes as she spat a spark towards his toes. Tobias quickly pulled back, avoiding her searing curse.

Still, she lowered her arrow. And looked closely at the strange pair.

"You speak of the Messenger," said the Fairy Knight. In her world, humans were not to be trusted. They were tricky and fickle and took whatever they desired, with no thought to the consequence. Vile creatures. "What do you know of her?"

"She is the Princess I have served my whole life," Tobias replied. His heart felt relief in speaking openly of Gabriella. "With luck and grace, she will be our Queen. But for that to happen, she needs her allies to stand with her and fight the great evil."

"Enough!" bellowed the Fairy Knight, threatening him with her firebrand. Tobias shut his mouth. He had no idea what he had done wrong.

"Are you mad?" hissed the Fairy Knight. "Never speak of that evil here. We have kept it at bay by keeping it from knowing we exist." The Knight shook her head. *Humans*, she fumed.

"I am sorry, my liege," Tobias replied. The Fairy Knight lowered her arrow, liking his respectful tone. Fairies might be shrewd but they appreciated a good grovel.

"We meant only to stress our need to help Gab –" The Fairy Knight tensed at the use of the Messenger's given name. Her gaze narrowed.

"The Messenger," Tobias corrected. "We are meant to meet her in Cardea. And we are running out of time."

"And that is my problem?" spat the Fairy Knight, sparks bouncing off her.

"Nooooooo," assured Tobias. "No. Of course not. But we thought you might wish to reunite her with the people tasked with protecting her."

"Clever human," smiled the Fairy Knight, tucking her arrow into her quiver. She looked Tobias over and noticed that he also carried a quiver of arrows and bow. She eyed him again. *For a human*, she thought, *you are not unattractive.*

Tobias shifted uncomfortably, sensing that he was being assessed. He was unsure where this appraisal might be going. Syrena suppressed a laugh, enjoying the tension.

We might have to sacrifice you to the Fairy Queen, she thought.

Oh great, he replied, *that hardly the Queen I wanted to serve.*

Potato, potahto, laughed Syrena. And Tobias shot her a side-glance.

"Ahem," announced the Fairy Knight. "We of the Fairy Queendoms believe in the Messenger's cause. We wish to protect these lands. And,,," She paused for dramatic effect. "We are prepared to aid those who support her."

"Thank you," Tobias said, with immense relief. Syrena nudged his, proud of him.

"Do not thank me yet, Hunter," the Fairy Knight countered. "We have terms."

Oh boy, thought Syrena. *It's okay*, Tobias reassured her. Though he was equally nervous. Maybe more, given the way the Fairy Knight had sized him up. If anyone was going to be the sacrificial lamb, it was definitely him.

Tobias nodded for the Knight to go on.

"I will confirm with my Queen," the Knight spoke in an official tone. "But I am empowered as her representative. So, we will guide you through a portal to Cardea."

Portal? Syrena gulped. *Yes,* Tobias replied. *Please be quiet.*

"You will, however..." the Knight paused, enjoying the discomfort felt by the two humans as she dragged out her price. She smiled. "Agree to having your memories cleared."

"Wait, what?" Syrena exclaimed. The Knight turned sharp eyes on her and Syrena shut her mouth swiftly.

Tobias quickly jumped in, "Our apologies, Wise Knight. We simply wanted to understand the fullness of your terms. Do you mean ... all of them?"

The Fairy Knight reveled in making the humans squirm. Until she felt the sudden disapproval of her Queen. *Nothing escapes her notice,* sighed the Fairy Knight. *Can I not have a wee bit of fun?*

Not at the risk of delaying the Messenger's cause, her Queen replied. And the Fairy Knight jumped.

"Ahem," the Fairy Knight regained her composure. "We fairies are civilized, unlike some creatures."

Syrena exhaled in relief. The Fairy Knight could insult them and humankind all year long if it meant she got to keep her memory.

"And still," she continued. "A price must be paid. Magic is not for the weak-hearted, as you both know. Do you wish to help your Messenger or not?"

"Yes," replied Tobias. "Of course, but..."

"But?" snapped the Knight. "But? You would negotiate this help?"

"No..." Tobias said. "But how can we help her without our memories? We will not know who she is."

"Fair point," replied the Knight. "Then you shall remember

the Messenger. You will know her. And your mission to help her. All else must be left behind."

"No!" exclaimed Syrena, jumping to her feet. The Fairy Knight rearmed her bow, aiming the firebrand at Syrena's heart.

"I..." Syrena sputtered. "I cannot forget my love. My Hannah. Please..."

The Fairy Knight paused, eyeing this feisty witch. Wishing she could take her back to their realm where such a magical creature belonged. "I wish I could change the terms. But I cannot. Take them and go to Cardea. Or leave them and stay here. You choose."

Tobias stood and looked into Syrena's tear-filled eyes. "I know," he whispered. "My heart breaks, too. But we have little choice."

Syrena collapsed back onto her rock. Feeling her spirit torn in two. Tobias sat gently beside her. *Maybe we will find a cure. One day.* He offered to her. *Do it for Hannah.* Syrena looked woefully into his eyes. And nodded.

Tobias turned to the Fairy Knight. "We accept your terms."

"You must both say it," commanded the Knight.

"We agree," Syrena and Tobias said together.

"The Queen gives permission to take you to Cardea," the Knight spoke officially. "You will forget all but the Messenger. And will land safely by her side in Cardea."

The Knight snapped her fingers and in a flash of light, A Fairy Guide appeared, iridescent in her airy beauty. The Knight whispered in the Guide's ear and the Guide nodded.

Tobias looked at Syrena. He clasped her hand. *We will find a way through this. I swear to you.* Syrena smiled sadly and nodded. She squeezed his hand but her faith was wearing thin.

"Excellent," replied the Knight. "Let the journey begin." She smiled roguishly and snapped her fingers.

The Fairy Guide swooshed around them in fast circles, weaving her magic.

Syrena and Tobias grew sleepy as she sped faster and faster. They leaned into one another, still clasping hands. They tumbled into sleep. As the Fairy Guide shielded them with an iridescent light.

And in a blinding burst of light, they vanished from the forest.

KATRIN SQUATTED on a wooden box in the narrow alley between two decrepit buildings. She ripped a bite off the rough, smoked meat that she had filched from an insolent traveller.

I am sure he stole the meat from a poor merchant. She tore off another bite. Katrin missed the thrill of thieving. Especially when it came with poetic justice.

The Vixen peered out from behind her legs. Katrin offered her some meat. The Vixen sniffed and turned away. *Why must humans dry and spice everything,* she growled.

The Vixen's stomach rumbled. And Katrin shook the strip at the haughty fox. "You need to eat something," said Katrin. The Vixen took a reluctant bite.

Katrin pulled her cloak closer, as they chewed and watched the night streets. She was not sure what she waited for, other than a sign. Some way of knowing how to find Gabriella's tribe.

She smiled at the thrum of life. Katrin felt more alive surrounded by rogues than she did princes and princesses. *With the exception of Gabriella,* she thought. *The Messenger must be part rogue or I never would have fallen into step with her.*

Cardea was no place to find beauty or love. Trade and

commerce were its lifeblood. Anyone who landed on Cardea's doorstep had a deal to make. Or a place to flee.

And thousands of people poured into the city on any given day.

Are we going to squat here all night? asked the Silver Vixen, barging her way into Katrin's thoughts.

"Yes," replied Katrin. "We are as likely to take a blade to the back out there as navigate those streets."

Speak for yourself, said the Vixen. *So we sit? Until when?*

"Until I know," Katrin growled. "You got me into Cardea. If that was your task, you can leave." Though, truthfully, she wanted the Vixen to stay. She liked her impudent company.

Not yet, said the Vixen. And Katrin's suspicious nature sparked.

"Why haven't you– ?" Katrin began. When a quick shimmer flew past, catching her eye. And the Vixen bolted from between her legs.

"What the hell?" asked Katrin, and shot to her feet. "Where are you going?"

The Vixen ran at top speed. Chasing the iridescent glimmer. *Follow me!* she bellowed.

Katrin hesitated, but her intuition screamed to shadow the fox. She took off running. And prayed that her intuition would not fail her.

The Vixen darted back and forth between legs and under wagons. Weaving so fast that drunken travellers assumed she was a northerly gust whipping through the square.

She moved so fast that Katrin did not have time to question. She could barely keep up. But that did not stop her mind from screaming at her that this was a trap. That she was trailing after a rogue fox and a spark of light in the most dangerous city in the land.

And yet, Katrin's heart soared. *She was following a trail of magic! In the most dangerous city in the land! What could be better?*

The Vixen leaped and swerved. Keeping close to the glimmer. Her nose twitching and her tail flying. As Katrin bolted after her, using every skill she had honed in all her years, to keep up. And still, she felt the Vixen's joy. Like the fox craved a pursuit like this with her whole being.

A feeling Katrin certainly understood. She felt the rush of the mystery. The thrill of the chase.

Her lungs burned from running. And the night streets were lit only by fire torches and barrel fires. Making her eyes ache with the strain. *Thank the stars for the shimmer trail*, she thought.

She twisted and turned to avoid the groping paws of drunk men. Wishing for a moment that she had the swift, discreet body of the fox.

But then, she thought with satisfaction, *I could not do this*. And she swung her hip hard into a slovenly drunk, sending him reeling into a trough filled with water.

Katrin grinned and ran faster, fueled by the night's vigor. Reeling horses and clamouring drunks. The howl of a shopkeeper after a thief.

Katrin ducked under the swing of a fist destined for the jaw of a fellow gambler. Then swerved hard to follow the bolting fox down a narrow alley. Keeping her gaze on the light and her ears alert for danger.

As she swerved right, seeking the fox, Katrin gasped and screeched to a halt.

Before her was a cloaked man with sharp eyes, clutching the Vixen by her scruff. The fox twisted and turned, fighting his imprisonment. And staring right at her.

Katrin's mind raced. She could run. She saw an escape route. And yet, she could not help herself. "Leave her be," she said. "The fox has not harmed you. Leave her and take me."

Her mind fought with her heart. Her mind screamed, *He is tricking you with magic! You cannot trust a stranger in Cardea!* And yet, her heart commanded her to stand.

"Wise thoughts," said the man, "You cannot trust strangers. Especially in Cardea." And he placed the Vixen gently on the ground. She sat quietly and contentedly. Peaceful at his side.

"But then," Adrian continued. "I am not really a stranger, am I Katrin?" And with a mysterious look, he pulled open the door to a discreet pub and disappeared inside. The Vixen swiftly darted in before the door closed.

Her eyes went wide. *He knows who I am. How? Gabriella? What did she say?* As fast as the thoughts rushed through her mind, Katrin felt her chance to know more closing. She needed to act.

"Oh hell," cursed Katrin, and yanked the door open.

She saw him stride toward a table tucked at the back of the pub. Katrin took in the small, yet packed room. Not a single soul looked up. Even the barkeep focused on cleaning a glass.

She moved nimbly towards the mysterious man. His eyes locked on her. No sign of the Vixen. *Traitor*, grumbled Katrin.

When she arrived, the man lifted an eyebrow and tilted his head to the left. Katrin spotted the Vixen tucked out of sight on the chair beside him. Katrin could swear the damn fox looked amused.

"Who the hell are you?" she asked, brashly. "And what do you want?"

He leaned in and spoke in a low voice that only she could hear. "I am Adrian. Companion and advisor to the Future Queen. And I want to defeat the greatest evil our world has known."

Katrin's entire body shimmered with the thrill of meeting Gabriella's wizard.

"Will you join me?" he asked, pulling out a chair without moving a muscle.

Katrin sat swiftly and gave a curt nod. Praying he would not change his mind.

PART IV
DESTINY

CHAPTER ONE

ADRIAN GESTURED DISCREETLY to the barkeep, as he held Katrin's gaze.

"I can see you have many questions," he said. "And our time is running short. But still, we need to eat." Katrin's stomach growled. She flushed at her obvious hunger.

Adrian smiled. He understood the demands of the body. Even more since he pushed too close to his own demise. He watched Katrin's attention move to the barkeep as he arrived with two tankards of cider. His helper followed swiftly with a basket filled with hot pumpkin bread.

Adrian gestured to the food and said, "By all means." Katrin grabbed the bread. Tearing off a piece and devouring it without shame. She had been starving for days.

Katrin had heard about Adrian from Gabriella. Otherwise, she would have assumed she was being bought. *And for a tankard and some bread, no less*, she thought. Then shrugged.

She downed her drink. And the barkeep's helper appeared, replacing it with another. "Will this go on all night?" she asked.

"We have too much to discuss," Adrian replied, as he sipped his dark drink.

Katrin felt like she was being assessed. Reminding her of a similar creature keeping quiet under the table. "Did you send her?" Katrin bit into another piece of bread and motioned to the pair of silver ears barely poking over the table's edge.

"No," Adrian replied. "She is her own mistress. But we have more important things to discuss. Like the coming war."

Katrin choked and looked around the bar. Every table was filled with questionable knaves. "And you feel safe discussing that here?" she asked.

"Safe is relative," Adrian said. "But yes. These people have no stake in what we discuss. And you, my dear Katrin, have a set of skills that no one else on our team has mastered."

"What might those be?" she asked.

"Instinct," he said. "Cunning. Boldness. And the ability to read people."

"I am flattered," she replied. "But how does that help in a war?"

A loud THUMP echoed through the pub. Katrin jumped and looked around. The barkeep exchanged a look with Adrian. "You will find out soon enough," Adrian replied and stood. "Follow me."

Adrian moved swiftly, disappearing behind the edge of the bar. The Vixen jumped down, trailing silently. Katrin grabbed a piece of bread and followed.

He pushed through a heavy oak door and held it open. The Vixen scurried through and Katrin paused, hesitant to be trapped in the back room of a questionable pub. Adrian waited but she felt the impatience under his austere expression.

I've come this far, she thought. And stepped inside. Adrian peered out then closed the door.

The dim storeroom was filled with casks and boxes, stacked to the ceiling. Katrin squinted and surveyed the room as best she could. But the shadowy corners and piles of merchandise made it tough to see anything.

She kept her back to the door, looking for what large creature could have made such a loud noise. Katrin leaned toward the door, when Adrian said abruptly, "Do not touch the door."

Katrin leapt forward a foot and asked, "Why?"

Adrian peered around another pile of casks. "I enchanted it to keep people out. It might hurt if you leaned into the spell."

Katrin calmed herself. Breathing deep. "I do not like being locked in a storeroom without knowing."

"Now you know," Adrian replied, then exclaimed. "Finally!" He took a giant step toward Syrena and Tobias, holding their heads and groaning.

"I was beginning to wonder if you would make it," he said. Katrin moved closer, curious who he had found. She stared at the two strangers and around the room. *How the heck did they* get *here*? she thought.

Syrena looked up, then around. She pushed back against the wall in a defensive stance, "Who are you? What do you want?"

Adrian pulled back and eyed Syrena and Tobias. He sighed and shook his head. "Did you consort with fairies to get here?"

Tobias stood up, holding his skull as though he woke after three days straight of drinking. "Maybe. Who wants to know?"

Katrin stepped forward, "Even I know that fairies weave a trick into every bargain."

Adrian was impressed. "She is right. Do you at least remember the deal you struck?"

Syrena and Tobias looked at one another. Tobias spoke, "Are we in Cardea?"

"You are," replied Adrian. "And the fairies delivered you to the right spot. That much I am grateful for. The loss of your memory, not so much."

"From all I have heard," said Katrin, leaning in to Adrian. "It wears off soon enough. They get their glee from the trick itself. Not the length of it."

"You have had some encounters with fairies?" asked Adrian.

"One or two," Katrin shrugged, looking at Syrena and Tobias with sympathy. "They play a mean hand of poker. And are not ashamed to cheat."

"Why are we in a storeroom?" asked Syrena.

"We had a meeting with someone," Tobias vaguely remembered, as he checked for his quiver of arrows, relieved they made the journey.

"With him?" she asked Tobias, sizing up the strange duo across from them. "What if I take the big one and you take the girl. We will be out of here in the wink of a maid's eye."

"We can hear you ––" said Katrin, until Adrian elbowed her and shook his head. "Well you might want to get some food in their stomachs. It will hasten the dissolution of the magic."

"Good idea," Adrian replied, and conjured up a tray of stew, ale, and bread. He walked over silently and offered the food.

Syrena eyed him warily. But the growl of her stomach made a powerful argument. Tobias took the tray and nodded his thanks.

"If we are going to fight," Tobias whispered. "You need the sustenance." Syrena nodded and hastily ate the bread.

"Give it a few minutes," said Katrin. "They will return to their old selves."

"Enjoy the peace while you have it," joked Adrian. And Katrin felt like she had passed some kind of test. A flood of warmth rushed through her as she imagined that Gabriella would be pleased.

Syrena devoured the food like she had not eaten in days. Chasing it with the full jug of ale. She swooned a little as though she might collapse into sleep.

When she looked up, her eyes were clear. "Adrian!" she exclaimed, leaping up to embrace him, except her knees buckled. He leapt forward and caught her.

"Easy, Syrena," he said. "Welcome back."

"What happened?" she asked. "And who is she?" *Wait,* Syrena said silently to Adrian. *Do you see her?*

I do, dear one, he replied. Rest your head. You have had a wild trip. One that included a fairy joke.

"Blasted fairies," Syrena cursed.

"They got us here," replied Tobias, still woozy. "You must be Adrian."

"I am," Adrian replied. "And this is Katrin."

"I remember you," said Tobias, warmly. Katrin nodded and smiled. She always liked Tobias, despite feeling sorry for his obvious crush on Gabriella.

Adrian cut the pleasantries short. "Gabriella should arrive soon. Let us hope she does. Our time runs short."

Tobias stepped forward. "You left her arrival to chance?"

"I did not say that," Adrian replied.

"You did," retorted Tobias. "How do we not help her?"

Syrena reached a hand back and steadied her friend. "Adrian meant when. When she finds a way. Gabriella always does." She arched an eyebrow at the wizard and thought, *Right?*

"Right," acknowledged Adrian. Adrian had been curious why Tobias felt fiercely protective of Gabriella. Now he understood that Tobias felt responsible for her. "She will be here."

Katrin watched this family of rebels and wondered, *What in all the Great Lands do I have to offer them?* A moment later, she grew woozy, as though a sudden squall was approaching.

She began to sway. *What is happening?* she wondered, and her thoughts blurred. All she could think was, *A storm is coming. A storm is ...*

Katrin's knees buckled. Tobias swooped in and caught her, as her body went limp. He crouched down, holding Katrin. He looked to Adrian, "She passed out." Adrian gestured for Syrena and Tobias to get down and take cover.

The air grew heavy. And the room fell eerily silent. A storm was coming.

A BOOM like the sound of thunder, CRACKED through the air. Sparks of light cut the darkness.

Slashes of lightning LIT UP the shadowy corners. And the rush of a sharp wind gusted through, shaking the walls and everyone inside them. Whipping their cloaks over their heads.

Adrian held strong, keeping fierce watch. Looking out for his tribe.

The wicked gusts grew unbearable. Adrian forced his eyes to stay open. Small slits to keep watch over the people he held dear. The wall boards rattled and the casks of ale threatened to break. He sheltered the others as much as possible in a gale force wind.

Magic crackled through the air. Adrian grew concerned the wind might knock the breath from his chest. His vision began to blur. And he was not sure how much longer he could withstand the onslaught.

When a cloaked figure appeared in the air above and dropped from the ceiling. Landing hard on the floor with a THUD. The room went silent.

Adrian gasped in air. Checking that Tobias and Syrena were safe. Groggily, they rose to their knees. Katrin opened her eyes. All three were alive.

He turned back and rushed to the cloaked figure. Adrian knelt beside her and pulled back the hood, exhaling with relief. "Gabriella," he whispered, touching her face. "You are safe."

Gabriella slowly opened her eyes and smiled. Seeing Adrian's kind eyes. "When has that ever been true, my love?" she teased.

"Every moment you are by my side," he answered. And helped her up.

<h1 style="text-align:center">CHAPTER TWO</h1>

GABRIELLA WINCED as the room spun. She had been in the storm for so long that she lost her sense of equilibrium.

"Give yourself a moment," Adrian said. As much as she wanted to argue, Gabriella did not have the strength. She closed her eyes.

"Is everyone here?" she asked.

Adrian hesitated. Catching Syrena's eye. *What are we to say?* asked Syrena.

What can we say but the truth? Adrian replied.

Better you than me, Syrena said. And moved an inch closer to Tobias.

Tobias was transfixed. He could not tear his gaze from Gabriella. She had been a ghost to him since her disappearance. *And here she is, a stunning woman and warrior,* he thought. Syrena elbowed him. And shot him a look.

You might want to relax the staring, Syrena said, only to him. *Blink, at the very least.*

Tobias dropped his gaze and bumped her back. *Fair enough,* he replied. *But truth be told, I began to wonder if she was alive. And here she is.*

She takes your breath away, Syrena acknowledged. He gave a quick nod. Syrena smiled. *She does that to all of us.*

Gabriella forced open her eyes. She gazed around the room. Her heart full of gratitude for every face she saw. *Adrian, Katrin, Syrena, Tobias,* she thought. Tobias! *What a lovely surprise. And a silver fox? Wait.*

She swept the room again. "Adrian?" inquired Gabriella. Fire sparked in her belly as she searched for her sister's face.

"Where is Hannah?" asked Gabriella. Her gaze locked on Syrena, who glanced at Adrian.

Gabriella caught the exchange. Her ire sparked, and she shook off his supportive hand. "Where is my sister?"

"Granamore," replied Adrian. Gabriella braced on a tower of wooden boxes. Her legs shook, whether from exhaustion or anger she was not sure.

"And why is she still there?" demanded Gabriella. She looked from Adrian to Syrena. *I can feel the secret you are hiding. Tell me.*

"Your sister defied your advice," said Adrian. "She was obsessed with finding your parents. And I believe that your ancestors called her home."

This caught Gabriella off-guard. "What? No. Why would they...?" Gabriella's lightning-quick mind flew through the possibilities. Chills rippled down her back.

"What happened?" she asked. Adrian reached out to steady her. But Gabriella pulled back.

"She is fine," Adrian assured her. "But she is trapped in a sleeping spell. That is why she could not come."

Gabriella exhaled sharply. She reached out to Hannah and caught a faint pulse. "I did not contact her for fear of putting her in danger," said Gabriella. "Could I have prevented this?"

"No," said Adrian. "You were wise not to draw attention."

"Then what in the stars happened?" exclaimed Gabriella, finally losing her calm.

Syrena stepped in. "Hannah heard your home calling to her for months. She was going mad from the voice that insisted she return. Every day, I fought to convince her to turn back, even as we travelled closer to Granamore. But she would not listen."

"When we arrived, we were attacked by thieves. We fought them off, only to have your sister fall into a sleeping spell when she stepped into your gardens."

"How can that be?" Gabriella asked. "Who could do that? The Palace?"

"We believe Hannah sprang a spell woven by your mother-line. She is fine. Better than fine. She is communing with your ancestors."

"So my sister is in a sleeping spell. Speaking magic with the ancestors." Gabriella aimed her fury at Adrian. "And you kept this from me because...?"

Adrian was relieved to see her rage. *She is healing.* Good. *She will need every drop of that fury in the weeks to come,* he thought.

"Because the spell protects her," He replied. "And it is waiting for the right time. Until then, there was no point in telling you."

"You are reaching," she accused. Her eyes blazing.

"He is not," Syrena added, getting excited. "Think about it. The spell affected her and not me."

"Or me," said Tobias, stepping forward. Gabriella turned to him and softened. She felt the bold, loyal heart beating in Tobias's chest.

"Tobias," Gabriella said. "Thank you for coming." Gabriella reached out and took his hand. He nodded, rendered speechless by her touch.

"Your ancestors did this for a reason." Syrena interjected. "I believe they want to reconnect Hannah to her magic. And keep her hidden until we need her."

Gabriella fell silent. Her thoughts drifted to a time when she and Hannah were children. Playing at the edge of the wild woods. Giggling and whispering, they called to the fairies. Tossing leaves and watching them burst into tiny flames. Throwing little starflowers into the air that promptly turned into snowflakes. They loved every moment.

Until their furious and terrified mother stormed across the garden. Hannah was still catching snowflakes on her tongue when Gabriella swiftly caught her sister's hand. And thought, *We must stop. No one can know.* Tears sprung to Hannah's eyes, as she nodded. *No one. I promise.*

The Queen grabbed both their hands and rushed them to the Castle. Safe from prying eyes.

"Hannah learned early to hide her abilities," said Gabriella, coming back to the present. "We both did. But she had a natural focus that I did not. I was driven to climb and run and fight, while Hannah had the patience to speak to the fairies and conjure subtle magics."

"And if you recall," a voice said from the corner of the room. "I played with subtle magics and spoke to the fairies. While you were determined to fight and conjure fire."

Gabriella snapped to attention. "Who said that?"

The Silver Vixen trotted toward Gabriella. And took a seat. "Do you not recognize your sister?"

"Not when you could as easily be a trickster in fox form," countered Gabriella.

"Wait," interjected Katrin. "You are Hannah? Why would you not tell me that?"

"And you would have believed me?" said the Vixen.

Katrin sighed with annoyance. "No. I would have called you a liar."

The Vixen turned patient eyes back to Gabriella. "Must I prove it to you?"

"Yes," commanded Gabriella.

"You made me swear never to reveal my magic," the Vixen said. "No one can know."

The words reverberated through Gabriella. Bringing tears to her eyes. She fell to her knees. "Oh Hannah! I did what I felt was right. Our mother was so frightened."

"You were right. We had to hide our magic for a time," replied the Vixen, rubbing her face against Gabriella's. "And now, we must use our magic. To show the Great Lands how to defeat the Palace. And call our people home."

Gabriella scooped the Vixen up in her arms. And twirled around. She beamed a smile at Katrin and the others. "My Goddess," said Gabriella, catching her breath. "How is it possible that we all made it to Cardea?"

The Vixen whispered in Gabriella's ear. Nudged her cheek. And jumped to a nearby box.

Gabriella exhaled and pulled Adrian in close. They hugged for several moments. Silent and intense. Making the others uncomfortable in such a small space. Finally, Gabriella released Adrian and called, "Come here," she insisted, waving them closer.

Her friends gathered. Gabriella hugged Syrena. Then she pulled Tobias into a tight hug. She whispered, "I missed you, dear friend."

Gabriella released him and took a moment to appreciate her fierce and loyal clan.

"So," said Katrin. "Can we plan how we are going to take out the Hidden Palace now?"

"Yes," laughed Gabriella. "We have a battle to plan," said Gabriella. "And not a lot of time to do it."

CHAPTER THREE

THE PRINCE GLANCED up at the clear starry sky from the back of another transport wagon.

The horses increased their speed as they saw the edges of the town. Knowing well that there was safety among the buildings.

"If only that were the case for me," said the Prince. And he climbed to the edge of the back of the wagon, preparing to jump.

He took one last look at the waxing moon. "I want to appreciate the beauty of your growing light. But it brings me only danger."

And he leapt, rolling against the hard road. Quickly getting to his feet to follow the back of the wagon as far as he could. Then slinking toward the back side of the central street running through the small city.

The towns grew larger as they got closer to Cardea. The Prince kept his profile low and looked for a safe spot that he might catch some sleep before jumping on another transport.

He had little time to spare if he wanted to catch up with Gabriella in Cardea. *If the rumours are true,* he thought. The

Prince was amazed how swiftly information travelled in the underbelly of his realm.

This truth rankled the old thoughts that still haunted him, his heart found it encouraging.

His stomach let out a loud growl. Reminding him that hunger ruled this moment. A sensation that disturbed him and made him feel alive, all at once.

The Prince slinked along the back alley behind stores and pubs. He learned quickly that dogs and rats would show the way to any source of food. If he was bold enough, or hungry enough, he could find something to carry him over to the next day.

I cannot risk my roaring stomach catching the attention of another transport driver, the Prince thought, wincing at the memory of being discovered and thrown off a wagon. He did not mind the bruises. It was how close he came to being recognized.

How low we have fallen, taunted his ancestors. *Why do you do this? For what purpose?* Their voices were faint. But they surfaced when he felt most vulnerable. A sensation that still made the Prince want to growl.

I do not know, he grumbled back. And ignored any more of their jabs.

The Prince learned that engaging with the voices only gave them strength. And that they showed up when he felt a surge of remorse for all he had created.

Hearing raised voices, he pressed quickly against the back of an old store. *By the pitch, they are children*, he thought, and his heart pinched. *They fight over scraps of food.*

He witnessed this occurrence in every town. Multiple times. *The witnessing is not the hard part*, he thought. *It is the cursed feelings that come with it.* Had the Prince known that on this journey the ugly feelings would far outweigh the pleasant ones, he might not have risked it.

Though, he thought. *Gabriella seems to inspire courage even in the hardest of hearts.* And sighed. He stayed out of sight as the hungry urchins battled over bruised apples and old meat.

How are we to fix all of this? he thought, as he listened to children snarl at one another. *This devastation was created over decades. I suspect it might take as long to set it right.*

These were the moments that he longed for Chancelry's company. *She would have a message of hope,* thought the Prince. *She would know what next step to take.*

The further he travelled from the Palace, the more the Prince discovered that he had only one choice. To find fortitude inside. Not to rely on others as he had his entire life. Finding hope when the struggle looked bleakest. That was true courage.

How many times had Gabriella faced hopelessness when she had no one but her steed? he wondered. He felt worst when he thought of the pain he had brought to Gabriella by devastating her family.

She might never forgive me for that, he thought. *I am not sure that I would forgive someone for such a betrayal.* Yet, the Prince felt compelled to find her. And he was not entirely sure why.

He gazed up at the moon. His one sure companion. And he saw that he did not have long to catch the next wagon to another rough town.

Such is the road I have chosen, thought the Prince, as he followed the sides of the building toward the main street. Peering to see where the next wagon was being loaded with goods.

Soon, I will be in Cardea, he thought. *Then I hope to know what this compulsion has in store. May the Fates be gracious with their choices.*

He ducked low, running along the edges of the boardwalks. Scurrying up into the back of the wagon filled with oak casks and boxes of cured food. Even as his stomach complained, he was grateful to be leaving.

The sooner he got to Cardea, the better his chances of understanding why he had cast his destiny into Gabriella's hands.

The Prince peered up at the stars. Wondering whether he would ever know a sense of home.

"I have longed my whole life to belong somewhere," he whispered to the moon, keeper of his secrets. "I do not know whether I deserve it. But still, I long for it."

He stared at the disappearing face of another lonely town. Praying that he might know peace one day.

C H A P T E R   F O U R

THE HIDDEN PALACE was confident that Gabriella would make her way back to her walls.

If only to make one last attempt at freeing the Great Lands, the Palace thought.

But that is where you will fail, laughed the Palace, as she toyed with the drunken humans still fumbling around the Prince's study. *You believe that my Prince will choose love over power. But I have human nature on my side. Ever the weak link. He will bend to my commands.*

As though to prove her point, the Palace pulled the strings of her human puppets. One man lunged at another. Wrapping his hands around this unanticipated enemy. His foe reached backwards and grabbed a silver candlestick, clubbing his attacker on the head.

First, I need to amass an army of weak-minded humans, she thought. *For while stealing back the Great Prince serves my future plans, I must leverage the present to kill the Messenger.*

As she was entertained by the fighting of the two men, the Palace considered her options.

I must gather enough wretched souls that I can fend off any

attack the Messenger might attempt, she mused. Though I trust that centuries of fear will keep most humans hiding in their pathetic towns.

The Palace laughed, as she thought of this coming opportunity. *Not only will I crush their heroine, but this is a glorious chance to extinguish any spark of fight. To assert my domain. And to determine the future.*

She felt a satisfying grumble in her bowels. Another weak-minded creature had died.

Ahhhh, she mused. *The starving wretches in my dungeons. They will be grateful for a reprieve. Their minds are tormented and filled with ruthless shadows. Their stomachs ache from starvation. And they have been hidden from their loved ones for months or years. Possessing them with a handful of bread and a few kind words will be easy.*

That is the beginning of an army, she thought as she provoked the two drunk women into a fight. Their animosity fueled her inspiration. Anyone within miles of my reach can easily be swayed to fight. But I need more. I need a plan to crush the Messenger's spirit.

As the Palace sneered at her pathetic humans, she got a brilliant idea. *I must turn someone she trusts! Cause torment from within. As she did with me. Oh yes!* The Palace thrilled at her evil notion.

And set her obsessive focus to how she would crush Gabriella's heart.

CHAPTER FIVE

GABRIELLA FELT the grim determination of her tribe of warriors.

She felt proud, as they swiftly gathered makeshift chairs into a war room. They were a rough and ready group. No one would imagine that they were fierce and powerful.

Gabriella saw that they were weary and hungry. Yet, they were ready to fight. Ready to die if they must. She reached for a chair and turned to place it at the head of their round table.

Adrian locked her gaze and dropped to one knee. Gabriella understood what he was doing, as each of her loyal tribespeople fell to one knee and lowered their gaze to the floor. Before her, every one of them, even the Vixen, waited for her to acknowledge her throne.

"Rise," said Gabriella. "I am honoured to be your chosen Queen and Leader."

Humbled, she took her seat. They rose and joined her at the table with the Vixen in Hannah's chair. Gabriella looked at the Vixen. *You are with me, Hannah. We rule together.* The Vixen nodded.

Gabriella looked around the table. "With the Prince gone, we must defeat the Hidden Palace. She has always been the evil behind the throne. Created by a Mad King and raised with foul intentions. We must determine her weakness."

The warriors at her table listened respectfully. For now. She could sense the questions and unrest inside them. And the need to fight.

"Years ago, my father attempted to negotiate with Evil," continued Gabriella. "He sent one daughter into the belly of the beast. While he trained the other to hide and fight."

She paused, swallowing her grief. Gabriella cleared her throat. "He wanted to reconcile with the Palace through peaceful means," she continued. "All that did was bring destruction onto our heads. The time has come to fight back. And to bring our lands back together."

She looked around the table. "That means this is not just our fight. The people must fight for what they want this land to be. They must step out of the shadows. And risk their lives for what they believe in. For the future that they deserve."

Gabriella paused. "Many will die. So, we must remember that without this fight, they are already dead. They might exist for a few more days or years. But the Palace will kill them."

The truth laid bare. They each felt the declaration ring in their spirit. They had been defeated for too long. This fight would reclaim their souls. And the vitality of their land.

Katrin cleared her throat. "I am with you to the end, my Liege," she said, formally. "But I need to know what you plan to do with the Great Prince?"

Is this what it feels like to be a Queen? asked Gabriella, exasperated by the tension of loving Katrin's challenge and wanting to silence it. The Vixen responded, *You know that it is. Our mother felt this tension every day.* Gabriella shot her a grateful, if fiery, look.

"Oh Katrin," Gabriella said. "I both love and hate that you asked that."

Syrena burst out laughing. Adrian grinned. Gabriella smiled, relieved. The whole room took a deep breath. Gabriella realized that her advisors did not want her to be any different as a Queen than she was as a Warrior.

"Well, my insolent ally," said Gabriella, raising an eyebrow. "That depends entirely on the Prince."

"A shrewd answer," Katrin replied.

"From a shrewd leader," said Gabriella. "The Prince will be given the chance to make amends for his deeds. He will have to choose which side he is on. The fight for liberation. Or the vile path of the Hidden Palace. If he cannot acknowledge the devastation that his ancestors have wrought on the Great Lands, we will have no choice but to imprison him."

"You would leave him alive?" challenged Katrin. Gabriella paused. She could see that Katrin was speaking on behalf of the family she had lost, and the homeland that was torn from her. She was speaking for herself and for every person at the table.

"I would prefer it," replied Gabriella, her heart pinched at this exchange. She held back her feelings for the Prince. "I do not enjoy taking lives, even in a time of war. But if he proves to be a bridge to evil, an opening for the Palace to keep hold on our land? Then he will be sacrificed."

Katrin nodded, satisfied. Syrena watched her friend closely. She believed her Queen's answer. And still, she felt the woman's heartbreak. The Queen would fight for the Great Lands, but Syrena feared that Gabriella's heart would pay the price.

"Do we know where the Prince is?" asked Tobias. "Is he a threat?"

"I have not seen him in my travels," answered Gabriella. "He is no longer at the Palace. but I do not know how far he has gone. Has anyone else seen or sensed him?" Everyone shook their heads.

"Adrian, would it be safe for you to check where he is?" asked Gabriella.

Adrian held her gaze. Jealousy sparked and he silenced it swiftly. "I fear that if I did," he replied, "The Palace might use it to target him."

"What if we assume he is close?" Gabriella asked. "Would that narrow the time you need?"

"Yes," he said, feeling her determination. "If I am quick, she will not notice. Especially if she is distracted by war preparations."

"Proceed," said Gabriella. "The sooner we know where he is, the better prepared we can be."

Gabriella had stepped into being a Queen and Adrian was grateful. He was free both to adore and advise her. Truthfully, he had been concerned that those roles might conflict. Now he saw that they belonged together.

Adrian closed his eyes and the room fell into a tense silence. No one wanted to interfere. They felt the danger. *This may be a magical room*, Syrena thought, *but who is to say it is strong enough to withstand the Palace?*

Gabriella heard Syrena's doubts and did not respond. *Once a decision had been made,* she thought, *there was no point questioning it. Our action is in motion.*

Adrian opened his eyes. And the Gabriella's Counsel exhaled. "The Prince has travelled far beyond his native mountains. He feels close to Cardea. Though I cannot say exactly how close."

The tension returned. Katrin's sharp gaze hit Gabriella like an arrow. Gabriella wanted to sigh. She had hoped to wait longer before having this confrontation.

"If the Prince is close at hand," she said. "We must decide if he will be our ally in battle."

And with that proposition, her Counsel erupted into chaos.

~

Every advisor at the table erupted into angry opinions. Speaking one on top of the other.

"He is unstable," Syrena said.

"You cannot trust him," said Tobias.

"He will betray us," added Katrin.

"You will never know where he stands," said Adrian.

Gabriella gave her Counsel time to air their objections, but Adrian could tell she had made up her mind. *You must speak your mind aloud*, Adrian said to her alone. *Let them understand.*

That hardly seems fair to you, she replied, and her heart ached.

Do not be concerned about my feelings, said Adrian. *I love you no matter how many times we disagree. Never doubt that. Never change your choices for fear of my response.*

You are my heart, she said, and her eyes softened.

And you are mine, he replied, and held his hand to his heart.

Gabriella turned back to her Counsel. "I appreciate your concerns," Gabriella said, and the table fell quiet. "We have a long history that proves only that the Prince has been cruel and calculated." Everyone nodded and murmured their agreement.

"And still," She continued. "I believe that he is an essential piece to our strategy. Even..." and she paused. "If he betrays us."

The Counsel erupted in anger, leaping to their feet. "No!" exclaimed Katrin. "How could you say that?" asked Tobias. And yet, Syrena did not pound or yell. She narrowed her gaze at Gabriella.

"You had a vision," Syrena said. And the others hushed and took their seats.

"Yes, my wise friend," Gabriella answered. I do not know why, but every time I see the battle, he is there. I have seen it in dreams and in waking, and still he is there.

"He has not been away from the Palace long," Syrena said. "He might be very unstable. He may not even know who he is yet."

"He might trade us all to save his own skin," interjected Katrin. She did not like this idea at all. "I will follow your lead to the ends of the earth, but this is beyond dangerous."

"I know," replied Gabriella. "And still, I have to trust the vision. Going against it will inevitably cause more harm than good."

"Perhaps he has knowledge we need," suggested Adrian. "Or he is a distraction for the Palace. That could be very useful."

"Or maybe he will betray us all," said Tobias. "And ruin our one last chance to defeat this unending evil."

The Counsel erupted again, arguing for and against. Gabriella understood. And still, this was her decision.

"I know," Gabriella said, loud enough to quiet her Counsel. "That I am asking you to take an unacceptable risk. I really do. And still, I must ask you to trust me. This is what the Divine wants. We may not understand why. But it will become clear. I promise."

She looked at her Counsel with compassionate fortitude. "I must ask each of you to acknowledge that you accept this choice. Or you will not join me in battle. If you agree, I will trust that I have your full loyalty."

As Gabriella looked around the table, each of her Advisors relented with a grim nod. Katrin paused the longest, then swore her heart to her Queen's plan.

"Thank you," she said. "These are hard times. With cruel choices. This will be the first of many."

"With that decided," said Adrian. "We need a battle plan. And a way to get to the Palace. As swiftly as possible, before she has gathered too large an army."

Gabriella turned to Tobias. "Tobias, I recall that you were an exemplary hunter and..." She paused, sensing the courageous man that he had become. "A fierce warrior, I imagine."

Tobias nodded. "Yes, my Queen. I have honed many skills, including outwitting hidden threats and anticipating the next attack by an enemy."

Syrena elbowed Tobias. He scowled at her. Gabriella watched their exchange. "What is it?" she asked. Tobias shook his head, dismissing their disagreement.

"Tobias has a unique connection to the nature spirits and fairy folk," Syrena said.

"I hardly think that is relevant to fighting a war against the Hidden Palace," added Tobias.

"That is where you are wrong," said Gabriella. "We are going to need all the help we can get. We will need the very land herself to stand with us. And if the fairy folk deign to help the creatures who brought ruin to their beloved forests, we would be much stronger for it."

"I would be honoured to ask for their help should we need it," said Tobias. He felt the burden in Gabriella's heart. Knowing that humans had caused pain and destruction to many innocent realms.

"We will need every skill among us and more," Gabriella said. "The Palace is a formidable opponent. Not only is she powerful, she is ruthless. So we will need to use every skill and every offer of help. If we can take any advantage that she might not foresee, we have a chance of winning. But we need more than our talents, we need to inspire the hearts of our people."

Gabriella looked around to each member of her Counsel. "I have seen the battle and it is hard. We have love and honour. And we need to fight like we may never get another chance."

"I believe that winning this war involves many fronts. Possibly even one at Granamore," Gabriella mused, as she looked at the Vixen. "And I trust that all of our gifts will come together to defeat the Palace. As long as we stay connected and courageous. I believe we will win."

"We must win," added Adrian. And the entire Counsel nodded.

Gabriella felt a wave of magic ripple up her back. Her heart began to pound, and a cool shimmer of sweat broke out on her arms. Only one person in the world provoked this reaction in her. *Not now*, she thought. *Not yet. I am not ready.*

A loud knock on the door startled everyone. The knock repeated two more times.

All eyes turned to Gabriella. She exhaled sharply. And told her heart to calm down.

She turned to Adrian. "You sent the lookout?" she asked.

"I did," he replied. "He was told to knock thrice when the Great Prince was found."

Fear rippled through the room. Each person secretly reached for a weapon. No one dared speak, but their hearts raced.

Gabriella looked to Adrian. And said in a commanding voice, "Let him in."

CHAPTER SIX

ADRIAN SNAPPED HIS FINGERS. Sparks flew from around the door, releasing the spell that kept them protected.

The door swung open and the burly barkeep stepped inside. He waited for a nod from Adrian and barked, "Bring him in."

Gabriella stood up. Her entire Counsel rose to flank their Queen.

Three hefty men threw a tall, wiry man to the floor. He landed within an arm's length of Gabriella. Tobias pulled an arrow in his bow and Katrin readied her knife.

Gabriella held out her hands, letting her Counsel know to hold their fire. "Leave us now," she said to the men. They dropped their gaze to the floor and backed out of the doorway.

As the door closed, the spell sparked and hissed, locking their protection back in place.

"Who dares to abduct me –" growled the Prince, until he looked up and saw Gabriella. His breath caught.

"Gabriella ..." he stammered. She was contained and regal, emanating power. *Only Gabriella could look more regal for being hidden in the back of a tradesman's pub*, he thought.

They regarded each other in silence for a long moment. The tension rippled through the room.

"I apologize for surprising you," Gabriella began, clearing her throat. "We needed you with us as swiftly as possible." She crouched down and took his hand. Struck by the tenderness in his eyes, and his humble appearance.

Gabriella stood and brought the Prince up with her. She was painfully aware of the many eyes watching their every move. They awaited a plan, and her direction. She did not have the luxury of taking time to connect with him.

"You have saved me the time of looking for you," he replied, with as much dignity as he could muster. Given that he was covered in dirt and soot.

He had not stood this close to her in a long time. And the Prince was overcome with the emotions rushing through him. He wished they were alone. He wished for any circumstances other than this. *Yet here we are*, he thought. *I travelled many miles for this.*

Adrian cleared his throat. "We do not have much time, your Majesty."

The Prince tensed at the title. As Adrian expected he would. The Counsel poised for The Prince's objection. Waiting for a reason to defend Gabriella.

He glared at Adrian. *You cannot bait me, Magician*, he thought. *I am here to serve just as you are. And we will see who stands at her side in the end.*

Yes, we will, thought Adrian. He cloaked his thoughts but not his rage from the Prince.

The Prince spoke to Gabriella. "You are headed to the Hidden Palace."

"We are," said Gabriella. "And we need your help."

"I will help as you ask," he replied. "But I will not return. I cannot."

"You must," Gabriella insisted. "I have seen you with us."

"No," he said. "You do not want me there. It is too great a risk. I have not been away long enough to trust that my mind will stay strong."

Katrin stepped forward, locking the Prince in her gaze. She wondered what the greatest torture might be for this man? "What if the Prince is right? What if he stayed here? He could atone for his offences by advancing the rebellion of his people."

Gabriella placed a hand on her friend's arm. "You have a point, Katrin. But I believe that is your role."

"You want me to stay here? To keep watch over the Prince?" Katrin asked.

"To raise the rebellion," Gabriella replied. "I cannot think of a better person to fill our people with courage than you. You have the fiercest heart that I know. They will need every ounce of your faith and fire to incite an uprising."

"Raise the rebellion from the city," said Katrin, as though she was trying on this role she had never even imagined. And yet, it fit.

"Yes," said Gabriella. "And word will spread. Every city, town, and village will be emboldened by what you do. The spark of courage will start many uprisings. We cannot win this without the people standing up and openly reclaiming their hearts and lands."

"I will do this," Katrin said. "I only wish I could also be at your side."

"I wish that, too," Gabriella said, taking her hand. "But I will feel your ferocity, no matter the distance." Katrin pulled her into an embrace, not caring an ounce for regal decorum.

"You must promise to watch your back," whispered Katrin. "And trust your intuition above everything. Even your heart."

As Katrin let go and looked fiercely into her eyes, Gabriella understood the warning was about the Prince. Her eyes flashed as she acknowledged the counsel. Katrin stepped back.

Gabriella turned back to the Prince. "You will come with us to the Palace. You must. We cannot defeat her without you."

"You know this is a risk," he replied, in a low voice. "I know you feel it."

"I do," she replied. "And still, I trust that it is the way."

"Even if she turns me back into what I was," the Prince said, his anger rising. "You would risk that?" His heart ached. But he could not speak that aloud.

Gabriella felt his heartache. *Yes,* she thought, as her own heart sank. *I must put this above all else. Above my own heart. And the safety of everyone I love.*

"I must," she replied. "The time has come for me to risk everything. Including my life."

For a brief moment, she let her armor fall and showed him the sorrow in her eyes. That she wished she could free him from this obligation.

The Prince caught her look. Her pain. And wanted, more than anything, to grab her hand and run. To flee to another land. To leave this battle behind them. He was about to speak when Gabriella pulled her armor back on. And became the Queen again.

"I need your agreement," she said swiftly, before the Prince could speak what he so clearly felt. "And your sworn allegiance."

The Prince felt his ire rise. Demanding his allegiance, instead of his alliance, meant she declared her right to rule. Above him, not with him. And the entire room felt it.

He swallowed hard. Forcing his pride down. Even this far from his home, he felt the screeching objection of his ancestors.

But if he wanted to prove himself to Gabriella, to claim he was worthy of her heart, he had only one choice. To show that he might be a better man, he must agree to what she asked.

The room hung in silence. As the Prince weighed one of the hardest decisions of his life.

"Then you have it," he said.

Gabriella eyed him carefully. Assessing whether he spoke the truth.

"You will help us defeat the Palace?" she asked. "And your father?"

"I will," he replied, even though he shook at the thought of being back in that prison of souls.

Gabriella wanted to throw her arms around him. To pull him close for his courage. For his determination to live according to his choices, rather than the ones dictated by his ancestors. More than anyone, she understood the strength that choosing your own path required.

"Thank you," she managed to say. "We are grateful."

I am grateful, she thought. *I will remember this forever.* Her face stayed composed, despite her aching heart.

She turned to Adrian, who watched the exchange closely. Gabriella stood between the only two men she had ever loved. And was forced to be a Queen.

"We need to get to the Palace," she commanded. "Now."

CHAPTER SEVEN

ADRIAN HAD WAITED years for this moment. The one he had seen in a dream.

Gabriella standing before him, claiming her role as Warrior Queen. He felt that strange sensation of knowing that the present and a dream united in reality.

He nodded to Gabriella and turned to the Prince. "The Prince can take us."

"What?" the Prince protested. "I came to Cardea by foot and wagon, Wizard. I know of no magic to get us there in less than a fortnight."

"You may not," countered Adrian. "But your ancestors do."

The Prince paled. He did not wish to converse with his ancestors. He shivered at the thought of the clutching ghosts in the forest and how narrowly he had escaped.

"What do you mean?" he managed to ask. His throat dry and his stomach nauseous.

"Much of your ancestry was evil," Adrian said. "But you have a few rebels among them. Some stayed hidden. And others spoke out. Over the years of defying your father's lineage, secret routes were forged. We might be able to use them. But they require a key."

"A key?" asked Gabriella. And she saw Adrian's gaze land on the Prince. *The key*, she thought. And Adrian replied, *Yes*.

"Only a person with their blood can access the hidden passages," said Adrian.

"I know nothing of this," the Prince said. "I cannot direct you through paths I do not know."

"You are wrong," said Adrian, enjoying a chance to defy the Prince. "I have seen the entrance to these long-lost tunnels. If we leave now, we can reach it before sunrise."

"And then?" asked Syrena, stepping into the fray. "How will we avoid being followed? We might get ambushed."

"You can only travel the passages with the blood kin of those who built them," Adrian replied. "No one can follow us."

"And you know this how?" asked Tobias.

"I saw it in my dream. I saw all of us, including you, Tobias. Long before we met." Tobias furrowed his brow but nodded. Adrian turned to Gabriella. "When we reach the hidden doorway, we will know it. The Prince's blood will sing."

"What does that mean?" said the Prince, his eyes wide.

"You will feel the song of your ancestors singing to you," Adrian replied. "And your hands will know what to do."

The Prince felt the skeptical eyes of every member of Gabriella's Counsel. He stared at the floor. His promise to return to the Palace was all too real. Adrian asked him to return now, before he had even had a night's rest.

And now I must ask the help of my ancestors, recoiled the Prince. *Is it possible that my rebel ancestors are less cruel than the despotic ones?* He raised his gaze to the only person he cared about – Gabriella. Knowing that she could not help him. And yet, needing to know that his choice, his sacrifice meant something to her.

Gabriella's gaze softened. She spoke only to his mind, *We need you, my Prince. I need you. I cannot surprise the Palace without your help. And if we wait too long, she will gain power too quickly, and we will have lost our chance. You, dear Prince, are our secret hope.*

Her plea melted his heart. The Prince realized that he would lay down his life for her. *And it might come to that,* he thought. *Who knows what the Fates have in store. For any of them.*

He turned to Adrian and declared, "Take me there."

Adrian was the last to jump from the supply wagon. They had ridden in under the cover of night. He slapped the side to tell the driver to ride on, and they disappeared swiftly.

The tight troop stayed alert. Adrian gestured silently and the pack followed. Syrena led the way, with Tobias at the back. And Gabriella tucked safely in the center, out of sight.

Gabriella had not felt that hiding her was necessary. But as they approached such a critical time, she could not be led by her pride. She relied on all of them. *A practice that will be essential in battle,* she thought. *I am no longer alone. I must think like a team.*

They moved up a rugged mountain path until Adrian veered off the worn track. He pressed up against a pile of rocks that appeared to be an old landslide.

"Are you sure?" whispered Syrena, sidling up to him. She eyed the pile of slate skeptically.

Adrian nodded. And directed her to strange markings on the far edges of either side of the rubble. Syrena had seen similar markings on the stone walls and even on trees in the lands surrounding the Hidden Palace.

A shiver ran over her spine, as she realized that she was headed back to the place she feared most. The Silver Vixen nipped at her cloak. Syrena jumped. *What the* – Then growled at the Vixen. *You startled me.*

You are a different woman, now, said the Vixen, and Syrena felt Hannah's love surround her. The love that had saved her life. *You are a stronger woman with allies. And magic.*

Syrena melted. She wished with her whole being that she could hold Hannah. *I am doing this for you.*

And I am doing this for you, replied the Vixen. Then added with a wicked grin, *And my sister*. Syrena chuckled softly.

The Prince approached the entrance and everyone fell silent. Tension filled the air.

"What do I do?" the Prince growled, looking to Adrian.

"You will know," Adrian replied. "Your ancestors will show you."

The Prince clenched his hands nervously. He felt exposed as he held his hands toward the blocked portal. He pressed his eyes shut, waiting for burning fire or searing pain. The cruel sensations that always accompanied his ancestors.

But the pain did not come.

Instead, a wave of shimmering light pulsed through his hands, arms, and legs. The Prince could have sworn that he was standing in the heart of his forest, feeling the rush of a warm Spring breeze. Eyes still closed, he revelled in the sensation of sunlight. Gently prickling on his skin.

I must be dreaming, thought the Prince. *Or I might be dead.*

You are alive, whispered his long-lost ancestors. *We have been waiting for the one with a benevolent heart.*

His eyes flew open. And he was standing, slightly dizzy, in the centre of the forest circle where he last felt the clutching hands of his cruel ancestors. A glimmer of sun caught the edges of the tree branches, breaking through to fall on his extended hands.

The Prince swayed, finding his balance. He felt the reassuring touch of Gabriella on his back. He did not have to look to know the feel of her hand. No one shimmered with light like she did. He savoured every second, until she pulled away.

He looked around to see that everyone had travelled with him. He did not know how. But the full rebel Counsel, even the Silver Vixen, was standing on shaky legs.

Getting their bearings in the centre of the forest only a short distance from the Hidden Palace.

CHAPTER EIGHT

THEY STOOD CLOSE TOGETHER, until their legs steadied.

Tobias searched for attackers. Syrena felt for the Palace. Adrian assessed whether magical adversaries hid nearby.

And Gabriella watched the Prince. To see if he changed this close to the Palace.

But the Prince only looked nervous. He did not feel ready to face his ancestors so soon. But he had no choice. The time had come and he must find his courage.

"We are being watched," whispered Tobias. "I can feel it."

"Tobias is right," said Adrian, looking around. "But it does not feel human."

"My ancestors attacked me here," admitted the Prince. "Spirits from another time. Cruel and unrelenting. I barely fought them off."

"But you did?" asked Syrena. She, too, watched the Prince. Of their tribe, he was the only one she did not trust. *All it takes is one traitor to lose the war*, she thought, eyeing him sharply.

"Yes," recalled the Prince. "It was nothing short of miraculous. I might have sworn that I had help, but I was alone."

"We need to understand what's watching us," said Gabriella.

"Surprise is essential to our plan. The Palace may expect us, but I doubt she anticipates us so soon. If a messenger alerts her first, we risk failure."

Tobias looked up into the far branches of the ancient trees. He had never seen a forest this tall. The trees were different from the forests of Granamore and he wished he had time to know them better. Even to climb one and look out over the mountains.

Recognizing a person of compassion and wisdom, the trees wished to know Tobias as well. "The hunter senses our power," said the Whitebark Spruce Oracle.

"And what are we to do with that?" asked the Regal Larch Queen. "They brought six humans to fight the greatest evil this land has ever known. They can hardly expect to win."

"Which is why they need our help," said the Foxtail Pine King.

"When have the humans ever heeded our guidance," snarked the Regal Larch Queen. "We may as well save the effort and prepare our clan for darker days ahead."

"We must make one last attempt," insisted the Whitebark Spruce Oracle. "Feel the power emanating from them, my Larch sister. They look small but their influence is mighty."

"She is right," added the Foxtail Pine King. "We have kept to ourselves long enough. The humans need our help. Even if they do not realize it."

"Fine," grumbled the Regal Larch Queen. "I like the one who looks to us. Who wishes to know us better. He shows promise. What would you suggest we do?"

"Speak his name," suggested the Foxtail Pine King to the Whitebark Spruce Oracle. "You know how to speak to humankind. Reach out to them, dear oracle. And let us see what happens."

The Oracle was pleased with this plan. She had seen this

gathering in her visions during the starry hours. And this one, this hunter, was special indeed. He had the potential to reunite the humans with their natural world. To heal the heartbreak of generations.

"Tobias," she called gently, as though wishing for a long-lost cousin.

Far below the tree canopy, Tobias heard the whisper. His eyes went wide and his skin shimmered with magic. He shivered from the iridescent sound.

"Be quiet!" Tobias shushed his companions. And he crouched toward the ground, listening close. The others quickly crouched with him, looking around.

Syrena drew close to his side. "Tobias, no one was talking."

"Tobias," called the Whitebark Spruce Oracle. "I wish to speak with you."

"There!" Tobias exclaimed, in hushed tones. "Who said that?" He looked at the confused faces of his tribe. Then cast his eyes up into the trees.

Syrena elbowed Adrian and gave him a knowing look. Adrian nodded.

"Tobias," said Adrian, "Tell me what you heard."

"My name," Tobias replied. "But in a far-off female voice. One I have never heard before. Except my heart knows her. I cannot explain how."

Adrian followed Tobias's gaze, sensing that the wise hunter knew where the voice came from. He had just not allowed himself to believe it. Adrian saw the shimmers of magic up in the tree canopy. The predominance of purple led him to realize he was in the presence of royalty.

"Tell me," Adrian said, "What are these trees around us. And do they naturally grow like this?"

Tobias sharpened his gaze. "I see larch, fir, and pine. And

they would easily grow together, except..." Tobias shivered from the realization.

"Speak freely," insisted Adrian. "Everyone else, keep close watch on the woods."

"What is happening, Adrian?" asked Gabriella.

"We are standing in the middle of a sacred tree circle," Adrian said with reverence. "One intentionally chosen by the tree elders of three clans. This spot holds ancient and powerful magic. Along with the spirit of collaboration."

"And these Elders have reached out to Tobias," Gabriella realized. "They know why we have come. And they want to help." Adrian nodded, his eyes shining.

"Tobias," said Gabriella, taking his hand. "Each of us brings unique gifts to this battle. These elders reached out to you for a reason. You have an affinity with nature spirits. I trust that they have wisdom to share with us. And we are lucky that they trust you with it."

Tobias glanced at Syrena. She nodded with encouragement. He gripped and released Gabriella's hand, grateful for a chance to serve her in this foreign place.

He looked up to the Tree Elders. "I am Tobias," he said, casting his voice to them. "I come with my queen, Gabriella of Granamore. We are honoured that you speak with us. What would you have us know?"

The Elders smiled. They had waited many generations for one who spoke their magic.

The Whitebark Spruce Oracle had foretold of a human who understood their language and would speak on their behalf. They had not dreamed that one would come in this, the most troubled of times. The disputes of humans had tried even the patience of trees.

They were relieved to meet one who was gracious enough to listen.

"Greetings, Tobias," said the Whitebark Spruce Oracle. "We have been waiting for you." Tobias nodded, intuiting that it was best to listen.

"We rule a powerful network of trees," said Regal Larch Queen. "And we come together in this sacred circle to share wisdom and forge alliances among our kind and the animal realms."

"We understand that you are here on a mission to battle the Hidden Palace," said the Foxtail Pine King. "While we cannot aid in the fight, we can assist you to get to the Palace undetected."

Tobias relayed their offer to Gabriella, then replied, "Thank you. We would be most grateful for your help. Can you support our cause when we are inside?"

"Unfortuntely, no," replied the Foxtail Pine King. "We have no influence within the man-forged walls of that place. But as soon as you are outside, you can call on us to help."

"Be aware that once inside, the Prince will need all the help you can give," added the Whitebark Spruce Oracle. "He will face many demons. His own and those of his ancestors. Do not allow him to fall down that murky well. Or you will fail in your quest."

The Prince turned pale hearing Tobias share the Oracle's words. The others might know that the Palace was formidable, but they did not understand the torment he had left behind.

"I should not go back," said the Prince. "Leave me here with the Elders. I will only risk your cause."

The others fell silent, unsure whether the Prince's proposal was wise. Even Gabriella questioned if they might all be safer if he waited behind in the forest.

"Do not mistake my message," added the Whitebark Spruce Oracle. "The Prince must go with you. He will never be free until he confronts the Mad King and all that his ancestors did."

"Is this part of defeating the Palace?" Gabriella asked through Tobias.

"We cannot say for sure," replied the Whitebark Spruce Oracle. "But I have seen that the Prince must be with you, or you will not end the Palace's reign. You will know when the moment to defeat her presents itself. Trust that we are here, in alliance with you."

Gabriella nodded her head in gratitude. Surprise was always key to their plan. She had trusted that the Divine would show them a way. And now, these regal trees risked their lives and their realms to protect her rebel warriors.

"Please relay our gratitude, Tobias," Gabriella said. "I understand the risk they take to give us a chance at victory."

"We are glad to be part of ending the torment of the Hidden Palace and her makers," replied the Foxtail Pine King.

"And now you must go," commanded the Regal Larch Queen. "Stay close to the cover of trees and we will protect you. The wood sprites will keep you cloaked until you reach the edge of the Palace compound. She will not sense you coming."

"Can we have time to assess how well prepared she is?" asked Syrena. "We need to know what we are walking into."

"We can provide you with cover while it is night," replied the Whitebark Spruce Oracle. "But the Prince's ancestors will awaken quickly to his return. Use the time wisely."

"We must adjust our plan," Gabriella said to Adrian.

"We will do that as we move," said Adrian. "Our time has come."

"Godspeed," said the Tree Elders in unison. "And good luck."

"Goddess knows they will need it," said the Regal Larch Queen, watched the small company disappear into the trees.

CHAPTER NINE

GABRIELLA and her companions hovered at the edge of the
forest.

Staring at the Hidden Palace, Gabriella trusted the cloak of
darkness and the shimmering magic that kept them hidden. But
once they stepped away from the cover of trees, they would all
be exposed.

And so they paused. Taking a breath. This would be the
greatest battle of our lives, thought Gabriella. And I cannot be
sure that we will all make it through. Though I pray that we will.

Her heart ached and she felt the weight of her choice. She
would give herself a moment to feel what she must, before
setting it aside and going into battle. The one truth that gave her
comfort was that she knew every person at her side was here
willingly.

They had chosen their tasks. Set a battle plan as they had
walked through the forest to arrive at the Palace. Yet as they
prepared to leap into the fray, Gabriella's stomach dropped at
the sight of hundreds of soldiers. Every last soul that the Palace
could manipulate into fighting, she had scrounged from the
belly of her dungeons.

As Gabriella recognized faces, she saw that the Palace must have emptied even the scullery maids and cooks were forced into combat. *Focus. You cannot think about the consequences of the battle, but the war that must be won. I will do my best to spare your lives*, she promised, as she looked at the vacant eyes of the Palace puppets.

She turned and locked eyes with Adrian and Syrena. Each would hold a different front of the battle. Gabriella shielded her heart and said to them, *It's time.*

They nodded and stood. Tobias and the Prince followed suit. And each leapt forward in a different direction. The battle had begun.

Gabriella wrapped a magical cloak around her and the Vixen. She would rely on her limited magic to slip past the hordes of soldiers. Once they were inside, she would cast aside the cloak. Knowing that the Palace would feel her anyway.

We must be wise about our energy, my wise Vixen, she thought. *We have a limited window to get to the throne room.* Gabriella restrained a shiver at the thought of returning to the belly of the beast. She kept her blade close at hand and the Vixen stayed near her feet.

She moved stealthily, sneaking through the soldiers and slaves. Knowing that while they snuck by, her dearest friends would be waging outright battle and risking their lives for their mission.

As are we, said the Vixen. *We just have not arrived at our moment.*

Fair point, replied Gabriella, as they clung to the shadows and avoided the rage-filled eyes of the Palace's soldiers. These men had fed on the Palace's lies for so long, they burned with bitterness and hatred. Ready to die for a rotten cause.

Though Gabriella felt compassion for their innate goodness, she could not risk the point of their blades. *We all make our choices*, she thought. *No matter the circumstance.*

She ran swiftly along the edge of the Palace walls, aiming for the front entrance. Her instinct told her the Palace would not expect her to bring her assault to her front gate. Yet somehow, Gabriella felt this was appropriate.

I may slink under the cover of magic as I enter, she swore, *but I will leave with my head held high for all to see.*

They crouched behind a stone pillar, waiting for a wave of soldiers to depart. Screaming and chanting, "Death to the Messenger!" Gabriella felt her will harden and her determination get stronger. Their curse only emboldened her.

As she sensed their opportunity to enter coming, the Vixen spoke, *This is where I leave you. Once you step inside, you will be accompanied by my spirit.*

Are you sure, Hannah? Gabriella asked. *This will not harm you?*

Not if we accomplish our task as quickly as we designed, the Vixen replied. *We will be safer and stronger inside if you see me in spirit form. I would not spend the effort until it was necessary.*

I trust that you understand your risk, Gabriella said, *as I understand mine.* The Vixen nodded.

Gabriella leapt up and dashed through the massive gates just before they slammed shut.

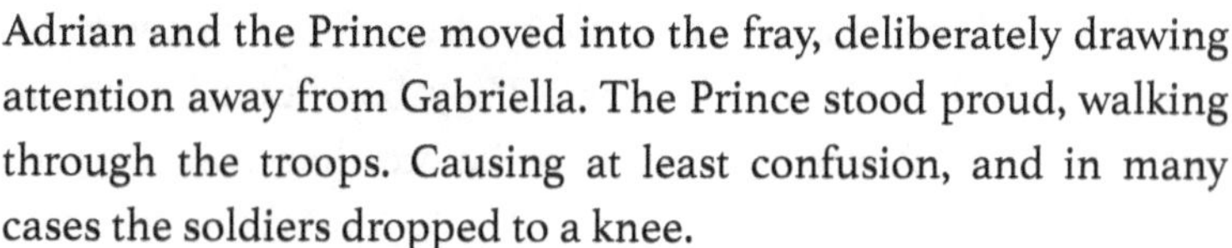

Adrian and the Prince moved into the fray, deliberately drawing attention away from Gabriella. The Prince stood proud, walking through the troops. Causing at least confusion, and in many cases the soldiers dropped to a knee.

The Prince shook on the inside, worried that the Palace would soon notice them. Adrian stayed close to the Prince, feeling his trepidation.

"She will know we are here soon enough," whispered Adrian. "We may as well hurry and get within her walls. Syrena and Tobias will distract her once we are inside."

"Easy for you to say," growled the Prince. "You did not betray her by leaving."

"No," Adrian shot back. "I only plotted a secret campaign against her."

He kept the Prince moving toward the side door that was their destination. Even if Adrian had to physically drag the Prince inside, he would not back away from confronting his father.

"Distract your people while I break inside," ordered Adrian, as he turned and set to picking the door's series of locks.

The Prince suppressed a growl. He hated being paired with the insufferable wizard. But Gabriella received a vision as they crossed the forest and approached the Palace. They divided their attack into three parties. With the Prince being stuck with her paramour.

No matter, he thought, attempting to stop his hands from shaking. *Once I confront my father, and Gabriella is crowned Queen, she will see that he is unfit to be her fellow sovereign.*

The Prince channeled his frustration into snarling at his troops and barking orders. Playing a part that used to come naturally and now felt like a suffocating hairshirt.

The door clicked open, and Adrian snuck aside. Pulling the Prince behind him.

"Unhand me," hissed the Prince. Adrian shot him a warning glance and the Prince fell silent. They both understood the danger of the Palace finding them before they reached their destination. And they had very little time now that they were inside.

They stood inside a servants' mud room. A dark and dank space filled with boots, cloaks, and belts. Adrian sensed that this cramped space would normally be buzzing with activity, except that any pair of hands capable of wielding a weapon had been sent to shoot the rebels on sight.

The Prince chose well, Adrian thought. He kept a sharp lookout in case the Palace had set traps and ambushes inside her walls.

They were on a mission to find the Mad King. Gabriella had seen him outside the Prince's private tower. If he was not there, it was up to them to figure out where he had gone.

Adrian had to trust his intuition and a reluctant belief in the Prince's desire to impress Gabriella. He was not entirely sure that ridding the Palace of the Mad King would undermine her strength, but he gambled that it would cause enough of a rift that they would get a chance to topple her.

The Prince crept forward through the mud room, and cracked open a second door that led into a servants' dining hall. He gestured toward a long staircase that led up several stories from the servants' pitiful rooms toward the highest floors where the Prince lived.

Adrian nodded, agreeing that taking the secret route was the best approach. As they crossed toward the stairs, Adrian felt the Palace waking to their presence.

And he braced himself for the imminent arrival of the fight of their lives.

Syrena wove a magical shield and charged forward into the fray of soldiers. Tobias stayed close, tucked behind her magic and firing arrows as he went.

They ran toward a massive barn far across the craggy front of the Hidden Palace. Syrena held fiercely to her spell and did her best to ignore the ominous presence of the Palace.

She glimpsed at the rage-filled, desperate faces of the soldiers fighting for their own survival. She remembered being lost in the fog of self-hatred and despair.

Now, she understood that the Palace found something inside each person to prey on.

If they could only find their need to be something more than a frightened slave, thought Syrena. Still, they had no choice but to fight as these hulking men attempted to slay them.

They battled their way through dozens of blood-crazed men. Syrena swinging a sword even as she held up the magical shield. Tobias fired off several arrows, clearing the path to the hulking barn.

Just as they approached, Syrena felt a shock go through her, as though she had been narrowly missed by lightening. *The Palace*, she thought. Then whispered to Tobias's mind, *She knows. She knows Gabriella is inside! We must hurry!*

They each grabbed a handle of the staggeringly large doors and pulled with all their might. The doors groaned and slammed back against the building. Syrena and Tobias ran inside with an onslaught of soldiers running towards them.

Tobias and Syrena looked at one another and nodded. *We will see what lengths of chaos we can create*, thought Syrena with glee.

Syrena leapt toward the paddock doors of cows and goats and donkeys. Setting them all free as swiftly as she could. The stampede of animals filled the barn and confused the soldiers.

They struggled to push through, but met with horns and hooves as they looked for the rebels.

Tobias and Syrena swiftly slipped out a side window. Tobias landed outside and pressed against the barn. Watching as the chaos distracted several companies of soldiers. He spotted a dead archer and dove to grab the quiver of arrows off his back. Then ran back to the barn, narrowly avoiding arrows and fireballs hailing down from the highest reaches of the Palace.

Tobias pressed back against the barn, as Syrena dropped to the ground beside him. He held up his bounty and she grinned. He pointed to their next target. The sleeping quarters for the groundskeepers, farmers, and their families.

Syrena nodded. Took a deep breath and created the magical shield.

Overhead! Shouted Tobias, and she adjusted her angle to protect them from the rain of fire. She grimaced as they ran, wondering how long she would be able to hold her magic.

Syrena focused on their target. And her intense belief that they could win, no matter the odds. Doubt and despair were the weapons of the Palace. She refused to give up her heart, or her hope, ever again.

So she ran faster. Keeping Tobias close. Pulling him along with her fierceness.

They landed outside the quarters. *What now?* Asked Tobias, as they crouched by the entry. Keeping an eye on the chaos they had unleashed only a few hundred meters away.

We need to find a leader, Syrena said. *All it takes is one or two to escape into the forest to spread word of the rebellion.*

The more people who flee, the more chaos, Tobias agreed.

And the more hope! Syrena realized, slapping Tobias in her delight. *The more chaos, the more fronts for the battle. We will weaken her grip. She cannot keep hold of so many at once.*

Too many fires to put out, Tobias said. *All we need is a few rogue fires to catch light and spread. Are you sure some will run?*

The ones who are left inside are the ones the Palace deemed too meek to fight, replied Syrena. *She underestimates the small rebels that lie await under her roof. At least, that was the case when I was still here. Let us hope it has not changed.*

Syrena grabbed the door handle when Tobias stayed her hand. *Speak to them as one who made it out,* he said. *They will remember you. And they will respect you for your courage.*

I escaped with Gabriella, Syrena retorted.

It does not matter, Tobias said. *You escaped and returned to help those you left behind.*

Syrena felt the truthful fire behind his words. She needed to offer her courage. As Gabriella and Hannah did for her. Syrena nodded. And Tobias released her hand.

She pulled the door open and they moved inside. Every woman and child was on their feet, panicked yet ready to fight. And Syrena felt the wrath of the Palace. She was sending reinforcements to cut her down. She had little time.

Syrena leapt onto a table and called out, "Hear me now!"

Their voices lowered but the overwhelming fear. Like cornered animals, Syrena felt they might attack at any moment. Tobias spotted a woman, pulling a blade from behind her. He loaded an arrow into his bow and barked, "Blade at the back! "

Syrena locked eyes with the woman and yelled, "Wait!" The woman glared and prepared her blade to throw. "I, too, was one of you," Syrena added. "A slave to the Palace and her cruel ways. I believed that the world was wretched and there was only one way to live. And die."

The woman squared her shoulders. Defiant, yet she stayed her attack.

"We are here to break the yoke the Palace has around your necks and all of the Great Lands," declared Syrena.

"You lie," declared the woman. "You cannot promise us freedom!"

"She can," Tobias shouted. "She has seen freedom. And she brought the True Queen back to claim her throne."

Whispers of hope spread among them. "Is it true?" the woman asked.

"It is," said Syrena. "Gabriella, Queen of the Great Lands is here. Inside the Palace walls. Bringing her rebellion to evil's door. She needs you to hold her flame. To run with it to the villages and cities. And spread the word so that the rebellion will grow."

"Now?" asked the woman, her eyes alight with terror. And hope.

"Now!" called Syrena. As she called out, she imagined sparks of courage lighting in the hearts of every person. They looked to the woman, unsure what to do. The bold woman decided she would never get a better chance to flee.

"I will run!" she yelled. "If you want freedom, run with me to the woods!"

Tobias pushed the door open and Syrena leapt down. Tobias let his arrows fly, protecting the people as they fled.

Syrena scooped up handful after handful of rocks. Swirling her magic to transform them into fireballs. And hurled them at the approaching soldiers, lighting their hair, clothes and beards on fire.

They screamed and fell to the ground. Desperately swatting at the flames.

Syrena and Tobias held the protective line. Raining down arrows and fireballs. As the fleeing rebels made their way to the woods.

Hearts ignited, headed for the cities.

As Gabriella slipped inside the foyer of the Palace, she dropped her magical cloak.

With the Palace waiting for her, there was no point cloaking herself. A shiver of fear rippled through her. The last two times she was here, it was to rescue a loved one or find answers.

This time, she thought. *We end this. One way or another.*

Gabriella closed her eyes, breathed deeply, and exhaled hard. She was ready. Her whole life had led her here. To this battle.

I will not let my homeland down, she thought. When she opened her eyes, Gabriella jumped and covered her mouth. Hannah's spirit shimmered in front of her, smiling.

Hannah! Gabriella exclaimed. She desperately wanted to embrace her sister, but she was also worried. *Are you safe? Can you spare this effort?*

You may be the Queen, but I am your sister, Hannah teased. *And I do what I wish.*

Gabriella blushed. *If I am not meant to be Queen...*

Hannah held up a hand. *We do not have time for this. I am not mad. Or jealous. I have always seen you as the Queen of our Lands. But – this battle is destined to be fought by us both.*

Spirit Hannah took Gabriella's hand. Strangely, Gabriella could feel the shimmer of her touch. She was flooded with the love that her sister brought into a room. Gabriella felt her strength.

Being in spirit gives me far more than it takes away, said Hannah. *So stop worrying about my wellbeing. Trust that this was meant to be.*

Gabriella nodded. Then felt the walls of the Palace tremble.

She knows we are here! exclaimed Gabriella. *We must hurry!*

Forever the bossy one, said Hannah. *Follow me!*

Hannah let go then vanished. As Gabriella looked for her, she felt the walls shake. Mortar crumbled and fell from the ceiling. Large pieces narrowly missed SMASHING into her. The debris covered Gabriella in dust.

Spotting Hannah's shimmering spirit, Gabriella sprinted down the hallway toward her. Giant stones CRASHING to the floor.

Gabriella heard the SHOUTS of soldiers. Yelling to find and capture her. As they ran into the Palace, Gabriella heard CRIES of terror and pain. Falling rocks CRUSHED into their skulls and limbs. Blood washed over the floor.

Gabriella stayed focused on Hannah. She could not look back. They must find the throne room. She did not know what awaited them there. But she had seen it in her visions of this battle. Every time, she ended up standing in the throne room.

She did not need to know why. Once she arrived and approached the thrones, Gabriella trusted that she would know what to do.

As rocks CRASHED all around her, they SMASHED the elegant tiles. Sending shatters flying through the air. Razor-edged projectiles slashed through her cloak and cut her skin.

She ran faster, dodging the flying weapons. Thrown by the Palace and by her guards.

The Palace LAUGHED, an eerie sound that echoed through her head. Sending shivers down Gabriella's spine. *Do you think I did not expect you?* She sneered. *Do you think I will let you leave?*

Gabriella ran harder. Her blood chilled by the madness that resounded through the Palace's words. *She was always torturous. But mad? That is new, and frightening*, thought Gabriella. As her lungs burned and her eyes stung from the mortar in the air.

She bolted through an elegant, neglected dining room. Past long-abandoned sitting rooms that never received visitors. She dashed through room after room that felt chilled by hatred and cruelty.

I will DESTROY you, Messenger! She cackled. *I will pull your limbs from your body and feed you to the rats in my dungeons. I will crush your people by spreading word of your defeat!*

As the Palace stormed, paintings SMASHED to the floor. Vases tumbled from marble tables. And SHATTERED into a thousand pieces. Soldiers rattled swords behind her. Emboldening each other to fulfill on the Palace's command, "Capture the Messenger!"

Gabriella ran harder. Flinching from falling debris and darting to avoid the crashing adornments. She prayed that her sister would get her through this.

Gabriella drew comfort from knowing her sister was safe. *If I do not make it, Hannah will still be here*, she thought. *We can still win.* And she sprinted toward the beacon of Hannah in the next doorway.

~

Adrian followed the Prince up the servant staircase, and felt the Palace TREMBLE. He gripped the handrail and braced, expecting the feeble wooden stairs to fall apart.

The Prince kept going, even though Adrian felt terror emanating from him with every step. He was impressed. *I underestimated his feeling for Gabriella*, Adrian thought, for he was sure that it was her face that prompted the Prince to keep going.

Adrian was grateful for the courage that it lent the Prince. He would deal with his other feelings if they made it out of this alive. *No point fighting a battle that has not been waged*, he thought.

The Prince caught Adrian's eye and kept moving with defiant loathing. He would not let the Wizard win. *We are lucky that the Palace is focused on finding Gabriella*, the Prince thought. *I must make the most of it and fulfill on my promise.* He gripped the rail harder and forced his feet upstairs.

As the Prince crossed onto the landing, he shook violently. Then gritted his teeth and pushed the door open, stepping into a bright hallway. A sharp contrast from the pitiful servants' lodgings.

Adrian flushed with the sensation of Gabriella's peril. *She will be all right*, he assured his heart. *She has handled far worse. Stay with the mission at hand.*

Just ahead of him, the Prince had frozen in place. Adrian did not see what had paralyzed his companion, but he felt a sharp CHILL in the air. *The Mad King*, Adrian thought, and his heart sank. *We are not even in his immediate presence, and this is how the Prince responds?*

Adrian had no choice. The Palace shook and crumbled, threatening to CRUSH their heads with an avalanche of granite. He resorted to the one thing that would prompt the Prince forward.

He drew close and whispered, "Gabriella's life is in your

hands, Prince. If you fail her now, we will all die. The Palace will win. And you will never get your chance to win her heart."

The Prince turned on Adrian, wanting to wrap his hands around his throat and end him. *Right now, right here*, he thought. *I would kill this man once and for all.*

"Yes," Adrian replied, standing boldly in the Prince's path. "Channel your fury. Then take that hatred to your father. And lay it at his feet. Defy all he has done. All that your ancestors have wrought. All that you inherited! Lay it at his feet and demand that he end this reign of terror!"

The Prince growled, still wanting to kill Adrian. But he took his lead and channelled the rage, charging furiously down the hallway. *Someone must pay!* he seethed. *My father must pay! I might have been a different man! I could have been something better!*

The Prince moved so fast, Adrian had to run to keep up. Following him down passageways that Adrian had travelled in spirit. The déjà vu shimmered through his body. *The Prince is running toward his secret tower*, thought Adrian. *The one guarded by the ancestral Queen.*

Adrian hoped he was running to confront his father. *Not to hide inside a tower while the world as he knew it crumbled and fell*, he thought. The Prince tore around another corner and Adrian ran after him.

He reached out to sense whether the Palace watched them. *She is strong*, he thought, *but she expected us to stay by Gabriella's side. She anticipated crushing us together. Not to have many battle fronts. So she keeps her gaze on Gabriella. And we must hurry.*

Adrian kept running. He also sensed the undercurrent of a rebellion. *And if the Palace lost control over the people*, he thought, she loses the mortar that holds her influence in place. Chills ran through his back. That's it! The people were the key all along. So if the Prince can free himself and his people from the –

Adrian turned the last corner and stopped. The CHILL in

the air was palpable. The Prince shivered, staring at the ghost of his father. Adrian did not know how many years had passed, but he felt fear and hatred emanating from the Prince.

The Mad King stared back at the Prince. They were locked in a strange spell.

Adrian drew closer, hoping this might be easier than he thought. Until he saw that the Prince's bitterness fed the King's power. A twisted grin appeared on the King's face.

"You came to confront your father, did you?" the Mad King scoffed. "You only wield power because I handed it to you, ungrateful wretch. You are not worthy of your ancestors' legacy. But you are the only child I had, and so you had to do. If only I had had a bastard. One I could have counted on to take my place."

A legion of cruel and twisted ghosts appeared behind the King. Drawn by the torment. Laughing at the Prince's wilting resolve.

The Prince shook with the COLD. He grappled to find his desire. His need to impress Gabriella. But he feared that if he could not confront the King, the Palace would soon claim back his mind.

"Do not give in," Adrian whispered. "You are stronger than he is."

The King laughed even louder. "Do not waste your breath, Wizard! I have centuries of power on my side."

As the King spoke, the Prince's ancestors surrounded him. Filling his ears with brutal and punishing thoughts. *Your only worth is in service to us*, they hissed. *And your legacy.*

The Prince shook and the air around him dripped with cold. He exhaled freezing clouds. And wrapped his arms around him. Forgetting that Adrian was even there.

The Messenger will never love you, his ancestors tormented. *No one loved you. You are worthy only of what we give. And what you take. Why would you throw yourself at the feet of a girl. When you can own all the lands. All of the people! Take it! Claim it! Throw them to the fire!*

The Prince fell to his knees, fending off their vicious, clawing fingers. And their cold and penetrating words. *Letting go is easier,* the Prince thought. *If I let go, I will be at peace. I will never have to struggle again.*

Adrian panicked. *We are losing the Prince,* he thought. *And we need him.* He could feel what Gabriella saw. As much as Adrian hated to admit it, Gabriella was right. Somehow, the war would be lost.

So Adrian crept closer. He felt for an opening in the heavy bank of foul energy that surrounded the Prince. He pierced the malevolence with a sharp bolt of light, and the Prince screamed in pain. Adrian doubled his efforts. A short-lived pain would not matter if he could get him back.

The Prince SCREECHED in agony. His ancestors fed on his pain. The Mad King cackled.

"Wizard, stop!" commanded a female voice. And Adrian's gaze snapped up. He saw the shimmering form of Chancelry. Powerful and kind, like the brave ones who forged the passageway.

She stepped between the Mad King and his son. The King raged and Chancelry stood strong against his BLAST of wretched, icy air.

Chancelry reached down to the Prince. "Those are not your only ancestors," she said, and the Prince raised his gaze to her. "You know that. You must choose which ones you will believe."

"Godmother," he said, tears springing to his eyes. "I have missed you." The Prince stood up, shaking but strong.

He wrapped his arms around her. And she whispered in his ear. "Remember that we spoke of this moment. That you would always have to make a choice."

She released him and stepped away. Even as he shook and had barely found his feet. "You must decide. Now."

The Prince gazed at his father. "I may be from you, but I am not of you." The King's spirit began to fade and the Prince gained more courage. Feeling that his determination held more power than his rage.

"Leave father," said the Prince. "You are not wanted here. And you have no power in my Palace. I am the ruler now. And I choose to align myself with those who speak generously. You are weak of spirit and without my fear, you have no anchor on this place."

"The era of cruelty is over," declared the Prince. "You do not belong here. Nor do your minions. I will have no part in their ways. This is a time for peace. And I will do everything in my power to ensure that the rightful ruler of the Great Lands will be protected until the end of her days."

"Heed the Prince," Chancelry added, placing her hand on the Prince's shoulder. Shining like a blazing star of love, the cruel and tormenting ghosts shielded their eyes from her.

They SHRIEKED and TWISTED. Shrinking back then vanishing. The Mad King grew confused. No one fed his fury. No one believed his lies.

The Prince stood strong. With Adrian on one side and Chancelry on the other, their combined power melted the remaining hold of the Mad King.

"We are in a new era," the Prince said. "I will atone for your actions. But I do not need your approval. Or your company."

And with that declaration, the Mad King vanished. Never to be seen again.

CHAPTER ELEVEN

Syrena and Tobias stood close to one another, shooting off arrows and fireballs.

Waves of soldiers continued to attack. Forced forward by the FURY of the Palace. Syrena was exhausted, wounded, and singed.

But we cannot wane, she thought, *we must keep fighting.* Syrena had felt a surge of hope only moments ago. She was sure that Adrian had reached his target. And the Prince had confronted his father. She felt hope in her heart.

So why are the soldiers still fighting? She thought. *Why are they more numerous than before?*

She glanced at Tobias, fighting valiantly despite little sleep and meager food. His determination reignited the fire in her belly. He fought like a man who did not care about tomorrow. All he cared to do was serve his Queen. And do right by the people he believed in.

Syrena drew on her deepening store of purpose. Her absolute belief that Gabriella and Hannah deserved to rule and would bring peace back to the Great Lands. A fierce grin on her face, she fought by the side of one of the most valiant men she had ever known.

They drew the soldiers out of the Palace. Taking on as many as they could. Syrena with her fire-magic and Tobias with as many arrows as he gathered from fallen soldiers. Between his bow and his sword, Tobias fought like a company of seven men.

Syrena and Tobias understood that their main task was to draw the attack away from Gabriella. They had sent off as many possible rebels as they could. Now they needed to keep the raging soldiers busy. But she could see that she and Tobias were weakening.

My magical light shield holds, but for how much longer, she wondered. *There is no shortage of soldiers. We cannot count on exhausting them by number.*

Syrena swung her sword and knocked back three more men. Far behind the hordes of rage-blind fighters, she caught sight of one or two who fled into the woods. *Somehow,* she thought, *they found courage. Or broke their bonds just enough to see another way.*

As she held back this latest front, she spoke to Tobias. *The soldiers do not weary from rage and fear. We need another way. If we can boost the people's rebellion, the effect might weaken the Palace.*

Tobias wiped dripping sweat from his tired brow. *You think this might weaken her soldiers?*

He fired at the man launching firebombs at them. The arrow pierced the man's shoulder and sent him reeling to the ground.

Yes, Syrena replied. *We have only so much strength left between us. Our endurance will fail. So we must find a way to break their chains. To free their hearts.*

How do you suggest we do that? he replied, as he fired a slew of arrows at the archers perched on a lower balcony. Then swung a sword at the men who approached clumsily from behind.

Use your influence with nature's messengers, she said, and gestured toward the ravens and vultures that had descended on the battle-field. Swooping among the beleaguered soldiers, they were arriving in droves. Spooking the most superstitious of the Palace slaves.

Tobias and Syrena drew closer to the birds. The fears pushing back the Palace's soldiers gave them a chance to find safer territory. And it meant Tobias had a better chance to make contact.

The corvids stayed despite Syrena and Tobias's approach. But he was doubtful they would listen to him. *I have no basis of trust with them*, he thought. *It is not as simple as speaking their language.*

Tobias shot off more arrows and noticed the Ravens watching him. He felt them calculating. Seeing that he provided dinner. And protection. *Perhaps if they believe we want their freedom*, he thought. *And to stop the Palace from killing off their kind, they might aid our rebellion.*

Watch my back, said Tobias. *I will not be able to fight while I do this. I need my focus.*

Syrena nodded, and doubled her assault on the rogues near and above them.

Tobias grew still and reached out softly to the ravens closest to them on the battlefield. They jumped and cawed a warning. But one made eye contact with Tobias. Intrigued by this calm man who spoke their ancient tongue.

"I wish you no harm," Tobias said. The other birds tilted their heads and muttered clicks. While the wisest kept Tobias in his sharp stare.

"We wage war against this evil realm," he explained, careful to keep his gaze respectful. "And we have a humble request of your kind."

The oldest raven hopped to the top of the pile of dead men and replied, "Speak your request, human. We will contemplate it."

Tobias nodded. "We wish for you to send messengers to the cities. Speak wisdom to the ones who will listen. No matter how old or how young. For us to win this battle, we need the rebellion to spread. We need a message of hope to reach their hearts. If the people, and the animals, take back our lands. We can defeat the Palace. For good."

The Raven tilted her head. Considering this man who stopped fighting during a raging battle to request their help. *The humans must be desperate*, she thought, and swung her black eyes to scrutinize the one keeping him safe. *The woman wielded natural magic unlike other*, she mused. *They are an intriguing pair.*

Her gaze shifted back to Tobias. She eyed him warily. *Perhaps humans had finally learned something. Perhaps they are ready to revere the old ways again. And listen to the ancestors.*

She heard the tumble of opinions rattling behind her. And shushed them so she could think. Tobias stayed quiet. Waiting for her answer. She liked that he did not cajole or bully. And she felt his warrior heart. *He will serve the Messenger Queen well*, she thought. *As was foretold.*

"I am willing to send messengers," she acknowledged, cautiously. "But I warn you that humans are obstinate and tricky. They will likely ignore our guidance."

"We can only try," replied Tobias, hopeful. "I am grateful for whatever you are willing to do."

He exhaled and came back into his body. Shook his head and swiftly re-entered the fray. Revitalized by the hope from the Raven clan.

The murder of ravens tilted their heads at the fascinating man. "If the Messenger Queen brings us more like him, humans may find their souls again."

The ravens clacked and clicked, expressing hope and doubt and intrigue and curiosity. As their Wise Leader tasked several of them to take to the skies. Carrying her message and magic.

Tobias and Syrena felt their heart's soar as two dozen ravens took to the sky. Flying in every direction with the promise of rebellion in the Great Lands.

A glisten of tears sprang into Syrena's eyes. She sent up a prayer of protection for the Ravens. And a desire that her people would find the humility to listen.

Then plunged back into the battle. Determined to see this land returned to a just ruler.

Katrin had worked tirelessly, spreading the word of rebellion in Cardea.

She had returned to Adrian's bar, where she felt safe. And clinked her glass of whisky with the barkeep. He understood the need for a stiff drink after a day of arduous work.

They downed their drinks. Katrin was not sure whether the flame of revolt caught. But she had spread the fire of intrigue. And that was at least enough a chance to turn the tide.

"I may not have set Cardea on fire," Katrin shared with the sympathetic barkeep. "But I sure as hell sparked the hay bales."

"We will pray that something fans the flames," the barkeep replied.

Even exhausted, Katrin laughed at her circumstances. She never expected to care about the Great Lands, not since the fall of Granamore. But the more she reclaimed her heart, the more she learned that caring came with heartbreak. They were natural partners in the game of love.

Katrin downed her whisky and asked for another. The barkeep filled her glass. She would stay and fight as long as she had fire in her belly and love in her heart.

And whisky in my blood, she thought, laughing.

As tired as she felt, Katrin felt a whisper of hope on the

wind. She looked up at the open doorway and saw a regal and iridescent raven fly straight down a main street of Cardea. Sending a shimmering light of hope in its wake.

Katrin felt the wave of enchanted courage ripple through her. As though three days of strength returned to her body. And a spark of hope leapt in her heart.

"Gabriella," she whispered. Then downed her whisky and leapt to her feet.

Katrin ran back out of the bar. She could tell that the Raven's magic was about to make her mission much easier.

And she was eager to fan the flames of rebellion.

CHAPTER TWELVE

Gabriella ran behind the ethereal Hannah as they arrived in the throne room.

They knew this room well. She had discovered her magic right here, years ago. And had since learned that this was the heart of the Palace. The source of its power.

That is why you were drawn to it, Hannah spoke silently to Gabriella. *That is why we end it here.*

Gabriella ran to stand in front of the throne and took her sister's hand. Regardless of Hannah's spirit state, the two sisters connected. Love and power coursed through them. Gabriella with her fierce spirit and Hannah with her compassionate heart.

They felt the magic of their lineage pour through them. And Gabriella understood why Hannah needed to be rooted in Granamore. She was the connection to their ancestors.

We are not alone, Gabriella said. *You are the conduit to our people. To the motherline.*

Exactly, replied Hannah. *You were never meant to battle the Palace alone. We are the continuation of a fight that has raged for centuries.*

"We stand here to end the battle of the ages," Gabriella declared aloud, knowing that she spoke for thousands. Those who had died and those who still lived. "We stand here to end the reign of terror. And to speak for those who fought valiantly against you."

"We call on the heartbeat of our ancestors," said Hannah. "We feel their power. We speak to their magic. We know they are with us to bring a new age to our lands."

Gabriella and Hannah stood strong, feeling the pulse of magic awaken. They called the magic that had been hidden and dormant for many generations.

Light radiated through their hearts. And pulsed through their hands. Sending wave after wave of dazzling sunshine rippling through the Palace. As though two magnificent suns had been released into the throne room.

The walls of the Palace shook. Mortar fell down around the two sisters. Crashing behind their feet and within a hair's breadth of their hands.

Gabriella felt the palace's RAGE and her delighted anticipation. "I have been waiting for you, Messenger," said the Palace. "You may feel invincible but your sister stands with you only in spirit. You are a feeble body that I can crush with an avalanche of my stones."

Hannah clutched Gabriella's hand. *Do not listen, Gabriella. You are more protected than you know. Together, we are far more powerful than the Palace understands.*

But as the stones fell, ROCKING the throne and SMASHING the wooden floors, Gabriella doubted. *I may die today*, she said to Hannah. *But you will be safe.* And Gabriella felt a surge of love, even as she shook with fear.

What if that is why we are twins? she said. *What if it was so there would always be one of us left to rule?*

Do not give up, Gabriella! Hannah insisted. *Claim your power.*

Stand strong with your fierce heart. I may be here in spirit, but I swear that you are as protected as I am!

Gabriella felt the surge of power from her sister. And saw the spirits of their lineage - from their mother to their grandmother and all the women of Granamore. Every spirit stood with them, sending their fierce magic.

Their hearts beat as one. And the pulse took over the cruel beat of the Palace. The Great Lands was ready to be released. To recover what had been lost.

The Palace ROARED in PAIN. The burning light pulsing from the sisters and hundreds of spirits seared her from inside. She had been prepared to take on the meek girls. *But this?* She thought. *This was trickery!*

"You will not take my throne!" thundered the Palace. Winds SURGED into the throne room, as though a vicious winter storm had been unleashed within her walls. The HOWLING gusts whipped around Hannah and Gabriella, pulling at them, and threatening to break their grip.

The Palace focused all her FORCE on their clutched hands. "I will break your bond," she howled. "I will crush you both and the people that stand with you. You will pay for what you have done. For generations to come!"

Gabriella's hair flew wildly, stinging her face. Even Hannah felt the CHILL and PIERCING HATE of the Palace. Hannah closed her eyes and focused on her sister's hand. The light pulsing from their grip grew BRIGHTER.

The Palace SCREAMED and increased the strength of her storm. Shaking the ceiling stones. Rattling the walls. Knocking Gabriella to her knees. Still, Hannah clutched her hand. Stronger than ever. As the VICIOUS storm SLASHED at Gabriella's face and SINGED her hands.

The mortar SHOOK and crumbled and CRASHED. Stone

after monstrous stone fell. SMASHING the solid, oak floors into splinters.

Shards of wood flew at Gabriella piercing her like vicious needles, tearing her skin. She squeezed her eyes shut and focused on her sister. On Adrian. On her family. On her people. She did this for herself and for them all.

"They are with me," she whispered, "they are with me." Like a mantra, over and over. She prayed and called and trusted. "They are with me. Be with me."

She would not fight this alone. Just like Hannah said. She had fought alone long enough. This was a battle for them to fight together.

Within moments, Adrian and the Prince rushed into the doorway. "The ceiling!" yelled the Prince, as he spotted the stones shaking loose and readying to fall on Gabriella. Adrian quickly held out his hands and threw a spell above Gabriella and Hannah.

The stones FELL and hung mid-air above the sisters. Suspended, as though an invisible net draped below the ceiling.

Gabriella opened her eyes, squinting through the assailing storm. She saw Adrian and the Prince, and a wave of hope washed through her. Gabriella forced herself to her feet, pushing against the FIERCE WIND. She stood with sheer determination.

Though the vicious howls, Gabriella heard a harmonious sound. A chanting. The sound was familiar, as though she had heard it in a dream. *The rebellion is growing stronger*, she thought. *Strong enough to send courage through the mortar of the Palace.*

Do you hear it? Gabriella asked. *The stones are singing.*

Hannah shook her head but smiled. *Do you feel the people coming?* Hannah replied.

Gabriella smiled and shook her head. *We are destined to rule together. I bring nature and you bring the community. Together, we unite the land and its people.*

The light shining from the sisters intensified. And the Palace redoubled her attack.

"You cannot free what is not yours!" declared the Palace. "Humans will always bow to fear and force. The ones who join you will feel the point of my sword. And when YOU die, no one will heed the voice of hope in the Great Lands EVER again."

The Palace intensified the WIND and shook loose the ceremonial weapons hanging on her walls. Freeing them from their stands. Swords and knives FLEW through the air, aiming for the hearts of Gabriella and Hannah.

"Gabriella!" Shouted Adrian. "Look out!" The wind drowned out his words. But the Prince heard him and, snatching a shield from the wall, he ran to the sisters.

The Prince leapt in front of Gabriella, holding the shield high. Waves of daggers STRUCK the metal and shook the Prince. He stood strong against the cyclone, even though his arms SHOOK and his legs threatened to buckle.

Syrena and Tobias appeared with a ragged group of determined soldiers. Fighting their way into the room against the fierce gusts. "Grab a shield," Syrena yelled. "And make a barricade around your monarchs!"

The soldiers YELLED and ran into the fray. Despite the gale-force winds, they felt the warmth of sunlight beaming from the sisters. They YANKED shields from the walls and LOCKED together like a wall. Forging a chain of courage and metal around their Queens.

Syrena and Tobias marveled at the magic pulsing from Gabriella and Hannah. They could see the vast assembly of ancestral spirits behind them. And felt emboldened.

They called more people into the fray, directing them to defend. Rings of soldiers protected the sovereigns. One ring holding shields before their chests. The next holding shields above their heads.

"I will crush you all!" promised the Palace. But as she reached for their hearts, they held strong against her clutching pain. Grimacing, they linked together tighter. Defying her hatred. Standing for all that is holy and true.

Furious, the Palace gathered her rage and focused it all on the Prince, bearing down on his heart with EVERY OUNCE of her HATRED and DETERMINATION. The Prince fell to his knees, as searing pain PIERCED his chest. He HOWLED in pain.

Gabriella lost focus. FURY leapt through her. The sunlight dimmed. And the Palace LAUGHED.

"That is right, Messenger," snarled the Palace. "I will crush him right before your eyes."

The Prince GASPED for air as the Palace seized his mind. *You are mine, Prince,* she declared. *You were sacrificed to me on the day of your birth. Your freedom in exchange for your parents' power. They made a pact to sacrifice you in exchange for ruling all that they desired.*

You were never going to be free, she mocked. *You are mine. Cursed. Never to be saved. Bend to me or die. This is your choice!*

As the Prince struggled for breath, Gabriella pulled at her sister's hand. *I must go,* she thought. *She will kill him!* Gabriella tugged harder, but Hannah held tight.

Search your heart, Gabriella, Hannah said. *Is that best? Or is that what the Palace wants? Look deep inside. Can you trust what is right to prevail, even if it is not your deed?*

Tears streamed down her cheeks. She felt the Prince's pain. Her heart was aching. Her mind was screaming. And still, she trusted her sister.

Gabriella closed her eyes. Feeling past the impulse to fight.

To a deeper place. A place of faith. She needed to trust others, as deeply as she trusted her ability to act.

This is the path of the Queen, she thought. *To believe in others. To trust them to choose well, to stand with her. For the sake of their land and their community. To feel the vulnerability of that trust. And to hold confidence that they will choose and act from love.*

She opened her eyes and saw the reflection of her understanding in Hannah's smile.

Gabriella looked at the Prince. Kneeling in pain. She squeezed her sister's hand and swallowed hard. Determined to believe in him. This battle for his heart was the Prince's to fight.

As he gasped, Gabriella prayed. She felt the loving determination of her ancestors. And leaned on their strength. Their courage. Trusting that every choice and brave act led to this place. The light shining from her and Hannah grew exponentially. Bursting forth like a stunning sunrise.

Chancelry appeared at the Prince's side. She smiled and nodded to Gabriella. She had been called forth by Gabriella's faith and shining light. Chancelry gently placed a hand on the Prince's shoulder. Standing for her lineage and giving the Prince strength to liberate his soul and lands.

Gabriella radiated love. Beaming it toward the Great Prince. Calling on their shared memories and history. She felt his courage and desire to be free.

As Gabriella directed all her love to the Prince, Adrian's focus stumbled. Fear of losing his beloved rushed through him and the Palace took full advantage. His protective spell waivered and the Palace RAINED stones. Skull-crushing rocks landed perilously close to Gabriella.

She winced and her eyes flitted to Adrian. And in this perilous moment, hanging between life and death, she knew. This was not merely a Wizard defending his Queen. This was a man risking his life for the woman he adored. Stumbling in the face of his own heartache and standing strong all the same.

Their eyes locked and Gabriella felt lifetimes of connection pour between their hearts. A knowing. A depth of understanding that she had never felt with any human except her sister. This man, this force of nature, was her true love. Her Soul's match.

Gabriella and the Prince shared a compelling history. An understanding of the perils of sovereignty and being raised by monarchs. But she and Adrian were warriors of the heart. They shared so much more than history.

When she looked at Adrian, she saw the man who loved her whether she was a Queen or a Commoner. He saw the woman she was. And believed in the desires of her heart. She held his gaze and knew he would follow her to the ends of the earth.

The power of their love overcame her. The fierce passion pulsing from him as he held back the crumbling weight of a Palace, broke her heart wide open. Piercing the room in BLINDING LIGHT.

Adrian's spell grew TENFOLD in strength. The stones FELL and CRUMBLED in wave after wave, as the Palace threw all that she had in an attempt to CRUSH the Prince and the Sisters. And the falling stones CASCADED into piles at the edges of the room.

The Prince pressed a hand to Chancelry's. He felt the line of ancestors who fought the evil. Who chose the path of defiance and gave their lives for benevolence. The Prince trembled and held back tears as he realized that he came from goodness as well as evil. Warmth flooded his heart.

With shaking legs, the Prince forced himself to his feet.

He stood in the face of shrieking winds and YELLED, "I never was your child. My father never claimed me. He rejected me. And so he could not give me!"

The Prince's stand grew stronger and he placed a hand on his heart. "My mother loved me. Every day until her death. In her name, I declare my freedom. Like her, you can kill me, but I will die a free man!"

He squeezed Chancelry's hand. "I liberate myself and all who came before me. I belong to my heart. I belong to my people. You will NEVER reign over me again. Be gone, evil ancestors who cling to this place. You are not mine and you are not of this land! We cast you to the depths of Hades!"

The Palace SCREAMED and HOWLED. The whirling WINDS of her storm SWIRLED up through the cavernous hole above the throne room. As they lifted, the winds died and her power was gone.

The Prince stood on shaking legs. And the stones of his Palace sang their liberation. The last treacherous tendrils of the Palace's magic bled away, deep into the crevices of the ground.

Gabriella and Hannah felt their light soar. Beaming into the night sky. They all gazed up to see the twinkling and peaceful lights of the stars.

As peace cascaded over them, the glow of dawn edged the sky. Casting a rose hue over the Palace. And the light radiating from Hannah and Gabriella beamed, turning the Palace into a beacon for every corner of the Great Lands.

Filling every heart with hope.

CHAPTER THIRTEEN

HANNAH FELT blood rushing to her fingers and toes.

The spell was wearing thin. And her body was waking.

Hannah felt Gabriella and their clan travelling with the fury of vanquishers back to Granamore. And for the first time in many months, a smile edged her lips.

She sighed, anticipating their love. Their arrival would break the sleeping spell. And she would be fully in her body. Awake. She could hug Syrena. And her beloved family, as her fore-bearers intended.

Her heart trembled as she sensed her ancestors leaving. *Will I be able to see you so when I am released from this spell?* she asked.

They smiled. But did not answer. And her heart fluttered with grief.

I do not want to lose this, Hannah said. *I have grown used to your comfort and guidance.*

The assembly of ancestors parted. And two figures stepped forward to speak. Hannah's breath caught as she looked on her mother and father. Her mother stepped closer.

Darling Hannah, she said. *We will always be close. What woke in you during this spell is part of you. You will not lose it.*

Her mother came to her side. *I am sorry for telling you to hide your gifts. For forcing you to lose the connection with your bloodline. I did so for your protection. But I am grateful to have played a part in returning your gifts and the magic of the lands.*

You set the spell, Hannah realized, wondering what her mother sacrificed as they fled all those years ago.

I did, her mother replied. *I could not leave without knowing that, one day, your gift would be awakened. I had a vision that these lands would need the unique magic of you and your sister.*

The ancestors began to shimmer. Gabriella and the others approached. Hannah's body prickled as her twin grew near. Along with the clan of her heart.

Your sister's arrival will restore you, her mother said. And her father stepped in, *We are so proud of you both. You will make superb rulers.*

Rulers? Hannah questioned. *But Gabriella is to be Queen.*

Her mother and father laughed. *Search your heart, dear one. You know as well as we do, that you are meant to rule side-by-side.*

Her parents leaned down to kiss Hannah's forehead. Then turned and disappeared into the gathering of ancestors. Hannah's heart squeezed as they faded into the mist surrounding the door. Just as the door flung open, and the greenhouse filled with whispering voices.

Sensation rushed into her fingers and toes. Prickling her all over, like a thousand tiny hornets. Hannah shivered and squirmed. And her eyes fluttered open from the heaviness of deep sleep.

She felt the warmth of a hand sliding into her right palm. And her heart burst with love. Another hand, that she had known her whole life, slid into her left palm. And she smiled.

Hannah sat up slowly, feeling dizzy, yet elated by the grinning faces of Syrena and Gabriella.

"Hannah!" Syrena said, relieved, pulling her love into an embrace. "I have missed you!"

Gabriella smiled, as a tear slid down her cheek. Hannah felt her twin's heart and relief caught in her throat. A matching tear streamed down her own cheek.

Hannah could not have imagined a more perfect way to be welcomed home.

As she struggled to stand, Syrena and Gabriella leaned in to help. "Gently, dear sister," Gabriella said. "You fought the war to end all wars while cloaked in a sleeping spell."

Hannah saw the smiling faces of Adrian and Tobias and Katrin and the spirit of Casmire, along with Gabriella and Syrena.

"Where is – ?" Hannah asked, looking only at Gabriella.

"The Prince stayed in his land," Gabriella replied, with a twinge of sadness. "He has many amends to make. And a lifetime of work to gain back the trust of his people."

Hannah squeezed her sister's hand. Knowing that her twin's heart ached. She had given part of herself to the Great Prince. A part that would forever belong with him.

She looked into Gabriella's eyes and saw a scene shared in the privacy of a remote tower in the Hidden Palace. Gabriella hugging the Prince tightly to her, tears streaming down her face. Her heart weighed down with loss. The Prince nodded, solemnly. Understanding, yet not accepting, her choice. Hannah's heart broke with them, as she turned from her sister to Adrian.

You understand the mighty responsibility of loving my sister, Hannah said. *She has sacrificed so much for her people, her sister, and her lands.*

Adrian nodded. *I do. It is the greatest undertaking of my life.* And Hannah smiled.

"Gabriella," Hannah said, glancing at the shimmer of light beyond the greenhouse. She was confident that she could strengthen her connection with their ancestors.

"Yes?" replied Gabriella. And Hannah took both of her sister's hands.

"You and I are now the rulers of our land," she said, softly. Gabriella understood immediately. And a sob lodged in her throat. Hannah nodded. "I saw their spirits. They have crossed over."

Gabriella's breath caught. She had known this in her bones.

When they returned to Granamore, she felt the grief in the forest and the pain in the castle. But hearing her sister say it aloud was another matter.

Adrian came to her side and she leaned on him. Still holding her sister's hands, Gabriella allowed the sobs of grief to take her. She had held onto hope for so long. Wishing for one last chance to say goodbye. Casmire's spirit shimmered near her.

"They will always be with us," Hannah said. "We can call on them whenever we need."

"We are meant to rule together," replied Gabriella. Hannah nodded. And both sisters sighed.

Gabriella reached for Adrian's hand. She encouraged the others to link hands together and stand in a circle. "To the beginning of a new era," Gabriella declared. "Ruled by Queens. And ordained by love."

"To love!" they exclaimed, raising their hands in the air. Casmire neighed loudly, making Gabriella laugh.

And the Great Lands shone with hope for the first time in generations.

～

Thank you for reading the *Great Lands* series! You can discover the *Fated* series with an excerpt of *Blue Moon* in the following pages.

DEAR READER

I hope you enjoyed Gabriella's brave quest to reunite with her sister and fight for the liberation of her home. The Great Lands is a magical world that inspires the courage and love of its powerful leaders.

If you enjoyed this series, please consider writing a review online or sharing your experience with me directly on Instagram.

You can review Queen wherever you made your purchase and on Goodreads.

Every review helps other readers to discover these stories. No matter how long, heartfelt reviews bring more readers to the Great Lands.

~

I love hearing how these books made you feel. And I am deeply grateful for every reader.

Thank you for spending your reading time with my books and sharing your experience.

~

Keep reading for an excerpt from *Blue Moon*!

With a glimpse into Blue Moon

Helen stepped off the elevator. She wasn't sure what drew her here. She had followed an instinct. Luring her up sixty-one floors to the top of this glass sky rise.

She stood for a moment in the entryway.

Gazing around, she absorbed that no man's land between elevator and business. Imagining how many people passed through this space. Matching what they wore to the finest details of the wallpaper, the door frames, the frosted glass. She smiled. Knowing these were the tiny specifics most people blurred past in their day.

For Helen, each detail was a clue. A fascinating mystery to be solved. She knew that someone had chosen each item, no matter how banal, to give an impression. To set a mood. Every thing selected to intimidate or welcome, depending on the business at the end of this passage.

Helen knew she stood on a bridge between worlds.

On her last birthday, Helen had created a game to follow any pull her instinct presented with enough force. No matter where it took her or how much talking she needed to do. She promised to follow.

Usually it involved picking an unsuspecting business or event, seeing how far she could get and how much she could find out. She gathered as many clues as she could before she opened their door, then kept the game going as long as possible. Other people went to movies. Helen invented her own little plots.

She knew Manhattan had millions of people, but it could be a lonely place at the best of times. Never mind expensive. So she created a fun source of entertainment to get to know the city, while meeting people she would never run into in her normal life. Not that Helen was remotely normal.

She had been on her way to a housewarming party with no intention of detouring into an Upper West Side skyscraper. Helen strode extra fast when she was forcing herself to a destination. She didn't like parties much, especially ones where she had to bring a home-oriented gift, but she reluctantly admitted they were a place to meet friends. Or potential job prospects.

She would have gone straight past the building had she not spotted the Logan & Associates logo. The moment she saw it, she felt a spine-tingling chill, and stopped in her tracks. The chill was her sign that there was something special about the place. Something mysterious.

Helen couldn't explain it. But she suddenly had to know who Logan was and why he needed associates.

She found herself pulled into the lobby by a curiosity so strong she would have sworn someone was tugging her blouse.

The building was remarkably quiet. She looked around but did not see a soul in the lobby. Even the security guard was strangely missing from his desk.

Helen didn't question her luck. She headed straight for the elevators, quickly checking the building's directory for Logan & Associates before disappearing through the elevator doors.

Now that she stood in front of their logo, emblazoned on the wall, Helen wondered what could have possibly enticed her up sixty-one floors.

Their conservative emblem announced their importance like a law firm yet with too much flair to be such a practical enterprise. Sparkling silver, the logo's material implied expensive services and the size laid claim to the entire floor. Yet the name was so banal, she would almost assume they didn't want anyone making the trip.

What kind of company offers high-end services to a limited clientele? Helen wondered as she moved her gaze from the logo to re-examine the entryway. She suddenly picked up on the missing washroom. And the lack of art on the walls.

They aren't looking for exclusive clients, Helen thought, *they don't want clients at all. Or, at least,* she corrected herself, *they don't want anyone who isn't invited.*

Helen smiled. Jackpot! And the chill shot up her spine. Just like when she saw their name. If she needed any confirmation, she had it. There was something mysterious about this place. Which made her game all the more exciting.

As she turned her gaze to the office behind the glazed glass, she wondered how to play this. The best approach was to let the receptionist take the lead. Helen preferred to be in charge, but when the dance was this unscripted, she knew to follow where other people loved to show the way.

Luckily, she had dressed for the party. Most days, she would never wear pants that required an iron, let alone a blouse discreet enough to be worn to a job interview. She glanced down at her flirty blouse, and shifted the shoulders back to adjust the plunge down her chest. Well, almost discreet enough.

Helen shook off her doubts and pushed open the glass door. She wasn't surprised to see the waiting area empty. But she had expected a receptionist. Not seeing anyone at the front desk, she moved lightly yet confidently into the quiet space.

As she moved past the simple, modern furnishings and the non-descript glass table, she was no closer to figuring out what this place was. Luckily, she spotted a pile of magazines in the far corner of the waiting area.

Helen was a pro at figuring out a business within five minutes of seeing their reading material. She walked straight past the front desk, around the edge of the waiting area, and reached toward the stack tucked in the corner. As though no one expected them to be read at all.

"May I help you?" a voice asked, in an unhelpful tone.

Helen practically jumped out of her skin. She whipped around to see the receptionist leaning out from behind an absurdly large computer monitor, looking far from amused. Helen wondered whether this woman was really a receptionist or a guard dog with her finger poised on an alarm button.

Helen smiled effortlessly and stepped toward her opponent. She didn't actually care what the woman's real job was. Helen reveled in the challenge. Hostile receptionists were like a rite of passage. If she hadn't piped up, Helen would have been disappointed to move past so easily.

"Why, yes," Helen began, approaching the front desk.

Helen's eyes swept over the clean, sharp lines of the white barrier between her and the reception area. The chest-height obstruction said much more than anyone else might imagine. Discretion. Restraint. Secrets.

Where others noticed simple elegance, she saw protection

and suspicion. Logan & Associates didn't want anyone sneaking up on their receptionist and catching a peek at her work. Helen smiled innocently and leaned in to create an air of intimacy with the cool guardian of the front desk.

"I have an appointment with Mr. Logan," Helen said, glancing over the barrier at the immaculate desktop. Not a sheet of paper in sight.

The receptionist gazed back without flinching. Then asked, "Which one?"

"Senior," Helen responded quickly.

She had no idea where that answer came from. Helen cursed her fast tongue.

Why did she say Senior? She should have opted for Junior. Helen always had better luck with younger men. Between her playful tone and complete lack of interest in their opinion, they couldn't help but be drawn to her.

"Your name," the receptionist demanded.

"Helen," she replied. "Helen Troy."

"Take a seat, Miss Troy."

As she perched on a white leather chair, Helen was nervous, but excited. She had secured an invitation inside this secret place. Not only was she going deeper into the labyrinth but she was officially rescued from her party.

Who knows, she laughed to herself, *she might even get a job out the deal.*

While she waited, she picked up one of the neatly stacked magazines. Intrigued to find an interior design magazine on the top. She glanced around surreptitiously as she flipped the pages.

No way this is a design firm, she thought. *Not a stitch of art. No minimalist yet pretentious furniture. No discreet yet oh so obviously placed awards for clients to notice.* She gazed down at the magazine. *Unless this is meant to distract me from whatever horrible problem I have by gazing at harmless, pretty pictures.*

Helen looked up, trying to catch a glimpse of the inside workings of Logan & Associates. No one walked by. No one showed up for appointments. No one called. She was alone with the sullen receptionist.

She began to wonder if anyone worked in this place. The more she wondered, the more the quiet grew unsettling.

Helen's mood shifted. She no longer felt excited. She felt vulnerable. She was alone in a strange office with one exit. If anything went wrong ... she glanced up at the door. Thinking about how quickly she could get to the stairwell.

Wait. Had she seen a stairwell? Or just the elevator? She wondered. *Skyscrapers had to have a fire exit. It must be code. But she couldn't recall seeing the door. Or the bright red Exit sign that lit the way in case of fire.*

Helen admonished herself. She was getting worked up over nothing. She must have missed it. Her instinct had never steered her wrong. That intuitive pull had landed her all kinds of amazing jobs, apartments, and even the occasional fun affair.

But she couldn't shake the feeling that this place was strange. Like whatever they did here was definitely *not* a game. And that feeling clashed with her reason for doing anything.

By her twenty-seventh birthday, Helen decided she'd had enough drama to last several lifetimes. That night, after many drinks, she swore on an invisible stack of bibles that she was never taking anything seriously again. Not love. Not money. Not even life itself.

As far as she could tell, life was some elaborate game played by the gods. Where dice got tossed and you had no say in the numbers that showed up. Helen had lost that toss too many times in twenty-seven years.

She was playful by nature. But she decided it was time to up the stakes — so her game was born. If life was a crapshoot, she was going to have as much fun as possible. Helen wanted to play life full-tilt, following her intuition. Life was for living. Not for getting attached. And definitely not for staying in one place too long.

Nope. Helen was about as far as you could get from every other twenty-seven year-old on the shores of Manhattan. Most twenty-somethings with enough chutzpah to get to this island, and afford the rent, were filled with more ambition than one human being had the right to carry. The very thought of it made her nauseous.

They were determined. Helen gave them that. Determined to climb any and every wall presented. To what aim, she had no idea. Their pathological need to prove themselves seemed just as random, and infinitely less fun, than her decision to let her intuition take her wherever it damn well pleased.

When she committed to her game, Helen was so excited she made the mistake of telling people at parties. She loved the idea of letting life lead the way! Pure adventure. Letting go of the reins. She was sure people would be inspired or at least intrigued.

Not so. The response she typically got was horror, confusion, or a blank stare. Not one ounce of curiosity. Not one person wanting to tag along and give it a try. She had expected more of people in New York. Especially the artists.

Somehow, her lack of ambition did not make her intriguing. Helen discovered that it made her suspicious. Like she made the whole thing up just to trick them and steal their gold when they weren't looking. Though she had ancestors who might have done that, she was still insulted.

Helen felt a twinge. Someone was staring at her. She turned to see a young associate waiting. Eyes flitting from Helen to the floor then back to Helen. She cradled a pad of paper in her arms like a shield and had a nervous energy that made Helen think of a startled fawn.

The jumpy associate did not ease her fears. Helen figured the young woman was naturally twitchy. But for some reason, Helen had a feeling she made the little fawn extra nervous. And the longer she waited, the more uneasy the associate grew. Helen had to decide. Either she was in or she was out.

They stared at one another for a very long moment.

When Helen thought the young woman was poised to bolt, she stood up and smiled. Then gave a quick nod.

The associate sprang forward down the hall without as much as a glance back. Either she had no interest in an introduction or she figured she would never see Helen again. Helen wanted to ask questions, to gather as much information as she could before getting launched into the interview.

But the fawn kept a far enough distance to discourage conversation. Helen shrugged off the awkwardness of being led without a word and used the time to look over the unusually silent surroundings.

She walked past stretches of secluded cubicles. Not so unusual, though Helen found herself a bit surprised to see people. She half expected the place to be as deserted as the lobby. Despite the number of diligent employees at their desks, not a peep was made. Only the hushed rhythm of keys tapping and papers shifting.

When she tried to make eye contact, not a single head glanced up. Every face stayed glued to the task at hand. Her presence was of no interest. Or they had too much work to worry about the new recruit.

Giving up on human contact, Helen caught sight of the tall windows above the cubicles, displaying the sun falling over the skyline. No matter which way she turned, her view was filled with light gleaming off elegant skyscrapers and landmarks. From this height, the city took her breath away.

But then, she had fallen in love with New York at first sight.

A fact that might have worried her ... for a few reasons. First, she had promised never to fall in love. And second, she was no romantic. As nostalgic as she sometimes felt for eras like the 1930s with their sensual approach to life, she knew romance was a fantasy. Even with a city, love affairs brought trouble. Setting you up for overblown expectations and crushed dreams. She preferred to follow the whims of her heart. Not someone else's.

Lucky for her, New York never stood still. If a place could be more restless than Helen, it was Manhattan. The city was always shifting, always changing. She had picked the perfect relationship. Like being with a new lover every night.

The associate stopped abruptly. Catching Helen off guard. She stopped as the young woman stepped aside, to the right of a heavy-looking wooden door. Helen waited. Thinking the fawn might lead the way.

But the young woman just stared. Blinking at Helen, like she should know what to do. Helen smiled and stepped toward the door. Glancing at her guide for any clue she had guessed wrong. Nothing.

Helen reached her hand out to grasp the doorknob. Turning slowly. Wondering, for a brief second, whether she really wanted to go through with this.

The latch clicked. And the associate bolted. Springing away in the flash of an eye. Leaving Helen alone.

Fair enough, she thought. *Into the deep end we go.*

And she pushed the door open.

Read more of Helen's adventure in Blue Moon, Book 1 of the Fated series. Order your copy today!

GRATITUDE FOR

My amazing readers for your generosity and support.
My friends & family for your loving encouragement.
My reader & editor, Kathryn Cottam. Your guidance is inspiring.
The talented Roberta Cottam for her gorgeous cover design.
The amazing Jacqui Nelson for her brilliance in layout.
The delightful Vanessa Mayville for her magical Great
Lands map.
The wonderful Kevin Corkum for your humour and wisdom.
And the Divine for trusting me with this tale.

ABOUT THE AUTHOR

Kate lives deep in the charmed realm of British Columbia, gathering inspiration in the woods. Her Celtic heritage inspires the poetic style found in the *Great Lands* and her second series, *Fated*. She is passionate about the mystical realms and the lost languages of ancient times. Kate shares about creativity, magic, and the mystical arts on podcasts and her YouTube channel. She offers wisdom about ancient mysticism for modern women through her company, *Venus Lessons*. Bringing her peaceful and playful spirit to daily intuitive and mystical practices. Find out more at www.venuslessons.com.

I love hearing from my readers and am deeply grateful for every kind review.

Join me on Instagram, Facebook, Twitter, and GoodReads.

instagram.com/katetremillsauthor
facebook.com/KMTremills
twitter.com/KateTremills
goodreads.com/kmtremills